T0161292

The Short, Happy Life
of Harry Kumar

The

Short,
Happy
Life

Asho

of
Harry
Kumar

Mathur

ARSENAL PULP PRESS
Vancouver

THE SHORT, HAPPY LIFE OF HARRY KUMAR
Copyright ©2001 by Ashok Mathur

All rights reserved. No part of this book may be reproduced or used
in any form by any means – graphic, electronic or mechanical –
without the prior written permission of the publisher,
except by a reviewer, who may use brief excerpts
in a review, or in the case of photocopying,
a license from the Canadian Copyright Licensing Agency.

ARSENAL PULP PRESS
103-1014 HOMER STREET
VANCOUVER, BC
CANADA V6B 2W9
arsenalpulp.com

The publisher gratefully acknowledges the support of the Canada Council
for the Arts and the British Columbia Arts Council for its
publishing program, and the Government of Canada through
the Book Publishing Industry Development Program
for its publishing activities.

This is a work of fiction. Any resemblance of characters
to persons, living or dead, is purely coincidental.

Text design by Solo
Cover design by Russ Bugera
Printed and bound in Canada

CANADIAN CATALOGUING IN PUBLICATION DATA:
Mathur, Ashok.
The short, happy life of Harry Kumar

ISBN 1-55152-113-X

I. Title.
PS8576.A 8286S56 2001   C813'.54   C2001-911423-0
PR9199.3 M397S56 2001

acknowledgments

Many parties provided me with the space and funds to work on this project: I am most appreciative of the Canada Council, not only for a writing grant that allowed me to complete this project, but for travel grants that gave me the opportunity to conduct preliminary research in Australia. I am also thankful to the Alberta Foundation for the Arts for a grant that allowed me to begin this project, and to the Alberta College of Art and Design which assisted in travel funds for my research in Australia and Aotearoa.

I am also indebted to the staff and board at Toronto Artscape for bringing me to the Gibraltar Point Arts Centre inaugural residency; and, as always, to Carol, Alexandria, and Christy at the Leighton Studios at the Banff Centre. Both these artists' spaces provided me with the luxury of uninterrupted time to focus on this project.

Friends and family have always provided me with the sustenance so necessary for any project like this that depends on the support of communities. I have borrowed, from my mother, her storytelling ways, and from my father, his sense of humour. Thanks to Perin and Parshottam. Special thanks, too, to: my partner, Aruna, not only for her unending love and patience as I flitted off from one place to another for research and writing, but for her keen editorial eye that caught up with my indiscretions around punctuation and unintentional word creations; my primary editor, Nalo, whose strength as a writer led me to believe, entirely correctly, that hers would be a fine set of editorial eyes for this project; and the crew at Arsenal – Brian, Blaine, Linda, Robert – for doing all that's necessary on the editorial and publishing side to make this happen.

Thanks, as well, to the camaraderie and friendship offered by those folks I'm used to having in my life: Hiromi (for always being able to share the same thoughts), Sharron (for how she lives in the world), Stavros (for the cooking, the laughter, the dancing, and the conversation), and Tamai (for teaching me how to chill out with a bag of ice after smoking in the boys' room). Also, all the folks participating in the Prairie Asians and Writers for Change tours: Larissa, Fred, Raj, David, Mark, Rita, Louise, as well as others previously mentioned.

the opening

*in which we fail to meet the protagonist but are introduced to
a scene that will occur much later in the novel*

Imagine, then, a rough, lunaresque landscape, dark for the moment, but still conveying the running figure of a dog, hurtling senselessly from one stalagmital silhouette to the next. Light bounces frenetically off the southern sky, refracting in the dawn, rather than allowing it easy entry to what now might appear to be Stonehenge-like remains were this not an entire hemisphere away and on an entirely different island.

This might be an encouraging perspective to the first sailors, intent on capturing this particular piece of real estate for crown and king, on the water for several weeks without sighting land, who were caught aghast at this site from the Indian Ocean – which, were we now to move forward to that period of daybreak when shivers of light actually glimmer off the tops of spires and radio towers and stalagmites of various proportions – appeared to them to be a veritable lake of construction or, perhaps, the remains of a construction much earlier abandoned, or, even possibly, that state of decay where all but the pillars and foundations are ground to dust, giving that very appearance of a splendid piece of architecture working its way skyward rather than the other way around. Picture this crazed canine, then, pitching back and forth between these erstwhile pillars, barking at its own remarkable pitch, and slavering all the while owing to the considerable heat it is generating by its own wild movements. Clearly the beast is in some degree of want, not just thrashing about between geological formations now, but veritably running up the side of them, defying not just gravitational laws but ones pertaining to species as well, dogs not being known for their perpendicular climbing abilities.

Now imagine the dog is not there, was, perhaps, never there, or was there only in your imagination, not as you imagine now, but as you were being told to imagine. Suspend all thoughts of canines in odd landscapes, but not the thought of the odd landscape itself, for these particular topographical formations are of considerable importance to the story that is about to unfold, or has unfolded in all manners of sequences, but is about to re-unfold in a particular order, although perhaps without logic. Light expands across the now-golden sand that comprises not just the sand itself, forming as it does the majority of the desert-like plain before you, but the odd and irregular abutments that

7

jut out of the sand like so many lawn darts, casually thrown and abandoned. These are geological formations, decidedly phallic to the common observer, but known locally and through tourist media as The Pinnacles, formed as soft material gives way to years of elemental pummelling, leaving the relatively sturdier and weatherproofed caps and all that lies beneath undamaged. Tourist cars, even buses, are known to traverse the rugged roads that spin through The Pinnacles, affording a spectacular view of sandstone phalluses to a plethora of eyes and camera lenses and travelling bodies that journey up the west coast of Western Australia to this particular spot by the ocean.

The story does not begin here, nor does it end at this delightful spot, but rest assured, The Pinnacles do figure, if not prominently, then with subdued distinction, in this story which is essentially built upon a quest theme, of losing and finding, of seeking and discovering, of going from a position of having to have-not-ing to having once again, as if anything were truly that easy. But no, yes, this is a great quest story and, being so, it must indeed begin somewhere, although that somewhere is certainly not here. So, dawn fully breaking over The Pinnacles, the first few tourists blearily making their way out of vehicles into the sky-kissing rocks, the musty smell of morning belying what will become a stinking hot day, we leave this area to its own generative devices, knowing full well we will be coming back to this very spot, perhaps this very time, only when we do, there shall indeed be a crazed canine running without thought to the conservation of energy, barking up every Pinnacle possible and over the top of some, panting furiously and quite doggedly, searching, searching for something lost, potentially never to be refound. That moment will come.

na, man

How we are compared to islands, hey? Or how we are not, as the case may be. As in, we are, none of us, islands. The human body, ninety-some percent water, so little solid inside of us it's a wonder we hold together, and yet we think of ourselves as so much more than liquid – flesh and bones, that's what we call ourselves, not mucous and saline. So, why islands, do you think? Why not lakes? No man is a lake, no woman either, now that would make some sense, put things in perspective, not in this constant backwards way we have of being.

Truth be told, I used to live on an island, me a lake of mucous and saline inhabiting a corporeal mass of stick and stone. But perhaps I'm being disingenuous. Perhaps we all live on islands, tectonically speaking, in that even our hugest continents are floating gently in a swirling sea. Arrogant, isn't it, to suggest that a land mass bordered north west south east by endless bodies of water, perhaps isthmused to another land mass by a moist sandbar or waterlogged peninsular arm, is not really an island? But we do have active imaginations to keep us sane, I suppose, and if history records us as islands living on non-islands, what business is it of mine to undo such stories? What business indeed. Well, I'll let you in on a bit of a secret. It is my business and it's been made my business because of what's happened before me, perhaps *to* me, and what's about to unfold all over again. It happened all backwards to begin with and I might as well be prepared for it to happen backwards all over again, but I firmly believe that we can reclaim that past in an altogether unfamiliar way. To be frank, I didn't like the way the story ended up the first time (is there any wonder?) so a little revisitation is just what's necessary to recreate this tale a bit more engagingly. Of course, to do so I need to remake myself, my history. I need to turn islands into lakes, men into women, palaces into prisons.

Yes, this is cryptic, but you see, if I were to decode everything here and now it would only happen backwards yet again, and I don't believe I could live with that. So I intervene, re-orchestrate, get my feet wet so to speak, stepping off my island and into the ocean, moving this once-tired and defeated body, this sack of mucous and saline with a taut covering the colour of pitch, back to its watery home to begin this story again.

We've met this crazy dog in the middle of the story and now it's time to meet him from the start. Madam, to begin.

the grotto

Harry Kumar is peering at the rockface. A shiny bit of rockface has caught his attention and it is at this particular piece of granite that Harry is now peering. It *looks* like it might be something, but Harry can't be sure. He tries to take a step closer but the forty-five-degree incline leading up to the rockface deters him. Harry is no mountaineer. As a matter of fact, his now-freezing toes, protruding as they are from two-year-old Birkenstocks, are trying desperately to maintain Harry's purchase on the pathway-ledge at the foot of the rockface, but they are fighting a losing battle and Harry keeps rectifying his backward pitch. Still, Harry continues to peer. He is absolutely certain he is looking, for the first time on what was his ninth trip to the grotto, at one of those pictographs he has read about. Pictographs or petroglyphs. He never was sure what to call them. They looked so clear in the large format books he likes perusing at upscale coffee shops and downscale art galleries. Pictographs (or petroglyphs) so clear they could have been painted yesterday, leaping off the rockface for all to see, declaring themselves as all-too-present in the world of living art. But that was in books. Here, in the bristling wind, in the icy grotto, he isn't too sure, after all, if he is looking at an ancient pictograph or petroglyph or the run-off deposit of iron ore. He isn't sure if he is looking at the figure of a man, hunched over and playing a flute, or the outline of a demon, arms flailing in a silent battle cry. Harry wants to look closer, but worn-out Birkenstocks and mid-autumn weather and a body that is just not cut out for this sort of thing all interfere and tell him to go back to his car.

Han, on the other hand, is more than happy to lope up the forty-five-degree incline and nearly scale the rockface, even though Harry is pretty sure Han has no idea why he might be performing such an absurd act. To an untrained observer it might seem as if Han were trying to retrieve the very essence of the age-old message drawn on rock, to bring it back to Harry for approval. But to Harry, this is just another example of Han acting like a crazy dog.

Han scrambles partway up the rockface for the fourteenth time in half as many minutes and looks back expectantly to Harry. Harry looks up at Han and sneers. Han looks down at Harry and yelps three times in quick succession, an act he somehow knows annoys Harry beyond belief. Han turns from Harry and half-heartedly licks the rockface, just about three inches below where the petroglyph or pictograph or iron ore runoff ends. Then he tumbles back down the incline and bowls into Harry's left leg, stepping hard on two of Harry's toes, the little one and the one right next to it, digging in sharply with Shepherd-Heeler nails that Harry should have trimmed several weeks ago.

'Goddamn ouch,' says Harry.

'Arf,' replies Han good-naturedly.

'Stupid mutt,' mutters Harry.

'Arf-arp,' replies Han.

'Say, that's a pretty healthy dog ya got there,' says a voice from behind Harry.

Harry turns around, not surprised that there would be another person out in the grotto on a day like today, but mildly alarmed that he has not heard anyone approach.

'What's his name?' asks the voice, which, Harry deduces, is attached to a middle-aged man, slightly balding and paunching, with a decidedly good-natured air to him.

'Han,' says Harry.

'Arf arf grrarf,' says Han, who never does like strangers coming up and talking to Harry.

'Hun? Like Attila the Hun?'

'No, *Hun*,' says Harry, emphasizing the short-u sound that, while spelled with an 'a' not coincidentally sounded out the first syllable of both his and his dog's name, 'like Hanuman.'

'C'mere Attila, ya crazy guy.'

'Hanuman is a monkey-god,' says Harry to the man and no one in particular.

'You a marauding Barbarian, are ya, Attila?' The man laughs.

'A monkey-god,' continues Harry, now certainly to no one in particular, 'from this epic story where he helps this princess Sita, well, really, he starts by helping Rama, but ...'

'Here big guy, you're not so tough, are ya, Attila?' says the man, reaching out his left hand in exactly the aggressive manner that competent dog books tell you not to.

'... eventually it's Hanuman who tracks down Sita and lets her know that Rama is on the way.'

'Grr arf grr,' says Han, which the man reads as a puppy invitation to stroke his head.

'He's actually a bit afraid of men,' says Harry, more to Han as a gesture of permission than anything.

'Who is? This monkey-god guy?' asks the man, somewhat surprising

Harry who thought his story was going pretty much unheard. But then, finding the dog much more interesting than the story or Harry, the man returns his attention to Han. 'That's a good boy, Attila ya Hun,' says the man, now patting Han on the head, now letting his hand slide under an apprehensive jowl.

'Grr yip,' says Han.

'No, not Hanuman the monkey-god,' explains Harry in a resigned tone, 'but Hanuman *my* dog, he's afraid of men.' Somewhere between the words 'afraid' and 'men,' canine teeth enter human flesh.

'Holy *shit!*' says the man, trying to extricate his hand from its new-found position as a Shepherd-Heeler pull toy. '*Ow*, boy, hey boy, leggo boy, *leggo* my hand, oh Jeez, *oh!*'

'Yip, grr grr grr,' announces Han in his new game.

'Let go of his hand, Han,' says Harry in his do-what-you-want voice. Then adds as an afterthought, 'Bad dog.'

'Owwww.'

'Grr-rrr-rr.'

'Enough, Han.'

Han releases the hand with mild surprise, licks his lips expecting, perhaps, a doggie treat.

'*Ow*. Jeez. Ow, he sure had a grip on me there. Hooboy, I guess I deserved that. Can see why ya call him Hun!'

'I'm terribly sorry,' says Harry humbly, 'I don't understand.' Harry pauses briefly, then continues in an all-too practised manner. 'He's usually so friendly. He's absolutely never ever done anything like that before.'

'Hey, that's okay,' says the man, rubbing his hand in the opposite armpit. 'My fault. No harm done. Take 'er easy,' and he trots off deeper into the grotto.

Harry turns to Han. He shakes his head slowly and Han looks up, somewhat admonished, but also clearly happy to have made some sort of interaction. Harry turns to go back toward the parking lot and Han bolts off ahead of him. Harry negotiates his way through the boulders carefully, no sense twisting an ankle out here. Maybe if he had four legs and was built close to the ground he, too, would scamper across the rocks like they were nothing at all. Harry watches Han come to a turn in the dry riverbed, look back furtively for Harry, then dash off around the bend. Crazy dog, thinks Harry.

'Arr-arr-arr,' comes the canine report from around the corner.

Shit, thinks Harry. He begins a pathetic little jog to get himself around the corner to see what sort of trouble Han is into. He hears the squeal of delight from another stranger, a woman this time.

'Ooo, what a cute dog,' comes the voice. Harry turns the corner, puffing ever so slightly. The woman looks up. She is dressed for a hike, no Birkenstocks on this one, and she beams up at Harry. 'What a cute dog you have here.' Han is sitting at the feet of a woman who is not altogether unfamiliar, plus he has put two and two together in his Shepherd-Heeler brain and figured out that the phrase 'cute dog' should inevitably be followed by a biscuit. 'What's his name?'

Harry watches the woman make the very same ill-fated manoeuvre of fast-forwarding her hand toward Han's face.

'Um, Attila. His name is Attila.'

'Attila? You mean, like the artist?' She doesn't slow the velocity of her hand. Han quickly ascertains that this fast-approaching hand contains neither a delicate treat nor even the smell of meat, but how could it, for the owner is a vegetarian and doesn't even let her fingers touch the canned tuna she religiously dishes out to her two overweight cats every evening.

'No, like the Hun,' says Harry, watching as the woman's scentless hand, carrying no familiar smells after all, makes initial contact with Han's left eye, an unintentional slight, but one that any good canine cannot leave unpunished.

'Arrrrr,' roars the woman as Han bites down.

'Arr-arr-arr,' growls Han to his newest pull-toy.

'I'm terribly sorry,' says Harry humbly.

'God, that hurts!' complains the woman.

'Yip,' responds Han, releasing the hand smelling vaguely of mint lotion but definitely no meat. He licks his lips. Definitely a meatless taste.

'I don't understand,' says Harry, his brain on auto-pilot. 'He's usually so friendly.'

The woman rubs her bruised hand, flashes a hurt look that suggests to Harry that she's never owned a dog – violent creatures, not docile like cats.

'He's absolutely never ever done anything like that before.'

young Kumar

So now we watch Harry walking out of the grotto with his hapless yet happy dog. Harry has his mind working on three things at once. He is thinking about re-enrolling Han in obedience school, although he knows he will have to find another one since Han was involved in too many, well, incidents at his last school and will not be welcomed back. Harry is also thinking that perhaps he should keep Han on leash, or at least warn people when they approach that his dog is an over-anxious animal prone to sinking his teeth into strangers. Yet it seems so much easier to pretend that Han is as people would have him be, a loyal, obedient, friendly dog with no predilection for biting or other monkeyshines. It does not occur to Harry, as it does to me, that he has things backwards yet again, and that his overused lie might start to sound as insincere to others as it now does to Harry himself.

The second thing Harry is thinking about, sparked by his relating of the core elements of the *Ramayana* to Han's first victim, is Sita – not the Sita of legend, but his friend Sita for whom, it suddenly occurs to Harry, Han might have mistook his second victim, both women being of the same height, build, and hair colour, although the similarities ended there. Harry had invited Sita on this walk, but her father was in town for a brief visit so Harry and Han had gone off by themselves, a not entirely unfamiliar story since neither man nor dog had a great surfeit of friends. Harry determines he shall call Sita later, since her father would be on a late afternoon flight back to California and Sita might feel like some company.

The third thing Harry is thinking about is his own father, a stalwart Hindu civil servant who had emigrated from India in his late twenties to find his fortune in England where he had, in the heady, hippified, anti-establishment days of the mid-sixties, met and married Harry's mother, a white Londoner who was desperate to refute her aristocratic and colonialist heritage, which she did admirably by 'embracing a world of downtrodden difference' (her words) or 'marrying down' (her parents' words). It is this last thought, not so much of his parents as a couple, which they were until Harry turned ten when they divorced with some initial, though not lasting, animosity, but of his father in particular that occupies Harry's musings as he and Han walk back to the car. Harry had thought his father a proud man, proud of his lineage, his honour, his life's work, yet there was one conversation between father and son that

Harry just could not get out of his mind. It happened when Harry went back to England to visit his father – his parents had immigrated to Canada the year Harry was born, and while his mother made frequent trips back, his father had decided to return to London permanently when their marriage fell apart – just a few months before the elder Kumar met an untimely end.

'Harry, my boy,' his father had said to him as they stared out at a river that reflected the dismal sky, 'I was born within sight of the Ganges, did you know that?'

Harry had shook his head.

'Within sight. In the mornings you could see the wood gatherers making their way down to the ghats, begin to light their fires. The Ganges.' Harry's father nodded as if someone had asked him a question. 'And this is the Thames. You know what, boy? I should have been born within sight of the Thames, not the Ganges. This is my home. This is where I belong.' Harry's father looked at his son and, uncharacteristically, placed his hand on Harry's shoulder. His voice dropped to a hoarse whisper. 'This is where I should have been born, where you were born.'

Harry had looked at his father then, at his father's handlebar moustache, waxed daily, at his neat suit and tie, and Harry had realized, perhaps for the first time, that his father may have been proud of what he had become, but was actually ashamed of where he had come from. And for the first time, Harry looked at his father as an old and tired man, not a robust father who was always forceful, confident, and, yes, proud.

'Yes, I should have been born here. And this is where I will....' Harry's father had paused, turned aside as if he were about to have an emotional epiphany, then turned back to his son, arms sweeping open in a gesture of ownership. 'I leave this all to you, my son,' and the great man's eyes had shimmered, the closest Harry had ever seen his father come to tears. He had leaned in close to Harry and whispered, 'Leave all of *me* behind – I am no Dasharatha with royal offerings for my son – and take all of what your mother left for you.' Harry had been taken aback – it was not as if his father wasn't prone to pepper his conversation with allusions to Hindu mythology, just that he was never this emotional. And in a moment it was over and Harry's father had regained complete composure and suggested he and his son should stop for a cup of tea before returning home. From time to time over the years, Harry would think about the union of brown and white that was his parentage, how his father, for all his outward demonstrations of pride, secretly loathed the brown, and how his mother, for all her staunchly English ways, could never abide the white. All this left Harry haplessly in the middle and, as was his wont, hopelessly confused.

☾

Harry's father died of sleeping pills in the early days of 1983, just before Harry turned eighteen. An overdose? he asked the voice on the telephone. No, said the voice. Not an overdose. Just two sleeping pills, one of which managed to lodge itself in Harry's father's windpipe. So he choked to death? Harry asked the voice. Not exactly, for Harry's father flung himself across the room in a vain attempt to dislodge the offending pill, eventually flinging himself into a plate glass window, into and through a plate glass window that was made of the pre-safety-glass-era glass and which had the tendency to shatter into very sharp and deadly shards which could slice through a man's jugular like a knife through butter. Thus spake the voice. So, Harry sighed, he didn't die of asphyxiation, but of blood loss caused by glass shards? No, came the anticipated response from the voice. Miraculously, Harry's father's body had vaulted through the shower of glass shards virtually unscathed but for a nick above the left eyebrow and one just a tad over his left ankle, just beyond the protective covering of thick wool socks he always wore in the cool London evenings. He vaulted through the plate glass window, gasping desperately for breath, having dislodged the sleeping pill, whether by violent contact with the window or by sheer shock alone, and fell to the ground below. Harry, despite his young age, realized this narrative was not over but that he had a part to play with this non-corporeal voice lecturing him over the telephone, and so he asked, did the fall kill him? Oh heavens no, came the voiced reply, he was on the ground floor, your father, the window he went through was actually a patio door that led to a magnificent garden, roses as big as a baby's bottom and enough watercress to feed an army. No, your father fell flat on his face and was still for a moment, we all thought he was dead right then, but then he leapt to his feet, brushed himself off, and like a proper gentleman returned to his bedroom as if nothing at all had happened. But, asked the frustrated young Harry, you did say he was dead? Oh, yes, said the voice, yes, and I'm afraid to inform you that we have no reason not to believe his gunshot wound was not self-inflicted. No reason? thought Harry. Not to believe? Not self-inflicted? Did this mean his father took his own life, or that no one believed he took his own life, and why was this voice talking in such riddles? He sighed once more, steadied himself and asked: Did he, then, my father, kill himself? The voice ahhhed and paused and then replied: Oh yes, most certainly. Your father was always an excellent marksman. Damn, I suppose that was a rather insensitive remark. But true, so very true. I say, young Kumar, are you all right? Harry sighed for the third and last time during the phone call. I'm not sure, he told the voice. I'm not sure at all.

((

See, this is the way things happened to Young Kumar. All out of the ordinary. He simply could not expect a telegram: REGRET TO INFORM YOU YOUR FATHER HAS DIED. No, it always had to be convoluted. His life was a series of convolutions, he would often tell people. Once, upon saying this very phrase – 'my life is a series of convolutions' – to a young woman, she became greatly concerned, believing Harry to be epileptic, and commented on how awful that must be, never knowing how or when he would enter into a series of seizures. Perhaps she could help, she had said, gently massaging the left temple of her most recent acquaintance with her right index finger and middle finger the way she had so expertly learned. No, no, corrected Harry, convolutions, unnecessary complications to otherwise straightforward narrative events. Oh, she had said, leaving his temple for a moment, only to re-initiate the massage once her surprise had worn off, though still uncertain why this young man had insisted he was subject to convulsions. Perhaps she could still help, she said, more firmly pressing on his temple and allowing her thumb to trace a slight but erotic path along his upper cheekbone.

Young Kumar, while the furthest thing from a seasoned womanizer, was not unaccustomed to such attention, although he had no idea why he garnered such treatment at the hands of young, often quite attractive, women. In his own way, Young Kumar was himself quite handsome. Owing to a high metabolism and a genetic disposition, Harry was slender without looking gaunt. He had his mother's height, putting him at just five-foot-nine, but his long limbs and straight posture made him look fetchingly taller, and his father's smiling eyes that would radiate affection even when Young Kumar was feeling quite sullen and bored. His eyebrows, thick and mysterious, accentuated those smiling eyes and, when furrowed in a characteristic v-shaped gesture, led an observer's gaze down to a sharp, but not oversized, nose, and full, quite feminine, lips, which he was in the habit of licking frequently. It was Young Kumar's great fault that he rarely recognized the purpose of any attention cast toward him, often misreading it and acting accordingly. Such was the case with the temple-massaging young woman, and there were several minutes of small talk before Young Kumar became cognizant that this young woman had sat herself down, uninvited, at his table in a cocktail bar he was not used to frequenting, and slowly it dawned on him that perhaps her firm temple massage was a prelude to her day job, so to speak, and he pulled away from her in a hurry. I'm sorry, he had said, but this is what I mean. Nothing is simple. There are no easy answers or uncomplicated paths. I'm in the middle of the very type of convolution to which I had earlier referred, he kindly pointed out. Oh, said the young woman. Should she call a doctor?

Of course, Harry had hurriedly left the scene, not wishing to further involve himself in the potential unfolding of a scandalous scenario, not that it would have mattered to anyone since Harry hardly held a position of prestige or notoriety. Still, he felt awkward as he fumbled for his bills, insisting on paying for the young woman's drink as well as his own, mumbling about misunderstandings, getting things backwards (but not convolutions), and rushing himself out the door, pausing only momentarily to wonder what, indeed, would be so wrong in admitting to the young woman that his epilepsy was actually quite well in control and would she like to continue what her index and middle fingers had so eloquently started. But this was only a passing, fragmentary thought, for Harry's life was not one that could accommodate such transgressions, deviations from a norm that only he could perceive as being absolutely necessary and not at all dull. Nevertheless, things happened to him, whimsical things, and when his colleagues would say smirkingly that they couldn't happen to a nicer guy, what they really meant was isn't it amazing how such fascinating things were thrown upon an exceedingly uninteresting young man such as Harry. What, they wondered, sometimes aloud and in front of Harry, much to his irritation, would happen if Harry were to take up even one-tenth of the odd assortment of offers that came his way?

YVR

Transitional places, airports. I think that's why I like them so much. There's so much opportunity for change, for redirection, for backtracking. And, despite all efforts by airport authorities to redesignate such sites as actual destination points, places people go to eat and shop and generally hang around, airports are bound to remain transitional places. Oh, sure, we say we're going *to* the airport, as if we were visiting our grandparents up at terminal one, but everyone knows we really mean we are going somewhere else, or else going to retrieve someone from some place else, or else to deposit a friend or family member at the airport so that they can take off, quite literally, to some city far away from us, the airport, and the entire region. But even then, see, we're not entirely sure we will leave the comfort of the airport since anything can happen in such a transitional place. Engines break down, pilots drink too much and can't fly, and of course there's always, always the weather, turning on you in a moment, turning flights back in mid-air, throwing all things into reverse.

It is such a potential reversal for which two people now wait, a man and a woman sitting on stools at a decorative jade bartop that used to front a popular oyster lounge until the airport authority realized people did not actually spend much time slurping back oysters in this transitional place. The man is in his early sixties, his ruddy complexion revealing a life well spent in outdoor conditions, his straight back and square shoulders suggesting a fit lifestyle and, barring the unforeseen, a healthy number of years in his future. The woman beside him is younger, thirty-five I can tell you exactly, although a combination of smooth, coffee-coloured skin, long, straight, dark hair that makes it down to the fourth vertebrae above her tailbone, and deep brown eyes (shared, incidentally, by her elder companion) allows her to pass for a woman with not quite three decades behind her. The two of them talk quietly, occasionally laughing softly, touching one another upon the hand as those familiar with each other often do. Oh, and I sit at a jade table not ten feet behind them, slightly closer to the woman, and yes, I watch their every move, their every gesture, and I listen to every word.

'So how is Harry doing?' he asks.

'He's well. He's – well, you know what Harry's like. Not too many ups or downs, just normal, kind of.'

The man laughs. He touches his daughter on her wrist, weathered white hand on smooth brown skin.

'But Sita, really. I know you've told me that you and Harry, there's nothing–'

'Intimate?' Sita asks, her eyes widening and a smile appearing. 'No, nothing like that, just like I've told you.'

'But if not with Harry, is there anyone else?'

'Oh, Dad,' says Sita, sighing and touching her father's hand in return. 'No, nothing. Your daughter will end up in a house full of old ladies.'

'Might be fun,' says Sita's father, grinning at his daughter's joke.

'Ah, well I don't know about that,' says Sita. 'I think there's a guy out there for me.'

'Worked for me,' says her father, his smile broadening.

'Hm,' says Sita. 'And did you always know that? I mean, you never told me. Did you know that even when you met Mom?'

'Well, I don't know about whether I knew when I met her – a special woman she is, you know. But soon after.'

'Before I was born?' asks Sita. Her father shrugs, ponders this question, and is thinking this through when Sita's cell phone rings. She pulls it from her jacket pocket and looks at its face.

'It's Harry,' she tells her father. 'I'll just tell him I'll call him back,' and she presses the talk button. 'Hi, Harry?'

From where I sit, if I look past Sita, past her father, and look up toward-but-not-as-far-as the skylights that bring in the natural light responsible for illuminating the international terminal of the Vancouver airport during daylight hours, my gaze rests on a huge bank of video screens, nine deep and nine across. For the most part, what appears on these video screens are brief narrative blurbs, bits of sports and news and advertising, projected as a single image broken down into eighty-one distinct and discrete parts, recomposed in the viewer's mind as the optic nerve transfers these multiple sets of images to the viewer's brain. So what the viewer might see, if he or she were to truly analyze the stimuli, are indeterminate blobs of video imagery, but what the viewer *understands* he or she sees is something completely different, something that somehow makes sense of these eighty-one images, drawing them into a monolithic whole that imparts some capitalist, or at least cogent, message deep within the recesses of the viewer's grey matter. But what I see is not a series of news/sports/advertising spots, but a vast array of images: this one could be an incomplete nostril, that one a blurred antennae, and then there are strands of hair, a flash of a numerical keypad, an earlobe, a green slab of stone, several more green slabs in a row,

20

a fingernail and a portion of thumb next to it, a finger of rock piercing through the earth's crust, a piece of a monkey's tail, a tooth and the fleshy edge of a tongue, a bubble rising from a mudpool, a tree on a hilltop, a bit of lip, another wisp of hair, all of which I could recompose in my brain as an image of Sita talking into her cell phone if I were of a mind to recompose the image thusly, instead of luxuriating in the endless possibilities afforded by each and every one of the eighty-one isolated, island-like images, any one of which could really tell its own story quite well. But I will have to collect these images for the purposes I have in mind, take my treasure and travel with her from one to another, image-hopping in the endless hope that this time things will turn out differently.

'Hey, can I call you back in ten minutes, Harry? My dad's just about ready to board. Okay, bye.' Sita puts her cell phone down and says to her father that Harry said hello. But Sita's father is looking up toward-but-not-as-far-as the skylights, his gaze fixed on the multiple video screens. Images coalesce and resurrect themselves in his grey matter to compose an image of his daughter on a cell phone, but then as quickly as the image is formed it dissipates. Sita's father looks around, trying to find the camera or cameras that have so clearly focussed in on his daughter.

'They can't do that,' he says.

'Do what?' Sita asks, now also looking about her.

'Put surveillance images up in public like that.'

'Surveillance what?'

Sita's father points to the video screen. Sita looks up and just for a moment thinks she sees something vaguely familiar and worrisome, but then is watching eighty-one images coming together to record a swing and a miss at a Blue Jays pitcher's slider. Sita and her father both stare at the video screens for a second longer.

'Um, nothing I guess,' says Sita's father. 'I should board the plane now.' He stands and straightens his shirt sleeve, then looks at his daughter and, almost as an afterthought, raises an eyebrow and says, 'Hey Sita, be careful, okay?'

He has nothing to worry about. We'll be fine. After all, it's not going to happen the same way as before. Quoth I: never like that again.

the teller

Until about a year ago, they actually had those wrought-iron bars at each wicket, the type you see on television movies about banks in the old west, the type of bars that relatively decrepit and wizened tellers squinted behind and out from at the customers. The bars were ostensibly there to protect the credit union, although Harry thought they were relatively useless, at least they were in the old television movies, because the only time you saw the bars, the decrepit/wizened teller, or the interior of the bank at all, was when some lone gunman or outlaw gang was about to rob the institution. Then the bars did no good at all, except to cast ominous shadows onto the teller's face, either just before he handed over the bags of money in fear of his life, or was shot dead for refusing to do so or even for complying if the particular gunman or men were in a particularly malicious and outlaw mood.

Harry was actually tempted to wear one of those translucent baseball-cap-visors like the tellers did in the old movies, the type which cast a seasoned glow on their faces, a glow that were the film not shot in black and white would carry with it a greenish-bluish hue, Harry was sure. But Harry did not wear such a visor to work, nor did he ever tell anyone of his fantasy, because that was just not the sort of thing Harry did. Harry was the reliable one. The steady worker. The quiet yet polite one. Harry was notable in that he alone had never become visibly irritated with a customer, had never raised his voice in alarm, had never done anything that would warrant a call to Mr Peabody's office for a brief lecture on how to perform his duties for the benefit of all and why he should not yell at the credit union's clients, even if they were dumbasses. No, Harry had never been called into Mr Peabody's office, which meant, of course, that not only had he never been privately chastised, but Harry had also never been promoted.

Six years was a long time to serve as a teller. Most tellers were moved into managerial positions or at least supervisory positions by this time. Or at the very least they had seniority so they could claim the best holiday time. But not so with Harry. It wasn't that Harry was disrespected. Everyone was cordial with him, and they smiled when they passed him, and on occasion he was even the subject of silly schoolgirl fantasies by not one, not two, but three of his colleagues: Ms Daphne Manning, Ms Arlene Houle, and Mrs Agnes Kowalski. But the fact of the matter remained that Harry was pretty much a non-entity in the credit union which was his place of employment.

When Mr Peabody decided that the wrought-iron bars had to go, the decision pleased most everybody. Now that we're moving into a new century, they joked amongst themselves, our glorious leader has finally decided to let go of hundred-year-old remnants. Who knows, they said to each other knowingly, in another hundred years we might move forward another inch and get a digital timeclock! Mr Peabody seemed pleased with his decision to renovate the credit union, to replace the bars with a deceivingly open teller wicket (the deceit being that with the removal of the bars came the installation of high technology surveillance equipment that was able to monitor every square inch of that credit union and which was quite obviously an infringement on the civil liberties of the staff therein, even though Mr Peabody assured them the cameras were for their own safety). Mr Peabody even held a ribbon-cutting ceremony on March 21 of the Year of the Renovation to celebrate the dawning of a new age. Later that evening he was to watch videotaped recordings of that very ceremony from at least four different angles and he paid particular attention to credit union staffers who had been paying less than full attention to his speech, which he made a note of for his own reference at Christmas bonus time.

Mr Peabody liked the sense of control one gets when one's perspective is omniscient. Behind his locked door, off to the left of his oak desk, under a flip-down counter that, when flipped up, gave the impression of a singles' club bar, was a three-monitor console, each twelve-inch screen rotating images from the fifteen video cameras positioned throughout the credit union. Of these surveillance cameras, six were slow-pan units moving at a turtlian pace of five degrees per minute, completing their range of eighty-five to two-hundred-and-seventy degree angles (depending on where they were mounted) in seventeen to fifty-four minutes; four were fixed focus on the main teller units with an option of secondary focus onto the reception area and various behind-the-counter spots; another four were situated in each of the personal account manager offices, equipped with a manual pan range of only twenty degrees but with an amazing wide-angle to telephoto zoom that, set to max, could provide a large enough magnification to let the viewer count the lines in the queen's face etched on a ten-dollar bill; and one camera illegally installed in a heating duct in the ceiling of the unisex washroom. From his desk, with the flick of a fancy remote control, Mr Peabody could see three different angles at once and set up the frequency with which the cameras rotated, zooming and panning at will. Mr Peabody could spend hours in his office not compiling financial statement overviews, but watching over his flock, noticing their personal and sometimes quite revolting habits, figuring out who each employee talked to the most, how each one goofed off when thinking no one was looking (ha!), and even who might have that tell-tale glazed gaze which usually indicated a workplace sex fantasy that recent statistics suggested to Mr Peabody the employees had a rate of six per hour, forty-five per day, two-hundred-and-twenty-five per week, and eleven-thousand-and-twenty-five per annum (based on three weeks holiday and no sick days, as if employees never took sick days even when they weren't sick: all of them, except, of course, for Harry Kumar who, if Mr Peabody, had he bothered to review employee records, would find had not missed a single day of work except once two-and-a-half years ago for indeterminate reasons).

Mr Peabody was peering at camera no. 8 which was slowly passing by the visage and wicket of H. Kumar. Something was amiss, thought Mr Peabody, but he couldn't quite place what that was. Then, sussing out the scene by flipping from camera to camera, Mr Peabody ascertained what was the matter. Harry had just finished serving a customer and was looking out placidly at the dissipating lunch-time line-up which, as Mr Peabody could tell from roving camera no. 12 on its return journey, was a queue of one, that person being a middle-aged and portly woman with an upper lip apparently twice as thick as her lower lip, not by injury but by strange genetic design accentuated by the totally inappropriate application of *au naturel* lip-gloss that was supposed to appear as if it were invisible, that is, not to appear at all, except in her case the gloss was all too apparent, glowing, growing that upper lip so the woman looked like she was snarling which, as it turns out, she was, in a roundabout sort of way.

'Next,' mouthed Harry – for despite the quarter-of-a-million dollar visual surveillance, audio was not a feature, and Mr Peabody had been too intimidated to inquire into audio possibilities, particularly after he had to slip an extra c-note to the surly technician so he would install a high-tech cam in the toilet area no questions asked – in the direction of the lone line-up occupant. Camera no. 12 showed the woman stoically refusing to hear Harry's offer, her lip growing even larger if that was at all possible. Maybe, speculated Mr Peabody, the lip thing was a nervous disorder, like a verbal tic or bulging vein. Camera no. 8, with Harry now squarely framed in the centre, again showed Harry offering to help the next in line. This was better than tennis, thought Mr Peabody as he zoomed in on Big Lip Woman who still, although flinching noticeably when Harry hailed her, ignored his plea. What was going on? Had Harry insulted the client on a previous occasion? Did she have a favorite teller, Daphne perhaps, who was just finishing with a client, or Arlene, who always endeared herself to the clients because of her girlish lisp, something everyone loved even if Arlene hadn't quite mastered the art of correctly dispensing cash? Camera no. 8, with Harry now escaping off to the left, thanks to a Bergmanesque pan, showed the hapless teller once again yoo-hooing to the client and camera no. 12 closed in on the defiance of the unmoving Lip. Then, almost imperceptibly, the woman moved, moved out of the range of camera no. 12 but not into the frame captured by no. 8, no, but to the willing gaze of camera no. 3 which, at this moment, was a wide-angle shot of Daphne looking a bit confused for she, too, had noticed Gargantuan Lip standing her ground and refusing Harry's offer, only to approach Daphne's till as soon as she had finished taking in thirty rolls of change from the guy who ran the loonie store in the strip mall down the block. Mr Peabody was at once satisfied that his surveillance system had given him insight into his employees' working day, and dissatisfied for he had not a clue about what was transpiring.

Mr Peabody straightened his tie. He stood up. He tucked in the back of his shirt and zipped up his fly which was doing that nasty thing of edging down about a quarter inch, not enough to be noticeable to anyone but himself, nor enough to convince him to dispose of the pants or fix the zipper, but enough that it bothered Mr Peabody and caused him, rather neurotically, to check and tug at his zipper at least three times per hour, usually, but not always, when he was sure no one was watching. He cleared his throat. He would get to the bottom of this.

By the time Mr Peabody had settled his personal appearance and emerged into the credit union teller area (which Mr Peabody always called 'the floor' as if he were running a retail outlet of men's fashion in a chi-chi shopping district) Harry Kumar was busying himself with the afternoon's cheque stubs and Daphne was rubber-stamping two cheques for deposit for the woman with the Amazing Lip. Mr Peabody surveyed the scene, this time in human-eye panorama, and decided his best course of action was to approach Harry to determine if there might be a quick answer to this conundrum. He stepped up to Harry from behind and gently touched him on the shoulder. Harry turned to look at Mr Peabody. Mr Peabody looked Harry straight in the eye to detect any signs of discomfort. There were none.

'Trouble on the floor, Kumar?' A statement more than a question.

'Trouble, sir?'

'Yes, trouble on the floor.'

'No. No, sir. No trouble.'

'Ah, yes, well, you see,' began Mr Peabody, well aware all of a sudden that his employees didn't know about the extent of his surveillance and he didn't want to play such a trump card now, or possibly, ever, 'I was just coming out of my office, uh, and I couldn't help noticing, not really, well, that, well, there appeared to be trouble on the floor.'

Upon uttering the word 'trouble,' Mr Peabody gestured with his neck and head in the direction of the Humungous Lip Woman. Mr Peabody had fully intended this to be a subtle gesture, but owing to his own building excitement and his unfortunate habit of combing what little was left of his own hair, growing out of the left side of his scalp, over to the right side of his head and holding it in place with sculpting gel, the subtlety replaced by a remarkable gesture that saw Mr Peabody slingshot his head forty-five degrees in the direction of the Woman of Enormous Lip, energy subsequently transferred to his goo-covered hair, making it first stand straight up from his head in some sort of military salute, then pitch over and point, like a slightly chubby but nonetheless overzealous Irish Setter, not just at the client standing before Ms Daphne Manning, but directly at the Woman's Upper Lip, a perfect tableau frozen in time by the recording devices attached to cameras no. 3 and no. 8, both pulled back into a wide-angle shot, enough to illuminate this moment from two distinct angles.

All eyes and three cameras in the credit union focussed on Mr Peabody as his Irish-Setter-pointing-hair slowly gave in to gravity and languished to a decidedly post-coital retirement against his scalp.

'Her!' Peabody whispered hoarsely, nonchalantly wiping a drop of sticky gel from his eyelid. 'She refused to be served by you.' Owing to excitement and an inability to truly whisper, something that had got Mr Peabody into trouble repeatedly at the theatre and the opera, this last statement traversed the short distance to the Unsightly Lip Woman whose facial oddity had apparently been compensated for by divine powers endowing her with the hearing of an Irish Setter, and so she responded, loudly, clearly, and surprisingly articulately considering the enormity of her upper lip.

'I refused to be served by *him*,' she responded, gesturing to Harry Kumar in a fashion not dissimilar to Mr Peabody's recent gestural attempt but without similar consequences, 'because *he's* a *man*.'

The Mammoth Lip Woman let that sink in before continuing. 'He's a male teller and I refuse to be served by a male teller because *they* always get promoted in a wink of an eye. They never know what they're doing because they refuse to listen to their women trainers, yet their male managers promote them out of their fucking wickets so they can join the boy's club and play squash or whatever it is they do once they are no longer mere tellers.'

She looked around, anticipating applause for what she perceived to be a feminist intervention, and perhaps she would have received such had the credit union not now been empty of clients and personnel save for Harry, Daphne, Henrietta, and of course, Mr Peabody, who was desperately wishing he had never left his video console.

To her credit, Henrietta did put on a slight smirk and placed her hands together, not so much in absolute applause, but in a tableau that would have appeared as someone caught in the act of clapping, had someone photographed this moment.

The Woman of Gargantuan Lip stared right at Harry now and finished with her *coup de grâce*: 'I won't be served by you because they'll promote you up and out of your position, asshole.'

Harry cleared his throat. He nodded as if in agreement, but muttered under his breath: 'I don't think there's much of a chance of that,' but no one, including Mr Peabody and the Woman of Large Lip Glory paid him any attention and, within a few moments, the client had left, Mr Peabody had returned to his videodrome, and Harry was left staring at Daphne who smiled gently at him as if to reassure him – although neither of them said anything of this incident then or at any time in the future – that she supported him completely.

Sita and Harry

It might seem exceedingly irregular that a quirky, not unattractive but certainly no film star in appearance or confidence type such as Harry would have struck up such a close friendship with Sita Simpson. On the surface about all they had in common, to the casual observer, was that they shared a similar family lineage in a similar fashion; that is, they were both products of differently-raced parents (one Indian, one white) which endowed each with a complexion that seemed all the rage in the fashion industry these days where being mixed-race was somewhat akin to the buzz created in earlier times when a dark-skinned immigrant could be called 'exotic' without a trace of irony or admittance of racism. But apart from this 'half-Indian' thing, they had little going that would have linked them, except that they obviously liked each other a great deal. In contrast to Harry's father, an ambitious and anglicized civil servant from India, Sita's father was an ex-cop who, after twenty-five years as a homicide detective, had emerged from the closet, left his wife on fairly amiable terms, and moved to a small town in the California redwoods where he set up a dog-training school – this from a man who had firmly disallowed any pets from darkening the doorway of the family home – with a gentleman lover only five years older than his only child. Sita maintained a good relationship with her father and her new-found 'father-in-law' and visited them often, as did her mother – the first member of her family to marry a white person since her Punjabi great-grandparents came to the Fraser Valley at the turn of the century – who, while saddened to lose her faithful husband of a quarter-century, secretly admitted to her daughter that at least the husband and father had left behind two women not for another female, but for a pursuit that had long been denied him when he worked in a macho and undisputedly homophobic police department.

Her father – whom she and everyone she knew referred to always and only as 'Simpson,' as if no one was aware of any given name he may once have possessed – was a common subject of discussion with Harry, who was not just a good listener, but an engaged listener who proved an apt advisor and confidant as well. So Sita would maunder on about her father, how their relationship had developed until he had come home one day and sat both her and her mother down, and with a tear in his eye and a retirement gold watch in his hand, explained to the most important women in his life that he was about to undertake a rather extreme departure from what would otherwise have been a fairly conventional retirement. Not that their relationship had ceased development, she would tell Harry, once her parents separated and her father began wearing turtleneck sweaters that actually fit him rather than the always ill-measured suits that had become his stock as a police detective, just that it had veered radically as if she was developing a relationship with a father she had never known, and that's what made things so different and so special.

'He's a lot like you, you know,' she once said to Harry, 'in that he was always a thoughtful man, but there was something so close to the surface, something brooding, and it took twenty-five years for it and him to finally come out. Don't let it be that long with you, Harry.'

This latter statement she said teasingly, but it still made Harry splutter and bluster and wonder aloud.

'Do you think, perhaps,' Harry stuttered, 'that maybe I am confused about my sexuality?' at which point he paused and looked up at the ceiling, wondering, for he himself could not discount that possibility, even while he did not think, really, that such was the case.

But Sita laughed and touched him gently on the shoulder in that way of hers that always stirred him, even though neither of them said anything about such feelings.

'No, Harry, that's not what I mean. But there is something about you, something that was in my father too, something under the surface that I can almost see but not see. Like refraction, where I know and can recognize you under the water, but I also know that the light is playing tricks and where I think you are, where your head and shoulders are supposed to be, you really aren't. And if I were to reach out and touch you like this, I wouldn't touch your lips, but your chin or your nose. You would be there, but you wouldn't be there. That's all.' And Sita laughed sweetly and Harry joined her in laughter, although his was somewhat more circumspect.

Sometimes, memories of her father would make Sita cry. She was not a woman given to indiscreet tears and Harry never did see her cry to the point that she was unable to talk clearly and coherently through the entire episode. Harry always thought this rather strange, for he had acted as confidant to more than a few women in the past, though none for several years now, and with the exception of one woman who steadfastly refused to cry at all, these women would never be able to carry on a conversation as did Sita, through tears. It was as if, Harry thought, that Sita were crying in another place and time and the conversation she was having was right there with him, uninterfered with by the crying. Her tears, large and bul-bous, would emerge from her eyes and slip down her full cheeks, then continue passage down to the corner of her lip or, with extraordinary effort, leap off her cheekbone to fall to her lap or to Harry's kitchen table-cloth or to the sofa from which they were watching sitcom reruns. At such times, Harry was still an attentive listener, but a very small portion of his brain could not help but focus on those tears, drifting down Sita's face, affecting her composure as little as a ray of sunlight might, in that she might brush it away in an unforeseen and undiscriminating manner, more a slight bother than a real issue. When she finally spoke, she would tell Harry her sorrow came at remembering how sombre her father had been when she was a girl, and how much of that might have been because he was thinking of a life that might have been. She knew, too, that her father was torn in that he would have never, not for the life of him he insisted to her, chosen not to have a beautiful daughter that he loved very much. Still, Sita would share with Harry, things might have been so different for him had he chosen a different path rather than deferring these decisions to his twilight, or certainly late afternoon, years. This comment, like so many sequiturs between them, would lead Harry to speculate on the metaphor of a day to one's life.

'We are thirty-five,' he said, nodding to Sita, who, indeed, was the same age as he, only born three months ahead and thus his literal senior, some-thing she used to great effect when she needed the upper hand. 'At thirty-five, where is that in the great day of our life? Is it early afternoon already, the time set out for us somewhat short before supper, after-dinner activi-ties, and then the inevitable bed time? Or, considering those first twenty, or at least fifteen, years were more or less training time, would we be more or less in mid-morning, those introductory years being mere moments incurred after rising and having little to do with the way the day proceeds?'

Sita interrupted to suggest that they could not know the way of the world. 'Perhaps I am already in my pre-midnight splendour, for who can tell if the next uptown bus will coincide with my penchant for jaywalk-ing? Or, the opposite, if the remainder of my life is such a sprawl yet, that this moment is barely a few seconds into my day? Should we determine the day in linear, chronological increments,' she asked, 'or should we decide this by accomplishments and goals?'

'Indeed,' Harry responded, 'how arbitrarily would we look at our day and, of course, is it worth looking at it from our limited perspective at all? Can I see your day more clearly or can you see mine better, or should we only look, solipsistically, at our own?'

This they discussed at great length with great lip-pursing and at one pensive point Harry was sure Sita was about to cry, but then realized it was he himself who was shedding a tear and, unlike Sita, he was given to uncompromised and inconsolable sobs. So their conversation finished on a decidedly morose note, Harry grieving and heaving on Sita's welcoming shoulder. Neither of them wondered, aloud or to themselves, why Harry was crying. He simply was and that was enough. They were good to each other this way.

One might think, from the description of Harry and Sita's relationship so far, that they were bound for great intimacy, perhaps a splendid wedding in the offing, a spruced-up condominium in their future, maybe even a child or two. And the likelihood of that is still promising, but that's not where the story is going, nor should you try to take it there. At least not now, not yet. Why, it's not even lunchtime.

((

Sita and Harry had first met at the aquarium. Unlikely as that sounds, it's exactly what occurred. It was the type of chance meeting that had Harry muttering about convolutions and that had Sita laughing uncontrollably, apologizing for her gales all the while. It was mid-October and Harry, recovering from the type of fall cold that never goes away thanks to Vancouver's damp environment, was celebrating that his cold had, amazingly, disappeared almost completely on this, his Wednesday off, and had decided to take himself out to the aquarium. He had bused into the west end of the city, choosing to walk into Stanley Park since the day, threatening rain, was not yet wet and Harry felt he needed the exercise. He was by himself, as he usually was, having little use for close friends – this was when he was thirty-three years old and had been at the credit union for long enough to realize he was going to be there for a long time to come – so he walked into the park quite happily by himself, convinced he would be leaving the same way.

He strolled into the park and to the aquarium, and was busying himself watching two beluga whales standing on their noses in a way that again made Harry question the logic of nature. He was there for a good twenty minutes when he felt something zing by his head. A peanut. A peanut nearly clipped his ear and bounced off the plexiglass of the tank. He almost didn't register this as an actual event, thinking it some freak of nature or an errant child, and would have dismissed it as such had not another peanut caught him squarely on the back of the neck. Still not turning, Harry rubbed the back of his neck quizzically and wondered how coincidental it might be to have two peanuts fired toward him in such short order. It was then he heard the gales of laughter that would turn out to be Sita's. He turned in the direction of the laughter, curious, for it did not come from the point from which he presumed the peanuts were being launched. He was correct. Sita was sitting with two co-workers, on their lunch break, and while her two comrades shared an intimate conversation, Sita, lost in thought, had suddenly noticed the young man at whom peanuts were being thrown. The next peanut clipped Harry right on the temple, the same place where that woman had been massaging just last week, causing him to burst out with an uncharacteristic 'ow,' which only served to heighten Sita's amusement at this whole affair.

Simultaneously, they both turned to view the assailant, no doubt a small child with no disciplinarian in sight, but could view no such being. It was not until a fourth peanut vaulted through the air, clearly sent from twenty feet up a red cedar, that the culprit's position was revealed. This peanut zoomed over Harry's head. Sita laughed. Harry began to shout, but then laughed too. He kept hearing Sita repeat, I'm sorry, I'm sorry, I shouldn't laugh, it's just so funny. And before he knew it, he too was bent over in laughter. Sita's friends, their conversation temporarily interrupted by the laughter, looked up, smiled, and politely excused themselves so they could continue their conversation elsewhere. Harry still eyed the red cedar and thought he could determine a shadowy form swinging from the bough to a nether tree, but he could not be certain. He dismissed it. Probably a squirrel or crow, perhaps, playing with peanuts and inadvertently shooting them out at him. After all, as much as it looked like one, it absolutely could not have been an actual monkey. 'Hey, I'm Sita,' said Sita.

'I'm Hari. Or Harry.'

'Well, Hari or Harry. What a way to meet someone.' And she doubled over in laughter. 'Listen,' she said, staring into the green eyes of this brown man, the first time she had seen such an iris shade on a person of colour, and she was intrigued and attracted all at once. 'I'm being completely rude by laughing this much. C'mon. Let me buy you a coffee or something.' Sure, Harry smiled, and took her up on the offer, certain that he had not really seen a monkey and enchanted by this woman who introduced herself with by laughter.

((

Now, now, I can hear you saying to yourself, why, this is a Hollywood romance for sure, how can it not be, two lovely young people in a chance encounter, definitely the stuff of the silver screen. And I must admit that it seems improbable, to be sure, that such a chance encounter and attraction (for Harry was as drawn to Sita as she was to him) would not come to an inevitable pheremone-drenched relationship. But, as before, we both get ahead of ourselves, and must draw in the reins, so to speak, because regardless of how much love might appear to be in the air, it is not in the text immediately following. So, so be it. Nevertheless, Sita and Harry did strike up a marvellous and ongoing friendship, the likes of which neither had before experienced. From that first coffee on, while the adjective 'inseparable' would hardly be *à propos*, as both had responsibilities and other factions of their lives which required attention, but they did see a lot of each other in the following two-and-a-half years. It turns out both had a healthy disregard for mainstream films, meaning they met often to view these films and took every opportunity, after and sometimes during these screenings, to cement their ideological positions with and for each other.

'I may not be a die-hard Marxist,' Sita would say to Harry, 'but does every American commercial film have to be about capital?'

And Harry might respond, 'But I wonder if that film was about class at all? Didn't you think the gender and race representations were what the director was getting at?'

Their post-film sessions could run well past midnight on weekday evenings, and far beyond that on Friday and Saturday nights. Their first encounters, following that fateful aquarium day's coffee, were somewhat subdued as they checked each other out, wary that each one's individual politics or prejudices might be offensive or irregular to the other's. Fortunately, such was not the case, and while disagreements were prevalent, this only sparked lively debate and did, in no way, hinder their continued assignations.

Hindrances, however, were in their near future, for it was some time into this congenial relationship that Sita, having broken up with a previous boyfriend only three weeks before the Aquarium Day, finally embarked on a date with an acquaintance she had made through her line of work (which was, incidentally, a Granville Island architectural firm where Sita was a competent and compelling office manager).

'Let's go to a movie this Saturday,' Harry said to Sita, more as a weekend planning comment than a question. 'There's a premiere of that film shot in Calgary last year and I think we could get into an early show.'

'Omigod,' replied Sita. 'I forgot. I have a date this Saturday.'

'A date?' Harry traced a mental note back to the time he and Sita had met to ascertain that she had never had a date since they had met.

'Yah. A date.'

'With who?'

'This guy. A client at the office. Well, not exactly a client, but a tiling supplier.'

'A tile supplier. How'd you meet him?'

'Long story. He came by to meet up with one of the independent contractors who knows Bill. A bunch of us ended up going out for lunch.'

'And then he asked you out on a date?'

'No. That was two weeks ago. He called a couple of times to try to track Bill down. Then he came in on Friday and he and Bill had a coffee with me after their meeting. I guess he asked me out then.'

'And you said yes?'

'Yes, Harry, I said yes. I know, I haven't dated in a while. But he seems nice and maybe it's time, you know?'

'Yes, I guess.'

'What about you, Harry? How come you don't date?'

Harry laughed as if this was a very funny question. 'I don't know. I don't know. I guess I've never dated.'

'Never? You never told me that.'

'Didn't I? Sure I did. I told you about high school–'

'But that was high school.'

'Things haven't changed much since.'

'Oh, Harry, we really have to work on you.'

'So what are you going to do, on your date?'

'I hadn't thought. Maybe see a movie.'

Harry's face registered disappointment. Sita laughed, the same laugh of the Aquarium Day, the type of laugh one produces when a dog is sleeping and his paws are aquiver with dreams of rabbit-chasing.

'Oh, Harry, I won't see *that* movie, if that's what you're worried about. C'mon. Let's see that on Friday, okay? Then we can chat about the film and you can feed me interesting lines about what to say on Saturday on my "date," okay?'

Harry laughed. Yes, that was fine with him. So they saw the movie about Calgary on Friday and went out to the west end for coffee later and talked until they shut the shop down. They quickly exhausted the topic of the film, which they both enjoyed, and true to Sita's word moved onto the subject of her upcoming date.

'You should wear something more revealing, Sita.'

'I don't want to look like a slut.'

'Nothing slut-like. But something that gives a hint of breasts.'

'Hint of breasts? Sounds like a perfume.'

'Or a made-for-TV movie. But really, something casual that has skin involved, that's what you need.'

'Are you trying to get me laid?'

Again, Harry laughed. 'Not at all. Just something to keep him interested.'

It was Sita's turn to laugh at the insult. 'So, you think I'm not interesting enough?'

'Ah, for me, yes. But we're intellectually compatible. What if he likes watching football? What will you talk about?'

'If we can't talk like you and I talk, then why would I want to keep him interested in my body?'

'Good question. Maybe you'll be interested in his body?'

'Good point. Harry, when was the last time you had sex?'

'Geez. I think it was two years ago. Yeah, two years.'

'Two years? Gawd. I thought I was out of practice at eight months. Two years. Was it on a date?'

'I told you. I don't date, never have. It was a friend – from high school actually, so maybe that qualifies as a high school romance, except she was the sister of a friend. Anyway, it didn't last long.'

Sita looked at Harry, then past him at the window of the coffee shop, then back at him. 'Well, I don't know if this will turn into sex. I don't know if I want it to.'

'Well, do let me know.' And Harry smiled.

☾

Yes, yes, this all sounds like a smouldering romance between Harry and Sita, but I kid you not, nothing of the sort was bound to happen. I say this now because what happens next in this narrative is going to make you say, oh come on, this has got to be a budding romance between H and S, let me flip a couple of pages and find the sex scenes. But, no, I swear, you can flip all you like. Despite what happens next the two of them, Sita and Harry, Harry and Sita, do not engage in any sort of naked extravagance, even as much as you, perhaps even I, might wish.

On that Saturday night, Harry made himself a big bowl of popcorn, the gourmet variety that you make on a stovetop, none of this hot air or microwave stuff for Harry. He had stopped for some noodles on the way back from a dogwalk on the beach, so he was only a bit peckish as he put an extra handful of popcorn into the now-steaming layer of oil in the stovetop pot. Han waited expectantly, not because he particularly liked popcorn, except for the ever-present salt that Harry added to it, just that, as a dog, he felt it was his role to sit and wait. Table scraps and tossed offerings were a way of life, a type of routine that Han and Harry had settled into soon after the two of them became housemates. Harry spun the freshly popped popcorn in a metal bowl and flicked two kernel fragments onto the floor. One made it to the linoleum, the other was seized mid-fall by the waiting Han. The other piece had bounced only twice, fluffily, on the kitchen floor before Han had scooped it up, fulfilling his duty by actually chewing three times and gulping down the warm flakes, one of them getting lodged in his throat causing him to gag and hack for about ten seconds before Harry called his name, shifting Han's attention and thereby allowing the offending kernel to slide down his throat. Harry shook his head at his animal companion and headed off to the living room. He was half-way through his pirated copy of *Casablanca*, just at the part where the Nazis shoot the slimy character played by Peter Lorre in the back, bang bang, when ding-dong, the doorbell rang. Harry looked at the clock on his VCR. It flashed at twelve. He hit the display button on his television to find it was actually twenty-two minutes later than his VCR was flashingly informing him.

'Who could that be?' Harry asked Han.

Han ducked his head, blinked, and licked his lips, apparently hearing an offer of food in Harry's voice.

Harry hit the stop button on his VCR and watched a too-loud music video fill the screen. Han growled at the intruding musician on the television screen and was satisfied he had warned the stranger off when Harry hit the mute button and asked again, 'Wonder who that is?' and lifted himself off the couch to make his way to the front door. Living in a particularly safe neighbourhood and never one to frighten himself unnecessarily, Harry was perfectly content to unlock the door and swing it open without checking the peephole.

It was Sita.

'Sita.'

'Hi, Harry.'

Sita waltzed in without asking. She was wearing a black dress, by no means low cut at the breast, but somewhat more revealing than what she usually wore, and Harry smiled to himself that Sita had, after all, taken his advice.

'Smells like popcorn. Any left?'

Harry gestured toward the living room. Sita left him to close the door and headed for the couch and popcorn bowl. 'Hiya, Han. Save some for me, guy?'

Han wagged his tail, stretched slowly, and burped before a quick lick hello.

Harry locked up and followed Sita in. He sat beside her.

'How was the date?'

Sita had hit the play button and was watching Peter Lorre die in front of Humphrey Bogart. '*Casablanca*? Saturday night and you're watching *Casablanca* with a bowl of popcorn and your dog?'

Han wagged his tail again. As with the previous utterance from Harry, Han again heard the offer of food in Sita's voice, plus he always associated the sound of 'dog' with the oft-appended adjective 'good' preceding it, which frequently resulted in a cookie.

'You're a sad case, Harry.' Sita filled her mouth with popcorn.

Han, suddenly inspired with a play prospect, stuck his snout under the couch and emerged with a blue rubber ring which he proceeded to deposit in Sita's lap.

'You too, Han,' said Sita, and she took the ring with her left hand and fired it down the corridor where Han pursued it until his feet gave out from under him and he rolled across the hardwood floor into an umbrella Harry had left carelessly against the wall. The offending umbrella landed on Han's head and he yelped, glared at the attacking instrument, then decided his left hind foot was in dire need of licking.

Harry continued to look at Sita who was smiling and shaking her head at Han's antics.

'The date,' she said finally. 'The date was fine. Ended a bit early, I guess. What time is it?' She repeated Harry's action of hitting the display button. 'Well, not that early for a first date, I guess.'

'So, what was he like?'

'Ah, it was okay. He's funny, you know, made me laugh. Cute, too.'

'But no sex?'

Sita swallowed her mouthful of popcorn. 'Nah.'

'Not tonight, or not ever?'

'I dunno. I'll see I guess.'

Harry nodded affably. Sita licked an errant popcorn fleck from her lip.

'Hey, Harry? Will you kiss me?'

☾

There are, essentially, three major elements involved in kissing: the lips, the teeth, the tongue. A less important element, but important not to forget, is the nose. When Harry was in grade six, the homeroom teacher was encouraging the class to think quickly and critically. Mr Southam, whom the students had nicknamed 'Southpaw' for no other reason than students like to nickname teachers, had given the students an assignment: each one would come to the front of the class, stand before her or his peers, and Southpaw would give that student a topic. Said student would have to talk, without pause, on this topic for thirty seconds to win a prize. This was the cause of much mirth and some embarrassment for the students, but it did get them to think on their feet, so in the end, Harry supposed, it was all worth it. He remembered one girl, Connie, the sexiest and sultriest girl in the classroom, who had stood in front of the class only to be absolutely stymied by Southpaw's topic for her which was, as it turned out, to talk about 'How to Kiss without Getting your Nose in the Way.' Poor Connie had hidden her blushing cheek in her hand, then giggled, then hidden her entire face behind spread fingers, then giggled and looked away, then looked at Southpaw, giggled some more, and then finally at the class. She found herself utterly powerless to begin her topic and the smiling Southpaw (who two years later, Harry remembered hearing, was summarily dismissed by the schoolboard for some unnamed but inappropriate action involving a teenage girl at the local high school, giving new resonance to his accidental nickname) took pity on Connie and let her choose another topic. Nonetheless, since that time Harry had often wondered about that subject, How to Kiss without Getting your Nose in the Way, and that grade six incident would always catapult to the front of his mind anytime he ever saw a stage or screen kiss and watched as the primary actors tilted their heads to one side or the other to kiss without getting their noses in the way. And it was this that Harry began thinking about when Sita asked, 'Harry, will you kiss me?'

Once past the nose, or, rather, the thought of the nose as obstacle, Harry began to reflect on the role of the lips, the teeth, the tongue, in the role of kissing. He looked at Sita. She looked at him. He was about to ask her why she had asked him, apparently out of nowhere, such a question, surmising it had something, of course, to do with her date, but he was so perplexed that he just continued to look at her. One might say he was in a bit of a dream-state, but not paralyzed, when Sita moved a surprisingly soft and gentle brown hand to his chin and cheek, turning his face ever so slightly so as to move his nose out of the way, and leaned in to press her lips to his. Harry felt the impression of her teeth pressing against his lips as well, and he felt her tiny tongue enter between his lips and swiftly explore his upper right incisor before contacting his own retracted but willing tongue. It was a short kiss, by any measure, and it was deep or intense by no means, yet it was an affirming and wondrous kiss for both of them. When Sita retreated a moment later and her eyelashes brushed Harry's eyebrow, Harry realized that he had not, as was more or less expected during such intimate activity, closed his eyes to enjoy the kiss but, rather, had stared unfocussed at Sita's left ear, noting with some surprise that she was wearing a pair of earrings (or at least one) that looked somewhat like a lost member from the childhood game Harry remembered as Barrel of Monkeys.

After the kiss, Sita and Harry looked at each other. Sita's hand slipped from his cheek and fell lightly on his hand before withdrawing to her lap. Harry continued to look at Sita even after she, in a moment of shyness perhaps, turned to watch Humphrey Bogart sipping bourbon.

((

Okay, all right, yes, this has all the makings of not just a love story, but a serious romantic interlude, and if I had more time, perhaps we could even go there. However, and I hate to repeat myself, but I feel that I must, when I say that despite this not altogether dispassionate meeting of lips, Harry and Sita did not strike up a hot and bothered relationship, either that evening or in that immediate future. But here I go, alluding to the future of this narrative when I should be concerning myself with the present. Sita smiled as she watched the classic film and, without looking at Harry, explained that as she was now dating, apparently, and since she was so close to Harry, she just wanted to see what it would be like to kiss. More precisely, she noted, she wanted to see what it would be like if *they*, Harry and Sita, kissed. And now that they had, she knew. Harry was mute and apparently unfazed, although his mind returned to that incident many times in the next few weeks, weeks that turned out to be more than a little tumultuous for Harry Kumar.

Athnic Long

Athnic Long was the sort of fellow who instantly took over a room. It wasn't that he was vain, or loud, or obnoxious in even that faintly boyish way; rather, it was Athnic's effusion. Athnic effused energy, excitement, anticipation, and it all came through in such a way that entire rooms full of people would stare at him, rapt, waiting for the next smile or nod or winkish utterance that came from Athnic Long. This was not something that Athnic understood, but then neither did he not understand, since what is there to understand? If you have always been treated a certain way, such a way normalizes itself so much so that not being treated in that way, however unique or aberrant that might be for someone else, you would think to be an odd treatment. So Athnic expected to take over a room, much as a cab driver expects to get behind the wheel and would find herself baffled if a fare were to sidle a foot over to clutch in, or a short-order cook expects to be the one behind the grill flipping bacon and squashing it between slices of toasted bread and would be utterly dismayed if he were to find a customer, clad in business togs for instance, busying himself away behind the greasy hotplate, looking for the salt or a tad of mustard. There is a place for everything and everyone in a place, so the saying sort of goes, and Athnic's was as a leader and manager and effusive taker-over, all in a good and natural way and not anything at all nasty about it.

Athnic was the sort of person people would ask for the time, even if they had already determined Athnic wore no watch (as he never did) and even if five other people in the room wore watches and even if there was a clock as big as a harvest moon positioned roundly over the door. Not only that, but Athnic would never say, should such people ask him the time, that he wore no watch, or that he didn't know, for Athnic was a helpful and gregarious sort and he would immediately go about determining that time, whether it was by looking up at the obvious wall clock or by reading someone's watch upside-down (and at such times no watch-wearer would ever volunteer the time either to Athnic or the time-asker, but might proffer a wrist supine-like, pulling a cuff back furtively perhaps, knowing, the watch-wearer that is, that this was her or his lot in life, to allow Athnic to read the hour so he could turn to tell, helpfully, the time-asker, what said person had asked for). So, this was the sort of attention Athnic garnered, even whilst he had no idea no others garnered such attention, at least not while he was in the room.

It should come as no surprise, therefore, that Athnic would always find himself in various leader-like or, at the very least, public roles and occupations. When he was twelve, on his first summer job, Athnic was a newspaper boy, like so many others, except he took it upon himself to not just deliver and sell the news, but to *deliver and sell* the news. His delivery route began at four-thirty in the afternoon, this being at a time when there actually were afternoon newspapers and people could wait until they made it home from their working- or middle-class jobs to find out what had happened the morning or night before and what was planned for the next little while. So, with a route that began at four-thirty, one might expect Athnic to show up, as did his peers, at four-twenty-five, pick up his bundles, toss them into a red pull-wagon, and shove off down the road, completing the route in forty-five minutes. No, Athnic would show up at four PM sharp, and before bundling his load, neatly took the top copy and began reading from the top left of the front page all the way down to the bottom right, a process he repeated on page three and then page two (having been taught that the important news was always on three before two) and so on until his colleagues rolled up at four-twenty-five, at which time Athnic would follow their lead. Then, Athnic would take at least ninety minutes to complete his route because, unlike his counterparts who couldn't wait to get home, play some street hockey or watch TV, Athnic would make small talk, make conversation, with all the customers on his route, not because he was naturally talkative but because, even at the tender age of twelve, people just wanted to engage him since he seemed so energized as he crossed their yards.

The reason Athnic read the newspaper so thoroughly was that the common refrain he heard as he delivered papers door to door was, 'Hey Athnic, what's up,' a greeting that referred to his general state of well-being, but Athnic, always wanting to help in any way he could, took this to mean folks were interested in their newspaper boy as a bearer of news in more than one way, and so Athnic would reply, 'Hey Mrs Tinker, looks like the Watson bigamy trial resulted in a hung jury,' or 'Hi Mr Kersky, weather system moving in, might want to cover up those begonias,' or 'Yo Nancy, pretty scummy editorial advocating more cuts to pensioners,' which, if this all sounds quite mature for a twelve-year-old, well, that's because Athnic took it upon himself never to sound like a boyish boy, and while he took care not to appear pretentious, well, all that newspaper reading (and he was well-read in literature and history, too, or at least better read than his peers) took its toll and made him quite an interesting and engaging lad, meaning, of course, that his route customers found themselves making all sorts of excuses to be outside to collect the paper from him when he came by because, my, that Athnic boy was quite an intelligent fellow.

Perhaps all this interest in the news would have led another to become a journalist or a writer or a teacher of literature, but Athnic's career was not to be so. He kept that paper route until the age of fifteen, at which time he left to take a job at the Quality Inn, a quaint if unpretentious establishment in the very heart of the city which was to remain his place of employment until he turned thirty-seven when he, fully uniformed and pleasantly unaware of the bus bearing down at him at breakneck speed, stepped in front of the oncoming vehicle and was summarily struck dead directly in front of the hotel. Even at that culminative point of his life, interestingly enough, there was a minor squabble, when two paramedics approached his energy-ebbing body, about who would address the dying man first, and the winning paramedic found that Athnic, gravely wounded and obviously not to survive the trip to the hospital, was still at his finest form, nodding casually to the paramedic and causing the latter to ask the fallen man, quite genuinely, how he felt, to which Athnic responded, 'Not well, not well at all I'm afraid,' and then nodded again before expiring, leaving both paramedics with a certain sense of loss that they had never felt before.

However, it was while Athnic was very much alive and fully employed as the senior concierge at the Quality Inn, a position that had been awarded him at the incredible age of twenty-two, a promotion that might have made him the subject of some jealousy amongst his older colleagues had they not all admired the young Athnic quite considerably, that Athnic first made the acquaintance of Harry Kumar.

The circumstances of their meeting were curious, and while not critical to the telling of this story, interesting enough and with some bearing on this narrative that it is worth relaying such details here. Their first encounter was on Athnic's thirty-third birthday, some four-and-a-half years before his untimely death, when Harry chanced upon the Quality Inn while looking for a discount furniture store from which he wished to acquire more bookshelves, as his apartment was being overrun by the volumes of pulp literature that Harry kept lugging home. Sita had told him that this particular store produced some exquisite bookshelves at a reasonable price and its only downside was that the store was two bus connections away from where Harry lived. So, on this particular Saturday, Harry rose early, had his morning coffee, read the newspaper and finished off his latest pulp thriller, then took himself off to catch the Granville bus. He made his connection without too much difficulty and got off at the proper cross street, but was baffled when he could see no furniture store in the vicinity. And this is what drew Harry into the Quality Inn, for it was precisely at the place where Sita had described the furniture store.

He entered the hotel and looked around for someone to ask. The clerks were all quite busy, it being check-out time for the businessmen who had overstayed their Friday business dinner welcome, and Harry would have walked out if not for the soft voice to the left and rear of him which said, 'Can I help you with something, sir?' Harry turned and saw the uniformed Athnic smiling pleasantly, and Harry shared with Athnic his dilemma. Athnic smiled knowingly and explained that it was a common mistake, for the furniture store was indeed on this avenue but at a cross-street with a distinctly similar name about twelve blocks up the road. Harry thanked Athnic for that information and Athnic said, profusely, that Harry was very welcome. Then the two men stared at each other a moment longer and Harry finally said what Athnic was thinking, which was, 'I think I've met you somewhere before.' Athnic, of course, nodded in agreement and lifted an eyebrow in a way that so many of his friends found to be extraordinarily fetching, and both men struggled with their memories to find a common previous encounter. But neither could, not that they didn't battle with the problem for several minutes, until one of Athnic's bellboys passed by and nodded to Athnic as well as to Harry, passed them both by, then turned and asked, curiously, 'Hey Athnic, is this your brother?' To which Athnic responded, 'No, I have no brother,' but then he and Harry stared back at each other and realized their familial resemblance was exactly why they thought they had seen each other before.

No, they were hardly *doppelgängers*, mirror images, identical twins, but their eyes and lips (and to a lesser extent their noses and cheeks) made for a striking and siblingly connection indeed. Of course, Athnic, from good British, Irish, and Germanic stock, was somewhat lighter complexioned than Harry who carried, according to his late father, 'a pitiful haunting hint of your dusty and supercilious homeland.' Nevertheless, they could have been brothers and they both laughed at their foolishness at not recognizing this before. At this juncture, Harry bid Athnic goodbye on his search for the elusive furniture store, but, somewhat uncharacteristically, suggested he and Athnic get together later for a drink to discuss possible similar parentages. This, of course, was a joke, and Athnic laughed with Harry, but clearly both were struck by one another's presence and so, of course, Athnic accepted Harry's invitation. Thus, later that day, after Harry had purchased a five-shelf unit made of pine and set-up delivery instructions, Harry walked back to the Quality Inn and found Athnic getting off shift, just as he had promised Harry he would at that particular time, and off the two erstwhile brothers went to have a coffee, it still being too early in the day for a drink, and that was the beginning of a quaint friendship.

(

Harry and Athnic met frequently after that, usually once a week, to discuss their lives, their problems, their situations. In Harry, Athnic found someone who didn't treat him as an object of leaderly desire; and in Athnic, Harry found someone who listened with concern and offered practiced advice, even if he did find his new-found friend a bit mysterious, almost as if Athnic knew way more about the world than he let on, as if withholding deep, dark secrets. Still, it was a mutually beneficial friendship. Harry would talk about his go-nowhere career at the credit union, how no one seemed to notice him and while that was all fine and good, he longed for some sort of excitement, unwilling as he was to incite it; and Athnic would talk about how well-respected he seemed to be at the hotel, but that upper management was now pressuring him to transfer to the east, to take on managerial positions that would befit his talent, to leave behind his bell captain routine at which he excelled but which was truly beneath him. Looking at them together, two young men with similar facial features and body types, a casual observer would think they were well-matched colleagues; listening to them and their various woes and achievements, a casual listener would wonder what in heaven's name an up-and-rising-star like Athnic was doing with a – well – loser like Harry. But if a truly effective eavesdropper were to nurse a gin and tonic at the table next to the unlikely pair, such a covert ear would hear how absolutely and marvellously compatible the two were. Who better, after all, for a wallflower like Harry to share his stories with than the ebullient Athnic? And who could listen with more favour to the immensely likeable Athnic than the, let's say it, dull and what-was-that-you-said-sir Harry? A match made in some cosmological space, to be sure.

(

It is at one of their weekly sessions, this being long after Harry has spent enough time with both Sita and Athnic to consider them to be his dearest, indeed only, friends, that Harry confides in Athnic. This, however, he does not do without prodding.

'Okay, why the brood?' asks Athnic.

'What do you mean?' asks Harry, his gaze drifting back from the coffee shop window and onto Athnic.

'You're in one of those broods you get into,' explains Athnic. 'One of those spaces where nothing exists outside your own head. I could be swinging by my tail from a chandelier for all you'd notice.'

'Really?' says Harry, surprised and completely missing his friend's hyperbole. 'I didn't realize it was so obvious.'

Athnic smiles and nods. 'So?'

'So. Sita kissed me two nights ago,' Harry says as he takes a sip from his double espresso.

'You dog,' Athnic smiles from the rim of his latte.

'No, you don't get it. I mean, she had a date and then she came over later and she kissed me.'

'Oh, I get it. You dog.'

'But Athnic, we don't have that sort of – I dunno. We just don't.'

'But you like her.'

'Yeah, yeah, of course, I mean she's my best and closest friend.'

'Oh no, you're not going to get into that bit about how you see her as only a friend, are you?'

'No, I don't think so. I mean, I just never thought…. What would you do? I mean, you've had lots of girlfriends, right?'

'I've had girlfriends, but I wouldn't say lots.'

'But women love you. I've seen it. I mean, guys do too. Everyone loves you.'

Athnic smiles at this truism, but he is embarrassed by his friend's excessive compliment. Harry takes Athnic's silence as complicity and continues.

'I mean, should I go out on a date with Sita now or what? Hell, we can't really start doing that since we're always going out to movies and such. How would we start dating from that? And anyway, I'm not sure I want that. I can't do that.'

'Well, this is radical advice, but what does Sita say?'

'I don't know. I called her yesterday 'cause we were supposed to see a movie, but she said she had a cold and didn't want to go out.'

'She's avoiding it then? Or you?'

'No, I don't think so. She did invite me to drop by, but said she was going to hit the hay early.'

'And you went?'

'No. She said she didn't need anything, had made herself some soup, which is what I would've done for her, and then I figured why go over if she's tired and sick and wants to sleep anyway.'

'Hm. Sounds like you were avoiding the first post-game analysis then.'

Harry looks confused. He always looks confused when Athnic uses sports analogies for real life. Harry never watches sports on TV, nor does he play them. In fact, his only connection to sports is the bad memories associated with junior high school softball games. He is certain he went up to bat more than thirty times in grade eight and struck out every single one of those times. Finally, Athnic notices his friend's befuddlement and helps him out.

'I mean the kiss. You don't want to talk about it with her, do you?'

'Hm. I guess so. I mean, I guess not.'

Harry downs his espresso and considers ordering another. He thinks about Sita and her warm lips pressed against his. He wonders why he doesn't feel anything at all in particular, and that, truthfully, is what worries him most. If he felt excited, if he felt betrayed, if he felt jittery or otherwise nervous as he was wont to feel with any other personal matters, then he would be a bit more himself. But he truly was at a loss. He didn't know why Sita had kissed him. He didn't know if he liked it, disliked it, or if it didn't even register on his like-o-meter. Harry sighs.

'Perhaps you're right, Athnic. Maybe I just have to talk to her. But I don't even feel like we need to talk about anything. It's just like, it was and it is, you know?'

Now it is Athnic's turn to be confused. He was quite a master of sports metaphors, but when it came to vague philosophical statements, Athnic, who could thrust and parry wittily with the best of the cocktail set, was at a loss for words. He always felt that philosophical language, however appended it might be with question marks, always cul-de-sac-ed a conversation. At least it did with him. Even during his delivery route, where he could engage just about anyone on just about every topic, he had no good retort for the good-natured soul who would ask him, almost in jest, about the meaning of life, or whether god existed, or if people had a will-to-power, that sort of thing. So, Athnic takes another sip of his latte and stares across the table at his brotherly friend. Then, but only for a moment, the light flickers – Harry thinks this is a momentary energy loss in the restaurant, Athnic thinks a passing truck has briefly eclipsed the street-front window, but to the barista standing at the counter ten feet away, it is clear that the flickering light emanates from behind Athnic's eyes, from that place where consciousness resides. And, as the barista polishes a glass mug, she wonders if such flickering might indicate a transmigration of souls, although it is a thought that is quickly forgotten and replaced with an overriding desire to clean a calcium spot on the mug's rim.

Athnic looks up from his coffee and looks at Harry from a faraway place.

'Just ask her. And remember to trust in what she says, okay?'

Harry shrugs. Okay. This is an odd statement coming from Athnic, but okay. And he thinks of the lingering taste of coffee on his lips and the softness of another's tongue on his own.

the rep cinema

Harry waits outside the rep cinema, waits for Sita to arrive, waits for something intelligent-sounding to pop into his brain to edge out current thoughts that tell him to leave immediately and feign illness as a later excuse. But Harry continues to wait. He checks his watch. It is six forty-two and the film begins at seven. He and Sita agreed to meet at ten to seven and he knows she will be ten minutes later than that so he has eighteen minutes to wait. For the next fourteen minutes he will worry about what he is going to say to Sita after the film, and then for the four minutes after that he will worry that Sita will not show because she has forgotten to come, or has been in a horrific traffic accident, or has been kidnapped by an evil villain. Harry entertains himself with these negative thoughts, partly because he thrives on an overly active imagination to balance out his self-acknowledged overly dull real life, and partly because he is superstitious enough to believe that if he thinks of all the bad things that could happen in all their possible permutations, then not being one who is given to accurate predictions, none of these bad things will occur.

At six forty-seven it begins to rain, the type of big-drop Vancouver rain that happens sometimes, the type where if you look skyward it doesn't look like it's raining that much because so few drops seem to be coming down, but because the drops are so large you only have to be hit by a few to become drenched. Harry feels the first three drops hit the crown of his head, his left shoulder, and his right sneaker toe. His head feels like he has stuck it under a running tap, his windbreaker shoulder is shiny and already sticking to his skin, and his right toe feels moist inside its canvas surroundings. Harry looks skyward as Vancouverites are not wont to do, that action owing to exactly what happens next, which is that a huge raindrop, one of the biggest of the big-drop Vancouver raindrops, hits him right in the centre of the pupil of his left eye. Not off to the centre so that it washes into a tear duct, not a few degrees higher so that it is partly deflected by Harry's long, curly eyelashes, but square on the pupil, splashing there and spreading out across the iris, the sclera, the entire eyeball, creating a little wave pattern that washes up against the surrounding skin and then ebbs back toward the centre of Harry's left eye.

'Damn,' says Harry, abruptly averting his gaze from the sky and blinking profusely to shake loose the water from his eyeball. He takes a step back under the protective awning of the rep theatre and continues to blink and curse, although now he is not doing so aloud.

'Hey, Hari,' comes the call from his right. He turns to see, out of one eye, the slight figure of Gopal, the box office manager, leaning outside the booth. 'Aré Hari, have you no sense to stand out of the rain?' And Gopal, who knows Harry from his frequent visits to the theatre to take in subtitled Italian, French, Hindi, and Spanish films, cackles in his trademark laugh that many of his friends try to emulate because it is so startlingly different and characteristically Gopalian. Gopal is a bit like Athnic that way in that people want to like him and want to be liked by him, but Gopal is quite a small man and unimposing in a myriad of ways, so *unlike* Athnic that he is often overlooked in a crowd or even in a small room. None of this bothers Gopal, since he doesn't need to be noticed and has enough to do anyway without being inundated with requests for friendship, or the time, or what have you.

Harry laughs in return and moves closer to the booth, still trying to wring water from his left eye. 'Hey, Gopal. No, guess I've never learned the knack of staying dry.'

'Who you waiting for?' Gopal asks, making conversation, since most of his clientele has already arrived in that set who demand getting their popcorn-drinks-candy and seat themselves before the trailers start and even before the cinema lights are dimmed, or will be arriving between seven and seven-oh-four in that set who just want to make it for the feature and don't mind struggling to their seats in the dark.

'Uh, Sita,' Harry says, now wiping his eye with a shirtsleeve protruding from under his windbreaker.

'Oh, hey Hari, almost forgot. Cindy was working the afternoon shift and said someone called for you, a Vera somebody?'

Harry looks blankly back at Gopal. 'I don't know any Vera.'

'Just a second,' says Gopal, looking under the counter for the message Cindy has written out. 'No, my mistake. That's a last name, Varre. There's an initial here, looks like an A. Do you know an A. Varre?'

Harry thinks for a moment. Not only does he not know anyone by that name but he is entirely unsure how anyone would think to call him at the cinema. Why not call him at home? 'No,' he finally says. 'Man or woman?'

Gopal looks down at the note again. 'Don't know. Thought it was a woman but that was when I was reading "Vera." Think Cindy just said you had a call and that she'd written it down. I'll ask her tomorrow if you want.'

'Thanks,' says Harry and blinks a few times with both eyes to check out his vision. 'Probably not important.'

'What's not important?' asks Sita, who has just come in behind Harry, holding a magazine above her head to keep dry.

'Sita. Hi. Nothing, someone tried to reach me at the box office is all.'

'At the box office? You moonlighting? Who was it?'

'No idea. Um, you want to go in?'

'Actually, I was thinking, you wanna grab a bite to eat and see the later show?'

'Sure, that's good,' says Harry, although it's really not okay with him because, while he did want to sit Sita down and talk to her, he had hoped to make his conversational plans during the film and now it looked like he would have to think on his feet, something he was neither keen on trying nor competent at doing. 'Sounds like a great idea.'

Sita orders a bean dip and an order of chicken wings along with a dark beer; Harry decides on a spinach salad and a glass of red wine. It is an unspoken understanding that he will have two or three wings even though he tries to maintain a relatively meat-free diet and that Sita will supplement her dip with a few healthy forkfuls of spinach salad. This is their routine.

Harry takes a deep breath.

'Sita, about the other night–'

'Uh-oh,' says Sita.

'What?'

'Nothing. Just that, well, just that I thought you wouldn't bring that up.'

'Why not?'

'Um, 'cause you don't usually bring things like that up, is all.'

'I see,' says Harry, nodding.

'Anyway, go ahead.'

'Okay. About the other night, it got me thinking.'

'Okay, okay, okay. I know this conversation. We're friends and maybe I transgressed some boundaries or asked you to and you're wondering where all this is going, whether we need to talk about our current relationship, our friendship, and what we want to see out of it, where we want it to go, is that it? Well, good, I think we should talk about it, but Harry, don't expect any answers from me because, well, I just don't know. I know that sounds lame, and believe me, this isn't my "let's stay just friends" speech because I don't even know if that's what I'm saying, but Harry – oh god, I'm sorry, I interrupted you just when you were starting. But that was what you were thinking, wasn't it?'

'Well,' begins Harry. 'Actually not.'

'No?'

'Well, not entirely. I mean, yes, relationships and all, I guess we can talk about that, but what I was going to say, I mean, what I am saying here, is that I wanted to talk to you about me.'

Sita smiles. 'This isn't always about you, you know.'

Now Harry smiles. 'You know that's not what I mean.'

'So, what do you mean exactly, or even approximately?' Sita is now smiling her relaxed smile, putting Harry at ease, and he realizes the two of them really do share a comfort level that he has never experienced before. Momentarily he is driven to distraction, thinking about the possibility of a romantic liaison with Sita, spending time together in the way that lovers do, not making love, although that is part of it that Harry will not allow himself to think about right now, but the way lovers, partners, hold hands or talk to each other in restaurants, or have that particular look in their eyes that doesn't signify starstruck love but something else, compatibility perhaps, and then Harry realizes that what he is imagining is pretty much what Sita and he already have, that intimacy, that old-souls-together togetherness.

'What I mean, Sita, after that – the other night, I think I have to change.'

'Change, like in what way?'

'I don't know, in every way. I think I have to change the way I think, the way I am with people, the way I do things, the things I like. You know, cosmic change.'

'Wow,' says Sita. 'I've been told I'm a good kisser, but this is quite a response.'

'Oh, Sita, you know it's not just that. I mean maybe that got me thinking, but look, I'm thirty-five years old, I have no family since Mum died six years ago, I work as a nondescript teller at a nondescript credit union, I never travel anywhere, I don't have a lot of friends – I mean there's you and Athnic, but even there, I'm not like you or Athnic, you guys have lots of friends and do lots of things. I'm just – I'm just Harry Kumar, an ordinary guy who holds out promise to do ordinary things for the rest of his ordinary life. And I just realized that I despise ordinary.'

'I don't think you're ordinary.'

'But you're just being nice. I guess that kiss, you know, I mean I wasn't the guy who moves and shakes things and meets you on Granville Island and invites you out on a date. I wasn't even the one who even thought about kissing you, or even thought about not kissing you. I just don't know. And Athnic, he says I should trust in what you say, whatever that means.'

'Harry, I think you need a vacation.'

'Yeah, a vacation. Sure. I need a life from which to vacation.'

'Um, maybe you could go away. Hey, maybe I can arrange to get the same time off, what do you think?'

Before Harry can answer, Sita's cell phone rings. She doesn't move to answer it.

'Don't you want to get that?'

'Nah, I'll check the message later.'

'You sure?'

'Yeah,' Sita says, taking the cell phone from her bag and looking at its face. 'Don't know the number anyway. So, what do you think. Maybe we could go down to California. Hey, maybe we could visit my dad. He'd like to meet you.'

'Well, I don't know. Thing is, I don't even know if I like to travel. I mean that's part of the problem. You'd think at thirty-five I'd know whether I liked to travel or not, hey?'

Sita's phone makes an angry beep, suggesting a message and causing them both to look at it. Sita picks it up and sighs. 'Well, Harry, I think if you're feeling this way you need a change and maybe travelling isn't such a bad idea.' She looks at the face of the phone again. 'Odd,' she says. 'It's a text message – for you.' She passes the phone to Harry. Harry reads the message on the glowing green face:

```
4 H. KUMAR FRM A. VARRE
   YOU WILL FIND HER ON AN ISLAND
```

Harry passes the phone back to Sita and she reads the message again. 'Who's A. Varre?' Sita asks. 'And who's on an island?'

Harry shakes his head. He has no idea.

madam, I'm Anna

Okay, okay, okay, ya got me. Maybe there is something to be said about a romantic interlude between the now-trapped Sita and the soon-to-be-searching Harry. After all, how much more evidence do you need? Mysterious connection between the two, the sensuous Sita reflecting on this odd connection with her friend, Harry consulting with his peers about the next sacred steps to take, and all of this fitting oh-so-nicely into a modern-day romance. Boy meets girl, boy loses girl, boy seeks out girl, finds her, destroys evil on the way. If not a fairytale-storybook-loverslane novel, then at least a movie of the week. Stories of unjust separations and glorious reconnections, don't ya just love it? But what happens when separations don't give way to reconnections, what happens when the split parties wait years and years, decades, perhaps generations or centuries, for retribution, reconciliation?

Not all stories have happy endings, and perhaps this one doesn't either. Maybe that damned dog just keeps climbing after moonbeams and never does catch one in his teeth to bring home. Who has a right to swing on a star?

Not all stories are built on older stories, but most of them are, and this one is pretty much the rule to the exception, except the camera angle is a tad different, and maybe that forties diffusion gel has given way to something a bit cleaner, a bit pristiner, a look into the soul, so to speak. After all, if Bogart's pee-oh-vee was achieved from standing on a soapbox (from which he could deliver his sorry-assed maybe-tomorrows and other sad-sack lines), then think of this as a perspective attained by a quick Jet Li kick to the box boards, splintering the pedestal and bringing things back down to earth, a level playing field as they say. Or, think of such a martial kick as a destructive manoeuvre that always precedes a different kind of building up. Art deco arches give way to postmodern architecture, brick and concrete give way to glass and steel, water filtration plants of a particular ilk and politic and design give way to water filtration plants of a different ilk and politic and design, and the very words 'give way to' give way to more snug-fitting passives like 'are destroyed by.' Cycles are bi for a reason.

Sita's internal monologue

Sita had not gone to Harry's place after her date with the intention of kissing him. She didn't know what came over her and she certainly didn't want to give Harry the wrong impression. Trouble was, she wasn't sure what the right impression was. Harry was her closest friend, she realized, and what becomes of friends when they become lovers? Or what happens to the friendship when thoughts of intimacy, arguably always present, take precedence? Sita had gone to see Harry after her date because she wanted to debrief. Her date, Joshua, was a nice enough guy, but within the first five minutes Sita could tell it wasn't going to work out between them. No feeling in the pit of her stomach. She knew that was a ridiculous way to gauge relationships, but that's how it had always been for her. If she felt that feeling, that somewhat yucky but, really, not altogether unpleasant, dull thud in the pit of her stomach, she knew there might be some future with this particular person. It had been that way with every guy she had ended up romantically involved with. First meeting, introductions, then Sita would (or wouldn't) feel that stomach-pitty thing. Not that she always ended up connecting with those guys who gave her the stomach pit feeling. Often she would have a passing interest that was never fulfilled. However, it never worked the other way around. No pit, no relationship, plain and simple. That should tell her something, she thinks to herself, exactly thirty-six hours after she kissed Harry, that should tell her, since she never had the stomach-pit feeling when she met Harry.

Of course, she had been laughing too much to notice if the pit feeling was there, that creature, whatever it was, hurling peanuts into the back of Harry's head. But, no, she thinks, eating her lunch at her desk because it's her turn to watch the lunch-hour phones, Monday and Wednesday, her days to sit inside the office and speculate on her life, no, she never had that feeling with Harry. But she has had definite feelings. Same feelings, in a way, that she has had for her best friends at various times in her life. And she has never become involved, sexually or even remotely physically, with any of her best friends. There was that one time in her first year of high school that she had impulsively kissed her best friend, but that was different. She was so young then, she thinks, chewing her way through a spinach/sprouts/faux-ham on pumpernickel sandwich. So young. And now here she is, older, wondering why the pit of her stomach has not been active for such a long time. Joshua was fine as far as he went, a handsome media consultant who had turned to tile supplies when all the media outlets he used to consult for were bought out by the same petrochemical company. Joshua did not appear all that intelligent – not stupid by any means, just not possessing the wit and philosophical desire that Sita always found attractive. Like Harry, for instance. Whom she had kissed, with no premeditation, thirty-six hours and three minutes ago.

Sita is licking her lower lip and trying to remember that kiss when the phone rings. She lets it ring two times, three, four, before she has swallowed her mouthful and is in telephone-answering form.

'Good afternoon, Sita speaking,' she says into the receiver. She never answers with one of those pre-fab introductions that advertise the three-partnered name of the architectural firm. People who called the office knew who they were calling and if they didn't, Sita didn't mind if they felt mildly uncomfortable because they were usually canvassing in some way or another and Sita had no intention of making unsolicited callers feel unnecessarily welcome. Besides, all three partners really liked that she answered the phone with 'Sita speaking,' since their clients felt they were talking to a take-charge sort of office manager, not some temp who just arrived and who wasn't going to be there next week. Most of the firm's clients rather looked forward to talking to Sita since she knew exactly where everyone was, what they were doing, what sort of mood they might be in, everything a client might hope to know. But this time, it isn't an architectural client looking for a partner and when Sita answers the phone, all she hears, for several moments, is silence. But that is not what bothers her. What disturbs her is no sooner has she uttered her 'Good afternoon, Sita speaking' refrain than that feeling hits her, hard and immediate, no doubting its presence this time. That feeling in the gut, the pit of the stomach, so strong that Sita wonders if there can be such a thing as love at first cramp. After several moments, and after the initial shock of the stomach pit pain has dissipated, Sita speaks again.

'Hello? Is there anyone there?' Then, 'Harry...?'

A slow, deep chuckle comes across the line, across oceans and con-tinents, across eons and eras, over to mainlands from islands and through steamy geysers and roiling mud pits, enters into the phone line and is transmogrified into electronic signals recognizable only to fellow digital machines and by the decoding device that resides in the tele-phone receiver pressed up against Sita's ear, a chuckle that Sita identifies as androgynous, sinister, playful, and macabre, all in one, this low laugh that drifts smokily from the receiver and enters Sita's left ear, staying a while in the outer chamber before sliding deliciously over stirrup and cockle and tentatively vibrating an eardrum as delicate as moth's wings before finally, finally, transmitting its warmth and measure into the auditory section of Sita's temporal lobe.

Sita opens her mouth as if to speak, her mouth forming a round *O* and her breath, forced from her as if someone had playfully poked her diaphragm just hard enough to encourage a wisp of breath to backtrack up her throat and emerge over her teeth and tongue and out through her lips in a sound that is part gasp, part sigh, part exclamatory note of surprise, 'oh,' and all at once Sita sees her body floating between mainlands and islands, through roiling mud pits and steamy geysers, over continents and oceans, into past times and future possibilities. 'Oh.'

The voice whispers something into Sita's inner ear, completely bypassing the telephone receiver, and the whisper enters Sita's grey matter and explodes like a luminous dye throughout her temporal lobe, her cerebellum, her cortex, lights up her entire spinal column, and then dissipates as steam through her pores.

'Oh,' says Sita, her voice itself a whisper that does not fully exit her mouth but is blown back by atmospheric pressure into her lungs so she can hear herself half-whispering 'oh' as the sound makes waves through her abdominal cavity, through her liver and her pancreas and her sinewy heart muscle, and through the density of her bones. The chuckle emanates once again from the telephone receiver, this time whirling out like a miniature tornado, wrapping itself around Sita's skin, touching her all over in a whisper that tells of moist tropics and warm winds. Sita does not breathe, not because she can't, but because there seems no reason to, and the receiver remains held to her ear, not by her hand, but by the sheer draw of her body to that voice. And the tableau remains for a very, very long time, all through the next age and certainly to the end of lunch hour when Bill, the first partner to return from a seafood special on the wharf, walks into the office and sees, not Sita frozen in time with a telephone receiver pressed to her ear, but a simple if physically unnatural scene of a telephone receiver hanging in mid-air, positioned in such a way as to suggest it being cradled between someone's shoulder and ear, the receiver hanging this way in mid-air, no one around to hold the phone, and Bill stands there watching the levitating device and he can hear, or thinks he can hear, a slight breeze carrying the sound of what is either a cool mountain brook or an old man's phlegmatic chuckle, he can't tell which, and then Bill is part of the frozen scene until the sound and breeze abruptly stop and the telephone receiver drops with a force equivalent to the force of gravity, clattering upon Sita's desktop and scarring forever the maple top before bouncing onto the ceramic tiled floor and splitting its plastic casing.

'Sita?' calls Bill. And for a moment he remembers the odd levitational scene, but then it is gone. And for a moment, he remembers Sita coming to work this morning dressed in a long, flower-print skirt, but then that memory, too, is gone, and all Bill can seem to remember is that when he came to work today, Sita was not there.

Bill sits down to collect his thoughts, what remain of them. Was Sita here this morning, he wonders, then decides not. He picks up the cracked telephone receiver and looks at it. Did he drop it himself, he wonders, then decides not. He dials Sita's number at home and waits for the answering machine to pick up, which it does after eight rings, and Bill leaves a worried message. He looks around the office again and wonders what he should do next.

Harry's cell

'You're not being punished,' insists Daphne. Look, Mr Peabody even gave you an office – well, of sorts – to work on this.'

'I'm being punished, Daphne,' Harry explains patiently. 'Mr Peabody thinks I screwed up on "the floor" and now I'm being punished by being taken off the windows.'

Daphne is standing in front of Harry who sits at a medium-sized pine desk that Mr Peabody has stuffed into a closet of an office for Harry's express use. The room is exactly eight feet by six feet. Harry knows this because when Mr Peabody showed him to the office there was a maintenance worker kneeling along the north wall, measuring tape in hand and a pencil between his teeth.

'I don't know about this,' the maintenance worker had said to Mr Peabody. 'That desk is going to be a tight squeeze.'

'We'll make it work,' said a tight-lipped Mr Peabody.

'I don't know,' argued the maintenance man. 'Think you might need a smaller desk.' And he looked up at the north wall, back over to the east wall, and then down at the south wall before glancing up at Mr Peabody and Harry at the doorway on the west wall. 'That, or a bigger office.'

'Hm. Out of the question,' said Mr Peabody, although he had not meant to say that aloud.

'Whatever you say,' said the maintenance man. 'Say, maybe we can cut the desk in half or something.'

They did not have to cut the desk in half, but it did take two men the better part of half an hour to move the desk into the room, and while Mr Peabody would later insist the workers were scamming the credit union since they were being paid by the hour, Harry did point out that in order to fit the desk, they did have to rip the moulding off the south wall and they unintentionally broke the light fixture as they manipulated the desk through multiple geometric possibilities before sliding it into the office. Now, to get behind the desk, Harry had to shuffle by it on tiptoe, owing to the simple physiological nature of lower thighs being slightly thinner than upper thighs. Mr Peabody, Harry thought to himself, would never be able to see the view from Harry's side of the desk, since even Mr Peabody's lower thighs were, to say the least, of considerably more girth than Harry's upper thighs.

'Punished for what, though? Because one lousy client doesn't want to be served by you?' Daphne argues defensively from the doorway. That is the other problem with a medium-sized pine desk in a closet – visitors have to stand in the doorway.

Harry sighs but smiles at Daphne. 'I don't know. I guess. Anyway, Daphne, thanks for the coffee.'

'No problem,' says Daphne, smiling back. 'So hurry up and finish this thing Peabody has you doing so you can get back on "the floor" with us.' Then she leaves, shutting the door behind her, which always makes the room shudder a bit and hurts Harry's ears, presumably because the room is windowless and airtight and any time the door is shut, it changes the air pressure.

Harry stares at the computer screen. He is sure if the large-lipped woman were to return to the credit union and see him in this office, however pitifully small it might be, she would believe her prediction had come true, that Harry had been promoted because that's what happened to male tellers. But Mr Peabody had been quite clear on this when he called Harry into his office for the first time in Harry's career at the credit union.

'Kumar,' he had said, 'I think you need a change of pace. You've been working a wicket for what, three, four years now...?'

'Six,' said Harry, not meaning to interrupt, but after all, this was a credit union and it was his job to keep accurate tallies.

'Six? Are you sure? Not five maybe?'

'No sir,' Harry had said. 'Six.'

'Well then, even more of a reason for a change. Kumar, you've probably noticed the push head office has for technology.'

Harry had said nothing, but managed to glance up to his left where camera no. 5 was pointing toward the main wickets.

'Yes, technology is the buzzword of the day, the year, really, Kumar. And I've been thinking. We spend all this time writing memos, entering figures into computers, writing receipts and correspondence, and I thought – it's my initiative, really, and while I haven't shared this with head office, I'm sure they'll approve – wouldn't it be easier if we could just dictate this information and have it written for us?'

Mr Peabody beamed at Harry. Harry, who realized this involved him in some unpleasant way, managed a thin smile.

'Excellent,' Mr Peabody had remarked, slamming his hand down on the desk and leaping up from his chair. 'Come with me, Kumar. Remember, this is only a temporary assignment, just until you work the bugs out of the system. It's called *voice recognition* software and I've found the perfect package for us,' he had said, walking out of the room and indicating to Harry that he should follow. 'Now you wouldn't believe how expensive some of these software packages are, but I looked around and found one that I think will suit our needs more than adequately.' Such euphemistic language indicated to Harry that Mr Peabody had purchased, probably through discretionary funds so that if the project worked he could take full credit and if it failed he could write it off as sundry expenses, a piece of software likely not worth the CD it was burned upon. 'And you, Kumar, you're the man who will test it out for us.'

'Um, Mr Peabody, shouldn't that be for someone with computer knowledge? I mean, a software technician or something?'

'Ha, nonsense. We can do this ourselves. Fully staffed, no one on vacation for three weeks. Called effective use and distribution of manpower. Besides, those computer geeks charge an arm and a leg and probably spend all their time playing asteroid games.'

Mr Peabody and Harry were now near the back entrance and coming to a storeroom that, until that morning, had housed relatively unimportant files that were now on their way to a warehouse on the east side of the city where they would be stored for fourteen years, untouched by human hand, until Fireman Ezekiel Paglia was to sift through the ashes they had become after an insurance-fraud fire.

'You will work here,' said Mr Peabody as Harry peered in through the doorway and noticed a maintenance man stringing out a measuring tape along the north wall.

Now, some two weeks later, Harry spends his days in front of a vintage computer screen testing out voice recognition software that he knows will never be effective for the credit union, all so that he was off the floor and so that Mr Peabody could show his employees what happens when clients are distressed by their behaviour.

Harry adjusts the plastic microphone towards his mouth and speaks into it: 'Thirty-six dollars and seventy cents toward a monthly mortgage payment,' he recites. After a painful flicker, the screen begins to display the voice-recognition software interpretation: *Throw to six doors in send cents Todd amortize paid.* That's not bad, thinks Harry. The software is at least now using bank-sounding words on occasion, even if they aren't close to the ones Harry is dictating. This was what they called 'learning' software, but so far, Harry was convinced it was due for remedial classes.

'You're a piece of shit, you know,' Harry says, enunciating every word carefully.

You up eat a ship to no.

'I am wasting my time on this stupid exercise,' says Harry, a bit more quickly.

Yam haste mountain in these step up cries.

Harry pulls the microphone away from his mouth, hits the function keys that deactivate the software, and leans back in his chair. For the first three days of this futile task Harry read into the microphone reams of text the instructions required him to do to 'train' the software. He might as well be training a monkey to sing, he thinks now. Or Han to do anything. Harry smiles as he remembers Han's sad face as Harry left this morning, a look the dog has perfected in the years he has been with Harry. Every morning it's the same thing. Harry gets up and does his morning ablutions. When he gets out of the shower, Han is sitting by the toilet, waiting for him. Before breakfast, Harry lets him out into the backyard and before letting him in prepares a bowl of cereal for himself and drops a three-quarter scoop of dog food in Han's bowl. Then, cereal bowl in hand, he lets Han in. The dog totally ignores him and rushes to his food bowl. Sometimes Harry will say something cute like, 'I love you too, Han,' and then he will sit down to read the paper to the sounds of crunching cereal and dog food. When Han has finished eating he will come and sit by Harry's feet and wait for Harry to finish his cereal. When Harry is done he will put his cereal bowl down and Han will gratefully lap up the remaining milk.

Usually there is time, after Harry gets dressed, to take Han out for his morning constitutional, a route that takes them four blocks up the street to an off-leash area where Han can socialize with a number of his friends for fifteen minutes, then back down a side street to the bagel shop where Harry will buy a strong coffee and some baked goods if he needs them for that evening. But Harry is smiling as he remembers the particularly sad face Han will put on when they return home and Harry opens the door but does not take off his shoes. This will mean, for Han, that Harry will be gone for a long eight hours and Han will be left to fend for himself. To accentuate the cruelty of his human companion, and to convince him that staying in today is really a much better plan, Han will rush off and grab whatever toy is at hand. It might be his squeaky monkey or his gross tennis ball or a partially consumed rawhide toy, but more often than not it is his Sita-ring, a large blue rubber ring about twice the diameter of his snout, which makes for some very funny and picturesque moments. This morning it was the combination of the Sita-ring encircling and perfectly framing Han's sad face that almost worked, almost got Harry to take off his boots and stay awhile. After all, what would happen if he was late? But Harry did not take off his boots, although he did play a bit of ring-pull with Han, finally winning it from the dog and tossing it into the living room where Han made a spectacular leap, missing by a wide margin, but managing to take out a copper candle-holder an aunt had given Harry for his thirty-third birthday. Harry did not bother picking up the candle-holder, using Han's temporary distraction to escape the house and head down the hill toward his bus stop.

Sitting at the desk, remembering Han with that dismal face encircled by the blue Sita-ring, Harry remembers where the dog toy got is name. It was during pre-Christmas shopping last year and he and Sita had gone out to a mall. They had split up to do their various chores and when they reunited, they began to tease each other about what they had bought. Or, rather, Sita had teased Harry into guessing what she had bought for him. He had guessed at the standard items: gloves, ties, slippers, and each guess made Sita laugh all the more uproariously. You'll never guess, she had said, and she was right, for when on Christmas eve, just before Sita had flown off to visit her father, Harry had opened the package containing a perpetual hourglass – one of those items you see at science stores where a combination of flowing sand and magnetic weights ensures that the hourglass keeps righting and uprighting itself, a perfect comment on the pair's frequent discussions of time and continuity – Harry too had laughed uproariously.

But at the mall, when Sita asked what he had bought for her, Harry replied that he had long ago bought her gift. It was, Sita would find out later, a tailor-made salwar kameez not unlike the one Harry's mother used to wear daily, despite the glares she would receive on London and Vancouver streets. What was a white woman doing in a get-up like that, was what those eyes asked, what an odd way to go Indian – unspoken questions to which Harry's mother remained blithely oblivious or at least intentionally ignorant. Sita had commented so often on her lack of proper South Asian attire that Harry had commissioned this for her after phoning Sita's father for her measurements. Still, at that moment Harry was truthful when he had said that none of his purchases today were for her. Oh, come on, she had insisted. He must have bought something for her. Why else would he have insisted on splitting up when they shopped? Harry explained he wanted to spend some time in a pet store, an excuse Sita found completely implausible despite Harry's insistence on that being the truth. Come on, she had said, a pet store, really. What had he bought for her? Harry had finally said okay, okay, he had bought her a ring. A ring, she had repeated, somewhat surprised. Yes, a ring, he had said. A beautiful and extravagant ring. And since she already knew what she was getting, he may as well put it on her, he had said, but for that to happen she had to close her eyes. This she did willingly, always being one for surprises, and Harry had opened up the pet shop bag, torn through the packaging for what was to be Han's future favourite toy, and thrust the obscenely large rubber ring around Sita's entire wrist. This was, of course, the source of a great deal of laughter for Harry and Sita, enough to solicit stares from others at the food court, and they often referred back to that day, to their shopping excursion when Harry had anointed his friend with what they then always referred to as the Sita-ring, even after Han had claimed exclusive ownership from the very day he tore through the Christmas wrapping.

Harry sighs yet again, looks morosely at the computer screen, and decides to leave his memories for the time being and try to get the damned voice recognition package to work. He reminds himself, however, as he pulls the microphone to his mouth and reactivates the program, to give Sita a call at lunchtime to see if she's free for a dog walk after dinner.

'Check savings account number seven-seven-three-five-two-nine,' says Harry, wondering if missile defense programs were run this way.

Chuck saves and count numbers when when three hive tonight. Harry imagines the horror of ICBMs vaulting skyward because some technician has ordered two sugars in his coffee.

'Maybe I should just give up and call Sita now,' Harry says aloud since he is now dreadfully bored of reciting clerical details for the machine to mismanage. Harry is not sure what happens next, whether the office lights sparkle for a split-second, or whether he has blinked unexpectedly, or whether the computer screen has flickered with new energy. Whatever the case, Harry hears, feels, and sees a shot of light somewhere, somehow, and then notices the software has translated his last utterance.

May day should jest get out and Seeta is not around. Interesting, thinks Harry, interesting enough to try some more.

'If Sita is not around, then where is she?'

You should go to find Sita, and you need to do this now.

Harry jolts to his feet, the microphone pulling off his head because of the short cable. Harry stares at the screen. Slowly he sits down again and re-adjusts the microphone. He clears his throat. The screen registers the words: *Hymn often.*

'This software is way off,' Harry recites slowly and carefully.

Sita needs your help. And she needs it now.

Harry's nose is now inches from the screen and he puts his fingers to the lettering as if that would make a difference. Three letters begin to appear where his fingers touch, italicized, shimmering, a *b* and a *p* and a *j*. Harry stares at them and they glow, expand, and then disintegrate, leaving the original message intact.

Okay, thinks Harry, okay, there's got to be a good explanation for this. And he whispers: 'Why does Sita need my help?'

Strait of G, straight to G islands, straight to island G, straight to G for tea.

'That doesn't make sense,' Harry says and the screen does not respond in any way. 'That doesn't make sense,' Harry says louder. The screen flickers, then comes to life. The words now appear much larger than before, larger and almost shimmering.

Strait of G, straight to G islands, straight to island G, straight to G for tea.

Harry starts to panic. He picks up the phone and calls Sita's Granville Island office. The phone rings almost seven times before a man's voice comes across the receiver in mid-ring. 'Yeah, hello?'

'Oh, hello,' says Harry. 'Can I speak to Sita, please?'

'Um, Sita's not in today,' says the voice. 'Say, is this Harry?'

'Yes.' Harry recognizes the voice as that of Bill, one of the architects Sita works for. 'It's me. Is she there, Bill?'

'No, Harry, no she's not. I thought you might know where she is. She's not at home – I've called – and she just didn't show up for work today. She's never done that before, ever.'

The two men are silent. Harry's mind races around traffic accidents, hospitals, and worse. Clearly, Bill has already been there.

'So Harry, I've called the hospitals, the cops – nothing. Can you think of where she might be?'

Harry remains silent. He looks at the computer screen and the letters start to glow as if on fire. He repeats them in his head over and over again, committing them to memory. They become more luminous, redder, and finally the letters begin to disintegrate. 'Strait of G,' Harry repeats in his head. 'Strait of G, straight to G islands, straight to island G, straight to G for tea.' By the time he has said this to himself for the fifth or sixth time, he is closing his eyes and can see the letters on the back of his eyelids. When he opens his eyes, the screen is blank.

'No, Bill,' Harry says into the phone. 'I don't know what to do.'

'Okay, Harry. But call me if you have any ideas at all, okay?'

Harry nods and hangs up the phone. He looks at the computer screen and readjusts the microphone.

'Where can I find Sita?' he says softly.

The computer screen flickers, hesitates, then: *Where I can find Sita.*

Harry slaps the side of the monitor. 'Come on you worthless piece of crap, tell me what you told me before.'

The screen crackles to life and responds immediately: *Come on you worthless piece of crap, tell me what you told me before.* Even the punctuation is perfect.

'I can't believe this is happening,' says Harry and the screen repeats this letter for letter.

Harry runs his hands through his hair, then grabs a sticky note from his desk and writes:

> *Dear Mr Peabody:*
> *Something's come up and I have to take off*
> *for the afternoon. Will see you tomorrow.*

And he slaps the note on top of the computer monitor facing toward the door before squeezing past his desk and out the door himself.

the Gulf Islands

Athnic is listening to a ska band on his Peugeot's very impressive sound system. He taps out a back beat on the steering wheel, mouths the lyrics, occasionally joins in as a background singer. Harry stares out the open passenger window at the row of cars next to them. Han, hiding from the sun behind Athnic's seat, licks the carpet where someone, some time ago, dropped a splash of mustard. Athnic, Harry, and Han are in a Peugeot on Tsawwassen spit, waiting to board a ferry to Galiano Island.

'Why are we here again?' Harry suddenly asks.

Athnic interrupts his finger-tapping and lip-synching only momentarily to say, 'We're here 'cause this is where we gotta be right now.' Harry could swear there is a twinkle in Athnic's eye as he says this, and not a metaphorical twinkle, but a real-life burst of light.

'I see,' says Harry. This is one of those times – one of many in the next few days, as it will turn out – that Harry feels Athnic is less than forthcoming. They sit in silence, but for Athnic's music, for the next fifteen minutes until they are waved onto the ferry bound for Galiano. They drive on, park the Peugeot, and start to make their way cabinward. Han, looking forward to some sea air, is told he is not allowed on the upper deck and must remain in the car. He looks disappointed, but once Harry and Athnic have left, he hides his disappointment by immediately falling asleep on the passenger seat, a place Athnic never lets him sit.

Athnic and Harry go topside. The ferry pulls away from the dock and into the Georgia Strait. Athnic goes inside to see what he might be able to find to eat and Harry stays on the outer deck, leaning against the rail and feeling the breeze against his face. They are here to find Sita, he tells himself, but he has no idea why they are beginning their search on Galiano. He asked Athnic that very question, why they were beginning their search on Galiano, but Athnic only shrugged and said it was a nice island to start looking for her. They would find Sita on an island, they knew that much, and while Vancouver Island might be the obvious site, it was much too large and too difficult to get your bearings. But, Harry had argued, they don't know for sure she's even on an island, just that an island figures prominently in her current residence. And maybe she's on an island half a world away for all they know. Harry can almost hear his colleagues at work – there he goes again, our Harry, getting the oddest assortment of offers. However, thinks Harry, this time, for perhaps the first time in his life, he has taken up the challenge, perhaps only because the stakes are so high, but he has taken up the challenge nonetheless. And yet, he realizes, he has no idea how to begin. He is glad that Athnic is along – Athnic the irascible, Athnic the adventurous, Athnic the charmed and blessed. But at the same time, Harry is disturbed that Athnic is along – Athnic the secretive, Athnic the controller, Athnic the player. Harry loves his friend and he knows Athnic has only the best of intentions, but still, why does Athnic have to be so unforthcoming? And to top it all, there is something different about Athnic these days, something ... lighter.

This is all going through Harry's head when a purser taps him on the shoulder.

'Lozenge?' the purser asks.

Harry begins to say no, thank you, but then realizes there is enough ambiguity in the purser's voice so that Harry doesn't know if the purser is asking for or offering a lozenge. As for the purser's motivation, Harry has no clue.

'Lozenge,' the purser says again, this time framed as a statement rather than a question. The purser is about five inches shorter than Harry, but stockier, and good-looking in that ugly, seafaring kind of way. He has extraordinarily thin lips and tiny irises, which make his face look a bit caricaturish. His nose and chin dominate the lower part of his face, segmented by a thin line that might be a smile, and the sclera, shot through with broken capillaries, would give him an Orphan Annie look were they not punctuated with those tiny brown irises and pinpoint pupils.

The purser stares out at the strait, affecting a pose not unlike Harry's, leaning on the rail and feeling the breeze run through his hair. Harry has still not responded, but this does not seem to deter the purser. After a moment of gazing out onto the water, he continues.

'Yup, lozenges are good when you're travelling. Cabin pressure, see. Constantly changing, all those departures and arrivals. Lozenges keep your inner ear in balance.'

'Isn't that more for flying?' asks Harry.

'Yes,' says the purser. 'Yes, indeed. Very good for flying, lozenges are. Very good.' He pauses. Harry notes that while the purser was enunciating quite clearly, he was doing so while sucking on a lozenge, an action made clearer now that the purser opens his mouth, exposes a half-dissolved lozenge on his tongue, and peremptorily spits it out into the ship-generated wash.

'Guess lozenges don't do much for when you're at sea level,' the purser admits. 'Old habits die hard, though.'

'Oh,' says Harry, getting the picture. 'Did you used to fly? I mean did you work for an airline?'

The purser gives Harry a surly look. 'No chance. Hate flying. Never flown in my life. Might like it, I suppose, were I to try. But as it is, never having flown, I think I'd hate it.'

Harry looks at the purser in dismay. The purser smiles in return.

'Have a good flight – er, trip. Hope you find whoever it is you're looking for.' And he excuses himself and trots off toward the starboard side of the ship. Harry calls after him, wants to know how the purser knew he was looking for somebody. The purser doesn't turn around, just waves and shouts an aphoristic, 'Everybody's looking for somebody,' and then turns around the corner and disappears.

Harry goes in to look for Athnic. By the time he finds him, Athnic is involved in a very friendly conversation with a couple from Sweden, a teenager from Squamish, and a young girl of nine from Abbotsford, all of them rapt by Athnic's presence.

'Athnic,' says Harry, conscious that he is interrupting Athnic holding court, 'I'm going to check on Han.'

Athnic breaks off from his banter with his entourage and smiles and nods at Harry.

One of the Swedes becomes afraid Athnic will leave with his friend, so he quickly asks Athnic what time of day it might be. Athnic, noticing a watch on the Squamish teenager, arches his neck while the teenager accommodates by twisting his wrist around, and Athnic informs the Swedish tourist that it is three-thirty in the afternoon. Harry slips quietly away, always impressed by how Athnic can work a crowd. He runs down the metal steps to the car deck and sneaks up on Athnic's Peugeot, just to see if he can surprise Han. The dog, indeed, is sleeping on the passenger seat, so when Harry raps on the window, Han leaps to attention and growl-barks at the world in general. Harry laughs and opens the door, forcing Han to move over to the driver's seat. Harry plops himself down and looks at Han.

'What are we doing, guy?' asks Harry. 'How are we going to find her? God, this is crazy, Han.' Harry puts his hand on his dog's shoulder, lays his own head back, and falls into a fitful sleep.

❨

Harry wakes up when he hears the car door open and Athnic jump in. Because of his adoring fans, Athnic is the last driver to return to his car and he has to start the Peugeot in a hurry to acquiesce to the ferry traffic director's command to move along.

'Have a good nap, both of you?'

Harry nods. Han wags his tail. Athnic directs the Peugeot up the ramp and onto Galiano Island.

'How about coffee and a late lunch?' suggests Athnic as he inches the car off the rickety ramp and onto the smooth asphalt. Harry, well past the worried stage and into utter dismay, manages a nod. Han wags his tail. Athnic directs the Peugeot up the road and toward the gravel parking lot that acts as a common area for the general store and coffee house. He parks and the three of them hop out. It is warm for early October and Harry and Han happily sit on one of the picnic tables out front while Athnic goes in to drum up a couple of coffees and water to fill up the dog bowl by the table. Sending Athnic in by himself is a mistake, thinks Harry, since there's no telling what sort of folks will be overcome by Athnic's charm and try to waylay him, but Harry is in no rush since he hasn't the slightest idea where they will go from here. Han busies himself by licking the leg of the picnic table. Harry pushes him away, but Han persists.

'That's some dog ya got there,' says a gentle voice. Harry looks up to see a fifty-something hippie, the only hair on his head tied back in a bristly ponytail, ambling over to the picnic table. He sits down next to the leg Han is licking. Harry is momentarily worried that Han will take offense to this intrusion but the dog ignores the visitor. 'So what brings you to Galiano, then, a holiday?'

'No,' mumbles Harry. 'No, I'm – we're – looking for someone. It's a long story.'

'Ha,' says the hippie. 'This is the place for it. Looking that is. Dionisio Alcalá Galiano, he was looking, y'know.'

Harry says nothing, which the stranger takes as an invitation to continue.

'Looking for the Northwest Passage he was. Actually hooked up with George Vancouver round these parts in 1792 but turns out his Spanish boat was no match for George's, so he skippered around the Gulf Islands before going home. And know what his claim to fame was?'

Harry shakes his head. The stranger beams and pulls a leaf off an overhanging tree limb, begins to tear it along the veins.

'Went back home and wrote how there was no Northwest Passage. You can't get there from here.'

Harry is now puzzled. 'Can't get where from here?'

'Nowhere. Least, not the way you're going,' says the hippie as he stands up, drops the dissected leaf and saunters off across the asphalt and past a sign advertising sea kayak tours.

When Athnic returns – he didn't take too long although he does admit to Harry that two customers did ask him the time and an American from Florida engaged him in a conversation about fishing for pike – he sits down with the two coffees and pours a bottle of water into the dog bowl. Han laps half-heartedly at the water, then resumes licking the table leg.

'So, what are we going to do, Athnic?'

'Let's think about it, Harry. First, what brought us to this island?'

'That's just it, Athnic, I don't know! I show you this note and you say, "Right, let's go to Galiano, " and I have no idea why, and further, why you haven't told me anything.'

Han continues to lick the table leg, making it glossy with his dog-spit and with the loose drops of water from the dog bowl which didn't make it down his throat.

'That's the thing, isn't it,' Athnic says to Harry.

'I talked to Sita's father before we left,' Harry tells Athnic.

'Hm, so you said.'

'I told him I'd call him again tonight.'

'Good idea,' says Athnic, and puts a supporting hand on Harry's wrist.

'But what am I going to tell him? Why are we here?'

'The note. It said what again?'

Harry has it memorized: 'Strait of G, straight to G islands, straight to island G, straight to G for tea.'

'Right. So that's Georgia Strait, right, and that's where we are, in the Gulf Islands.'

'Uh-huh.'

'And then, "straight to island G" could only mean Galiano, see? And now for the kicker, this place we're at used to be called Gladys's Tea Kitchen. Get it? "Straight to G for tea," had to be a reference to this place.'

Han is getting quite excited by licking the table leg now, and he begins to gnaw a bit as well.

'So, Athnic, tell me, how did ya know we weren't going to Gabriola Island?'

Athnic furrows his brow.

'Good point. I didn't think of that, Harry. Think maybe we made the wrong decision?'

'I think maybe you should confide in me before you go dragging me off to all these G-damn islands,' says Harry.

Han yelps, partly from pain, partly from surprise. Harry looks down at his panting dog. Han has somehow got a sliver in the middle of his tongue. Harry notes that the table leg is slimy with dog spit.

'Oh, Han,' and Harry expertly plucks out the sliver from Han's tongue.

'Hey, Harry, look.'

Athnic is pointing to the wet table leg. Han's licking has brought out someone's knife etchings from what looks like years ago. Wet down by Han, it is now quite readable.

SITA WUZ HERE

This is done with a switchblade or some other fairly imprecise instrument. But below the inscription is a tiny, almost microscopic, yet perfectly formed engraving. Harry and Athnic have to get their noses right to the table leg to read it, encouraging Han who thinks they are finally about to do something useful and lick the table leg. But they don't lick the leg. Instead, they read aloud and in unison the remainder of the message.

Hanlan's Pt ferry, The Centre, last studio.
—Brasso Pilgrim Junta

Harry and Athnic turn to each other, nose to nose. 'I'll be damned,' says Harry.

'Would I lead you astray?' asks Athnic.

'Lick the damned table leg,' thinks Han.

But, instead, Athnic pulls out a scrap of scarlet paper from his hip pocket. From his shirt pocket he produces a pencil, places the paper against the lettering and gently rubs the pencil across the paper. Harry is not certain why Athnic feels it is necessary to do this sort of text transfer when all he needs to do is scribble down the important information, but as this is all quite confounding to Harry, he says nothing and waits until Athnic hands him the carbon-covered sheet which reads, in scarlet lettering:

Hanlan's Pt ferry, The Centre, last studio.
—Brasso Pilgrim Junta

'Okay,' says Athnic thoughtfully. 'Let's go.'

'Wait,' says Harry. 'What's this all mean?'

'They're directions,' says Athnic matter-of-factly. 'Let's go.'

'But this Brasso – what was it?'

Athnic checks the sheet again and frowns. 'Brasso Pilgrim Junta. Looks like a signature or name or something.'

'Meaning?'

'Who knows?' says Athnic, shrugging. 'Let's go.'

girl in the bubble

Oh come off it, there's no point pouting. Think of this as an adventure and it will all be fine.

'I don't understand,' says Sita. She is curled up in a fetal position and doesn't look up at me when she speaks. 'I don't understand what's happening or where we're going or any of this.'

No, I don't suppose you do, but all things in their own good time. Do you want something to eat? I can tell Sita wants to resist saying yes, but she is hungry and, despite herself, she nods. I give her some crackers.

'I have this feeling that – that is, I'm having this déjà vu feeling.'

Nonsense. Déjà vu is nothing but a misfiring of brain synapses, information reaching the brain through a couple of different routes, only the first and fastest doesn't quite register until the second comes through and then the brain tells you it's seen this pattern before. That's déjà vu.

'But then what I'm feeling…?'

What you feel right now is that all this has happened before. And you're right. No misfiring synapses, no missed signals. This has happened before. And it's happening again. Only this time it's going to be different.

Sita takes a bite of her cracker and chews thoughtfully. I imagine she is wondering why she is not more frightened or more angry, or maybe she is trying to remember if this really has happened before. Now she finally looks up at me. What she sees is a short, dark person, gender indeterminate, and I imagine she recognizes my face as a gentle one, a face that reflects the care I really feel for her.

'I know you,' she says slowly.

I know.

'I know you and the crazy monkey and the fire, but I don't know how I know all this or where I know it from.'

I know that too, Sita. I know that we were once together on an island, and I know that even while I was rather rude (though never transgressive, we both know that), you were more than kind to me. I know that I mistreated you but that you never mistreated me, even to your own peril. I want to change all that, Sita. I want to reach back into history and reclaim it for myself in an altogether different way. I want to do all this with you all over again but with a different end. Do you understand any of this?

Sita smiles at me, the first time she has smiled since we entered this place. But hers is a smile that is thoughtful and contradictory. 'You can reach back all you want,' she tells me, 'but history isn't yours to rewrite as you choose.'

And why not? Don't you know who I am, what I can do? Don't you know that history is no more than a few etches on a page, a pattern of imprints on a memory, nothing more? Don't you think that the past can be changed?

'Oh yes,' she tells me, reaching her hand out for another cracker which I drop into her waiting palm. 'History can change. It's just that you can't do it. Or can't do it alone.'

I don't think I like where this is going, but I nod and urge her to continue.

'You can't make all these reclamations by yourself. No matter who you are. There are – other players. You see?'

I nod again. She is right, just as she was right before when she said things would never work out according to my plan. Then, she had said, she would help me rewrite my plan, but I was stubborn and wanted it my way, the only way. I was wrong then. I don't want to be wrong again. *Other players? Yes, I see what you mean.*

I look out through the translucence that surrounds us. Perhaps there is still a way.

island at the centre
of the universe

The Air Canada counter agent smiles at Harry.

'Where to today, sir?'

'Toronto,' Harry says nervously, trying to keep his carry-on over his shoulder while he hands over the ticket.

'Toronto, eh? Everyone flies to Toronto.' He looks at Harry as if he is waiting for an answer.

'Um, I guess so.'

The agent continues to look at Harry, apparently expecting more discussion.

'Um, unless they drive, I suppose. Or take the train.'

'Ha. Drive, yes. Yes, I imagine you're right. Ha. They could drive or take the train.' He is in the middle of processing Harry's ticket when he pauses and looks up, lost in thought. 'You know, people don't take the bus like they used to. They always drive or fly or take the train.'

'Well,' Harry offers, 'the bus is still cheaper, really. It's the cheapest way to go, so I guess a lot of people take it because it's cheap.'

'Naw,' insists the agent. 'No one takes the bus anymore. Nobody.'

'Of course they do,' Harry mutters, alarmed at himself for getting into an argument over such details with the Air Canada agent.

'You think so, eh?' The agent frowns at Harry, then changes the subject entirely. 'You should visit Kingston. Ever been to Kingston?'

'Um, no.'

'Fine city, Kingston. Two of my brothers work in Kingston. One's at Queens, does some techie stuff, the other's up at the Pen. Max security, you know. Think you'll get to Kingston?'

'Oh, I don't think so, really.'

'Shame. I think you can take the train to Kingston,' says the agent, handing Harry's ticket back to him. Then he stares right into Harry's eyes and adds, 'Or the bus. Have a great flight.'

Harry is about to move away when he notices Han sitting in his cage looking miserable. 'Oh,' he says to the agent. 'My dog?'

'Just take him down to special handling, sir. They'll take good care of him.'

'Good. Thanks.'

And Harry wheels his luggage, including Han, down to special handling. He completes the paperwork and squeezes a finger into the cage to say goodbye to Han. The dog, ever hopeful, licks Harry's fingers in search of food.

'You be good now, Han,' Harry says. Han looks through the cage bars at Harry mournfully.

Harry goes through security and finds his gate. With ten minutes to go before boarding, Harry finds a phone and calls up the Bay area number he now has memorized.

'Yes?' says the voice on the other end of the phone.

'Mr Simpson. It's me, Harry.'

'Yes, Harry. Any news?'

'Yes … well, no. I don't know, Mr Simpson.'

'Simpson. Drop the mister. Everyone calls me Simpson, always has. Now, slow down and tell me what you've got.'

'Um, well, Simpson, you remember the note I got before?'

'G, gees, straight to gees, yeah, you told me.'

Harry tells Simpson about their eventful trip to Galiano, about stopping at the place that used to be called Gladys's Tea Kitchen, about Han licking the table leg and about the discovery of the second clue. Harry listens for any sign of anxiety from Sita's father, but there is none, and Harry puts this down to the practiced patience of a former detective.

'Hm, so this message said…?'

'Well that's what's so strange, Simpson. It was like Sita was actually there, I mean she, or someone, scratched "Sita wuz here" into the table leg. And after that it said: "Hanlan's Pt ferry, The Centre, last studio."'

'I see,' says Simpson. 'So you're off to Toronto?'

Harry is silent. How is it that everyone else seems to know more about what's going on than he does?

'Uh, that's right. I don't know why, but that's right.'

'Good. Good for you, son. I have faith in you.'

'But, Mr Simpson, one more thing. It's my friend Athnic. I can't help but think – oh, I don't know what I'm saying. It's just that he seems to know everything about where to go next, what to do next. I'm not sure – he's one of my best friends, Simpson, but I'm not sure if I trust him.'

'Trust him,' Simpson says firmly. 'Trust me, you should trust him.'

Harry nods into the telephone and then suddenly remembers a forgotten detail.

'Oh, and the message carved into the table leg, it appeared to be signed. It said: "Brasso Pilgrim Junta."'

74

Now it is Simpson who is silent.

'Hello? Simpson, you there?'

'Hm. Yes, I'm here. Brasso Pilgrim Junta. It just reminded me of a time long ago is all.'

'Then you know this Brasso—'

'No, not really. No, it's just that, you know when I said to trust me and to trust your friend Athnic? Well, trust yourself most of all, you hear me, son? Trust yourself and things won't go all backwards on you.'

Trust Simpson, trust Athnic, trust himself. Here was Harry all set to trust just about everyone and yet he had no idea what was happening all around him. Trust. Sure.

'All right, Simpson. Listen, should I call the cops when I get to Toronto?'

'No,' says Simpson, simply and firmly. 'No. Just trust.'

☾

When Harry boards the plane he finds he has been assigned a window seat at the very rear of the plane. He was going to ask his seatmate if he would like to exchange places, since although Harry does not fly that often, when he does, he prefers an aisle seat. However, Harry nixes this approach when he notes that his seatmate is not a man, but a woman, and one who is very pregnant. The woman glares at him as Harry looks at his assigned place beside her. He quickly glances around for an empty seat so as not to bother her, but the plane is absolutely full. Harry says nothing, as the woman gets the idea and struggles painfully to her feet to let Harry by. Harry remembers his aisle preference and begins to make an offer.

'If you'd rather….' he says, indicating the window seat.

The woman rolls her eyes as she finally pushes herself out of the seat and into the aisle. 'Oh, yeah, right. Look, I'm gonna be up and into the lavatory thirty-six times during the flight, so that's why I asked for this seat. Got it?'

Harry nods, not sure what he has actually done to elicit such an angry response. But the woman is not through. Once Harry has seated himself and the woman has flopped back into the aisle seat, she continues.

'So, you're probably thinking what the hell is this woman doin', going to Toronto when it looks like she's about to break water? Well, lemme tell ya, it wasn't my idea. Oh, no, I tell my husband no way am I flying any-where in this condition. Do you know how pregnant I am? Do you?'

Harry shakes his head.

'C'mon, try and guess. Wanna put your hand on my belly? Everyone's always coming up to me and touching my belly, like I was goddamn public property. What do I look like, a friggin' Buddha, touch my belly for luck? You haven't guessed how pregnant I am. I said *guess!*'

'Um, eight months.'

'Eight months! Ha. I wish it was eight months. You know when it was eight months? Eight weeks ago, that's when. Yeah, you heard me. Eight weeks ago. Do the math. I'm at ten months. You know how friggin' long ten months is when you're pregnant? No, of course you don't. Men have no friggin' idea about pregnancy. You wanna know what it's like? I'll tell ya what it's like. Think about carrying a two-four of beer around with you everywhere. Now think about doing that while holding a tennis ball between your knees. Got it?'

Harry stares at the woman, dumbstruck. The plane's engines have revved up and the plane is taxiing down the runway.

The woman reaches over and squeezes Harry's cheek between her thumb and forefinger. He grimaces. She smiles sadistically. 'Yeah, hurts, doesn't it? Well, life hurts, all parts of it.' The woman lets go of Harry's cheek and laughs and laughs. Harry, realizing this is most probably an inside joke, rubs his tweaked cheek. The woman allows this and continues to laugh.

'Yeah, so what am I doing flying, huh? Doctor was against it, airline wasn't crazy for it either. My goddamn husband, though, Harry, he says it's absolutely urgent I get to him in Toronto. Doesn't say why, doesn't offer to come out and be with me, just says, "Rita, you have to be here, now."'

Harry is shocked that the woman's husband is named Harry and he tries to think of a name he can make up should she ask him his, which seems quite unlikely given her rate of speech, but still. The plane reaches takeoff speed and the front wheels lift up, followed by the rear assembly. Harry hears the landing gear fold into the plane. He watches, past the pregnant woman, the cityscape giving way to water.

'Oh my god,' shouts the woman. She grabs Harry's wrist in a death grip. 'I think I'm going into labour.'

((

When Harry walks down the stairs toward the baggage carousel at Pearson, he is rubbing the feeling back into his wrist. The woman did not give birth on the plane, much to the relief of Harry and the other passengers. She did, however, down six double brandies, insisting such medicinal care would delay the birthing procedure at least until they landed. The flight attendants were understandably hesitant to serve a pregnant woman double shots of St Remy, but once she howled at them for their ignorance – didn't they know a fetus was at risk only during the first goddamn trimester and here she was entering her fourth – they allowed her a couple of drinks. It would have stopped there, but every time her glass ran empty, which was frequently, she would grasp Harry's wrist and utter a shout, 'God, it's crowning,' or 'Put on some goddamn hot water or get me a brandy,' or 'Trust me, the time has come,' or some such order that would have the flight attendants scurrying to provide her with more liquor. At one point she actually growled and showed her teeth in such a manner that Harry thought Han might have inhabited his seatmate's body, but such was not the case, of course. Han was quietly whimpering, berating himself for falling for that old trick, food in the cage, and trying to block out the whine of the engine.

The circulation in Harry's wrist is almost back to normal when he reaches special handling to retrieve his dog. There are three porters surrounding the cage and Harry's heart misses a beat when he notes that one of the porters sports a wrap of gauze around his middle finger. Fortunately, there is no anger present, only murmurs of calming voices.

'Poor guy, must be frightened, huh, I don't blame ya.'

Harry walks up and Han whimpers with delight. Harry looks at the porter and his finger and clears his throat.

'Hm. Is that, that is, did my dog, did he...?'

'Ah,' says the porter, waving it off, 'it's nothin' but a flesh wound. He looked so sad, I just poked a finger in to say "hi," but I guess that was the wrong thing to do!'

'I don't understand,' Harry mumbles. 'He's never done anything like that before. Have you, Han?' Han wags his tail blissfully and waits for Harry to let him out of his cage.

((

Harry collects the rest of his luggage and he and Han pile into a cab, after three taxi drivers have refused to take them.

'He's very friendly,' Harry offers to the fourth driver, who nods in boredom and lets them climb in. 'The Westin on Queen's Quay,' Harry tells the driver, then sits back and tries not to think about the flight. He fishes in his pocket for the scarlet paper with the neat lettering:

Hanlan's Pt ferry, The Centre, last studio
–Brasso Pilgrim Junta.

Harry closes his eyes and tries to imagine what this all might mean.

incarcinogen

I have to stay one step ahead, always an island hop away. I have to plan our final encounter and I have a good feeling this will all end where it began. Birthplaces can be death sites, pyres built above buried placenta. Wouldn't it be grand, just me and him in that final struggle, the entire junta watching in celebration as we battle on that sacred ground? Perhaps, someday, they will erect a monument testifying to our feud. But something nags about that place, that space. I watch Sita for answers, but she sits quietly in this, our secret place, while we wait for him. She feels me watch her. She looks up.

'This place is new to me.'

Yes. That's the trick. To go over old ground in new ways.

'It's a factory or plant of some kind, is it?'

They used to clean water here, enough for an entire city. But then it fell into disuse, forgotten by the citizens, and it was … it was claimed by others who had no right.

'Others? Which others?'

Does it matter? There are so many others. They came here uninvited and infested the place. They grew and multiplied like mutated cells.

'And so you tried to stop them?'

Yes. But not me alone. This type of work takes will and power. It took the entire Brasso Pilgrim Junta to remove the tumours and restore order.

'So this is how you plan to change history? Sounds to me like the same old story. Going back to the same places, the same feuds. How can you hope for different endings?'

She has a point. The story has to change its setting if the outcome is to change. Now do you see why she's so special? Now do you see why she's worth fighting over? I look over at her, see her watching me without hatred and that alone is enough. *Can I touch you?* She smiles, lowers her head.

'I am a prisoner here.'

A prisoner! Do you see iron bars? Do you see shackles around your wrists or ankles? Do you see armed guards or locked doors? A prisoner? Ha! You are here as my companion. Can you hate me with your heart?

'I see no bars, no shackles, no guards or locks, all this is true. And there is no hate in my heart for you.'

Well, then?

'But I am a prisoner here. Maybe you are too.'

Bah, this talk of guardless jails, barless incarceration, frustrates me to no end. I only want her to like me. Still, that might take time. And Sita has given me the clue I need, the change of venue necessary for the change of all things.

Toronto Islands

'We don't take dogs,' says the clerk at the Westin, watching Harry toting the dog kennel, Han trotting alongside

'Um, I know. Actually, I'm not exactly checking in.'

Han checks out a particularly expensive piece of luggage at the counter and Harry is silently glad he made the dog pee outside the hotel.

The clerk raises an eyebrow.

'You see, my friend, Athnic Long, from Vancouver's Quality–'

'You're a friend of Athnic's?' The clerk's demeanour changes. 'Sure, what can we do for you?'

'Oh, well, Athnic said since we had to head to the islands, you might be able to store our stuff, just for the day.'

The clerk is smiling broadly now. 'Of course, of course, no problem. Just leave it there, enjoy your day, and I'll take care of your bags and such. Hey, how is Athnic?'

'Oh, he's fine, fine.' Harry nods a thank-you to the clerk and he and Han make their way out of the hotel down to the ferry dock. He purchases a ticket for one ferry ride and then looks down, guiltily, at Han, but the ferry ticket officer pays the dog no attention and Harry soon realizes this is not the same as public transit. The next ferry, he is told, is in ten minutes.

Harry and Han sit on a bench and wait. In exactly five minutes, a gate opens and a man with silver hair flowing down to his waist calls out to the almost-empty terminal: 'October ferry to Hanlan's point,' and then cackles loudly. He looks at Harry who, not counting Han, is apparently the only passenger on this mid-afternoon run. 'Get it? October ferry...?' Harry stares at him blankly. 'Ah, it's a ferry joke.' The silver-haired man lights a cigarette and beckons Han and Harry on board.

'Say, good lookin' dog ya got there.'

'He bites,' warns Harry.

The man pats Han on the head fairly stridently, then pulls back Han's lips to reveal a healthy set of teeth.

'Good teeth,' remarks the man while Harry looks on in amazement as the ferryman pulls and prods at Han, who appears not just at ease with this process, but to be thoroughly enjoying it. The horn sounds and the ferryman finally leaves Han's mouth alone and lifts up the gate. Harry watches the terminal recede. He looks over at the ferryman who has just pulled out a dog-eared book of poetry. The ferryman senses

Harry's gaze and gestures with the book: 'Ever read this? Won a Governor General's award a few years back. Me, I've read this sucker backwards and forwards about forty times in the past two years, I'm sure.'

'Oh? What's it like?'

'Haven't the foggiest. Forty times and I still don't get what he's talking about. Poets, eh?'

Harry smiles congenially. 'How long is it to Hanlan's Point?'

'Hm. On a good day, four-and-a-half hours.'

Harry looks stunned and the ferryman cackles, takes another drag on his cigarette.

'Just kidding. It's only a mile across; we'll be there in a few minutes.' The ferryman looks intently at Harry and smiles. 'That is, if we don't crack up on the rocks.'

Suddenly, a look of terror comes across the ferryman's face.

'Damn,' he says, 'it's them again!'

He sets down his book and covers both ears with his hands, the cigarette still firmly clamped between his lips, so his one-word warning has a sense of urgency as it puffs out with smoke: 'Sirens!'

Harry stares at the ferryman. The only thing he can hear is the chugging of the engine and water falling away from the ship's bow.

'Sirens?' asks Harry. 'Like police sirens?'

The ferryman stares at Harry as if he hasn't heard him, which, of course, he hasn't, his hands clapped tight against his ears. He does see Harry mouthing something, though, and removes one hand to find out what it was. 'Eh?'

'What kind of sirens? Fire sirens?'

'Don't be a simpleton,' says the ferryman, clapping his hand over his ear again. 'And either cover your ears or lash yourself to something, man.' The ferryman shouts this at Harry, presumably because he can't hear how loud is voice is.

Harry swallows hard and stares at the ferryman who looks, for all intents, like a hear-no-evil monkey. Then, as if nothing at all unusual was happening, the ferryman removes his hands from his ears and picks up the book of poetry, flipping to a particular page.

'Never mind,' he says, removing the cigarette from his mouth momentarily. 'Think we're safe. They'll lead you astray, though, if you don't take precautions.'

'Who?' asks Harry. 'And where?'

The ferryman looks up at Harry and shakes his head in dismay.

'Makes no never mind,' he says slowly. 'If you don't believe the old stories, maybe you can't hear the old songs neither.' He shakes his head again and begins reading earnestly.

Harry, Han, and the ferryman travel the remaining five minutes in silence. Then the ferryman jumps up, puts down his book, butts out his cigarette and lights another, and begins the process of docking the ferry.

It is a sunny day and Harry and Han are both glad to be out of the city grime. As they walk off the ramp, Harry turns to the ferryman.

'Hey, where's the Centre?'

'Gibraltar Point,' the ferryman says in business-like tones. 'Can't miss it. First and only building on your right if you go straight ahead. Maybe twenty-five minutes.'

Harry and Han head down the asphalt trail. They make it about fifteen minutes down the path, encountering only a few other pedestrians and some cyclists on awkward tandem assemblies that remind Harry of the autorickshaws he would see in the streets of Delhi when visiting distant relatives with his father, when Han decides to take off after a squirrel. He runs past the picnic tables, past the tennis courts, past the sign informing the public of the approaching 'clothing optional' beach. And it is here, onto the smooth white sands of Lake Ontario that Han chases the squirrel, losing him in the tall grass but continuing the pursuit, sans target, right up to the edge of the lake. And Han would have thrown himself in and pursued his target to Buffalo had Harry not called him back. Han looks around to see Harry running along the beach toward him and a number of nude sunbathers looking up in distress at the antics of man and dog. One of them takes it upon himself to rise lazily and saunter on over to Han, who has decided to sample the drinkability of Lake Ontario. This fellow is taking full advantage of the optional beachwear, and it shows in all its splendour as he stretches out, displaying pretty much everything for all the world to see. Unfortunately, it is this particular gesture, followed by his leaning down and patting Han on the forehead a mite too hard, something the dog was willing to forgive in the silver-haired ferryman but not twice in one day, that inspires Han to grab hold as if in a tug-of-war the first part of this stranger's body that presents itself. As he chomps down, he can hear the nearby wailing of Harry, urging Han to just this once not to follow his instinctual inclination to bite.

'*Holy fuck!*' cries the man with the alarm of one who suddenly questions the good sense of clothing options in public places, 'Holy fuck fuck fuck. Leggo leggo leggo leggooooooo.'

'*Han!*' Harry is upon them now. 'Um, drop it.'

'Grrrr-grr-grrr,' says Han as he is wont to do when playing tug-of-war with Harry, although that was usually with less fleshy objects stuffed with cloth.

'*Holy....*'

'*Now*, Han!'

'Grr-grr.' Spit. Pant-pant.

'*Holy f....*'

'I – I don't know what to – I – um, he must have thought you wanted to play. I mean, he's never done anything like this before.'

After everyone calms down and the man, with newfound respect for Victorian swimwear, realizes that there is no permanent injury – not even broken skin since Han was only playing – there is great relief in the air. The man, who hastily, though tenderly, donned swimming trunks soon after the misadventure, is even kind enough to direct them to the Centre, a place which turns out to be the Gibraltar Point Arts Centre, a retreat for artists who would work at their craft in studios created from the old island school, saved and converted for just this purpose. Harry and Han follow the twisty bike path past sports fields and groves of mismatched trees, past the spire of what appears to be a somewhat anitquated lighthouse, until they come across a rather sprawling and definitely school-like structure, bound on one side by the bike path and the other by a hedge along the beach.

It is this Centre that Harry and Han now enter. A sign proclaims this to be a special open studio day, so while there are few visitors, those who are present are not questioned or challenged in any way to provide a reason for their presence. This is a good thing because Harry would be hard-pressed to explain how he got there and what he hopes to find. And he is quite at a loss as to how to go about his search now that he is this far. He had taken the Hanlan's Point Ferry. He had found the Centre. Now he is to look for something designated as the 'last studio,' but he has no idea what to make of that clue. Three artists are in the hall and they greet him, welcome him and his dog to the Centre. One of them is a painter, one a choreographer, one a performance artist. The painter asks Harry where he comes from and all are pleasantly surprised to find out he is here from the west coast, had just arrived that afternoon and had made his way, dog and all, directly to the Centre. She asks him if he is looking for someone in particular, and Harry hedges and hems and haws, until finally, meekly, says he did have a penchant to see the 'last studio,' though he isn't exactly sure what that means, to him or to them.

The artists, too, speculate on what that might mean. Was it the last studio renovated for the Centre? Or might it be the last studio to be occupied on a permanent basis? Or perhaps it was one of the studios in the portable units which were, after all, closest to the lake and therefore the last studios before heading out south into water and the United States?

But none of this sounds right to them until someone hits on the idea that perhaps the last studio is the last one a visitor would come to upon visiting the centre. This they all agree upon until someone points out that it all depends on which ferry one arrives on. The last studio from the Centre Island ferry would be at the opposite side of the building from the last studio from Hanlan's Point. Aha, says Harry, say I arrived at Hanlan's Point, which I did, what would be the last studio then? Well, the artists say in unison, that would be in what is euphemistically referred to as the 'writers' wing,' and they all point to the end of a long hall, which was indeed the way away from the ferry dock at Hanlan's Point. Thank you, says Harry, who starts making his way across the creaky floor to what he surmises will be the last studio. Han, however, is way ahead of him, scurrying down the hall and going past a doorway that clearly leads to the writers' wing. Unable to negotiate the ninety-degree left turn on waxed floors, Han hurtles his Heeler frame into the first of the studio doors with such a clatter that the resident of said room opens the door with great alarm. Han looks up at the resident who looks down at Han. Harry calls out to him, 'Sorry, my dog....'

The resident nods an acceptance and clears his throat.

'Mother died today. Or maybe it was yesterday,' he says.

Harry looks at him, shocked. 'I – I'm sorry, I didn't know.'

'Oh, no,' says the resident. 'That's Camus. From *L'Étranger*?'

'Uh, yes, of course,' says Harry.

'My new book is like *L'Étranger* except it's set in North Dakota. Angst-ridden protagonist who sleeps with prostitutes. Say, you're not a publisher are you?'

'No, no, I'm a credit-union teller.'

'Fair enough,' nods the resident writer. 'Fair enough. We all have our existential burdens to bear. The repetitiveness of the world. Good luck.' And he swings the door shut. For not the first time today, Harry looks stunned.

Harry catches up with Han and sees that along the left-hand turn are two more studios. The first one is shut, but the second one, which Harry assumes must indeed be the 'last studio,' is open, and Han has already poked his nose around the side. Harry can hear the clatter of a computer keyboard and as he turns the corner and pokes his own head into the studio, he sees the back of a person's head, shoulder-length black hair bobbing up and down as slender brown fingers type. Han and Harry stare at the Writer and, more importantly, they stare at the computer screen, or at least Harry does as Han is now quite licking a crumb of some ancient food type off the studio floor. On the screen, Harry can glimpse various words, and while he is slightly self-conscious about reading this potentially private work, he cannot stop himself.

'Islands,' he reads, 'islands and separations. Islands, separations, and prisons. Prisons are islands of separation. Islands are separated from mainlands as justice is separated from history.' This is pompous stuff, thinks Harry. Then his eye drops to the bottom of the screen and his jaw drops too when he reads: 'Sita is looking for you, too, but how can she find you when you're so busy getting lost? She's not here and never was. Here's the deal. Freo, Lot 150. Think about it. This may provide some answers to these conundrums of separation and islands. Freo. Lot One Hundred Fifty. Routed through the woolly coasts of Sydneysiders. Sita waits.'

Harry is still reading this when the Writer, whose face Harry has yet to see, and in fact, never will, holds down the command key and presses the letter p, setting into motion a series of gears and processes that end, twelve seconds later, with a single page of paper spitting out of a tiny printer connected to the Macintosh laptop that the Writer has been typing on. The Writer's left hand picks up the ejected paper while the right hand continues to type, working the keyboard a bit slower but still as efficiently. The left hand swings around the back of the Writer and fully extends, so that the piece of paper is now just a foot away from Harry. Han, taking this moment to be extremely useful, gently grabs the paper and, amazingly, turns his head to allow the paper to touch Harry's hand. Harry's fingers close around the paper and he reads the printout of what he just read on the computer screen. The Writer's left hand, meanwhile, resumes its position at the keyboard and continues to type at a furious rate.

Harry is dumbfounded. The room is silent but for the clacking of plastic keys. Then, without slowing the typing even a notch, the Writer speaks: 'You have what you want. You best get going.' Harry nods, even though the Writer does not face him. For just a moment, then, there is silence in the room as the Writer gives up the keyboard to pull something from behind the computer. He flicks something into the air, then returns to his intense pace. Han leaps up and does a perfect three-quarter flip before landing quite happily, his jaws wrapped around a sizeable dog biscuit the Writer has thrown to him. Han crunches once, twice, swallows, and takes the remainder of the biscuit out the door and down the hall. Harry continues to stare, at the Writer, at the screen, at his dog, and finally at the piece of paper in his hands. At the top of the piece of paper is the header, *Harry Kumar*.

Harry is still staring at the piece of paper when he and Han again encounter the three artists in the hall. The performance artist, Harry notices, has flattened his body against the wall near an extruding pipe.

'Did you find what you were looking for?' asks the painter.

'Yes, did you find it?' repeats the choreographer.

'I am Duchamp's *Fountain*,' says the performance artist. 'Use me. I am ready-made.'

'Oh, yes, thank you,' says Harry to the painter and choreographer, ignoring the performance artist. 'By the way, who is the writer in the last studio?'

'The last studio?' the painter asks.

'Yeah, the studio you directed me to.'

'No one in that studio. No one in that wing 'cept a guy who always goes on about Sartre and essentialism,' says the choreographer.

'Camus and existentialism,' Harry corrects.

'I am concave porcelain,' says the performance artist.

'Whatever,' interjects the painter to both Harry and the performance artist. 'The last studio is empty, has been ever since the ... incident.'

The artists all look at each other knowingly. Harry figures he should know better, but asks anyway.

'The incident?'

The artists tsk-tsk to themselves, the performance artists adds flushing noises, and the choreographer puts his arm around Harry and tries to explain.

'Sad case. He was here from Camrose or Canmore – somethin' like that – writing an adventure novel about white water rafting on the Great Lakes....'

'White water on the Great Lakes?' asks Harry.

'He was a visionary, a free-thinker,' explains the painter. 'Had a girl's name, though. Valerie, I think, and an odd last name, Mickey or Maki, some such thing.'

'A shame, such a great artist,' adds the choreographer.

'I am a dog implanted with fish genes,' says the performance artist, who wags his ass and makes fish faces. Han begins to take great interest.

'What happened to him?' asks Harry.

'You mean Val, the writer from Kamloops?' The choreographer shakes his head.

'The lighthouse,' says the painter, shaking her head sadly.

'Woof-blub-blub,' says the performance artist. Han begins an amorous dance with the performance artist's leg. The performance artist, not wishing to end his piece, makes more violent fish faces and tries to think of a way to incorporate this act of spontaneity into his performance.

'Yes,' says the choreographer. 'Mickey, or Mikey, he jumped from the lighthouse.'

'My god,' says Harry, remembering seeing the five-storey lighthouse just outside the centre. 'Killed himself?'

'Oh no,' says the painter. 'Door was locked so he couldn't get in. So he jumped from the front step. Only eighteen inches high, but he did it with his eyes closed and tried a backward flip. Sprained an ankle, had to go to hospital, never returned.'

'I heard he's back in Cargil telling people he injured himself on some number four rapids on Lake Ontario,' adds the choreographer.

'Quite possible,' says the painter.

'Oh, Christ, get off my leg, you miserable cur,' says the performance artist.

'C'mon, Han, let's go,' says Harry, leading his dog outside so they can do a quick check on this lighthouse.

to the lighthouse

When Harry and Han get to the lighthouse, just a stone's throw from the Centre, they notice two men with ill-fitting grey suits trying to wrap a measuring tape around the base of the tower. The men wear expensive Italian shoes, making their task that much more difficult, owing to recent rains which have made the ground surrounding the lighthouse slightly boggy. One of the men slips and almost falls, his sunglasses going askew so that when he regains his balance and stands upright, his glasses cover one eye and one nostril. He is the first to see Harry and Han. He calls to his partner.

'Stan … *Stan*, there's someone here.'

His colleague notices Harry, turns his back as if it were the most logical thing to do, and covers his mouth with his wrist as if to stifle a cough, although Harry and Han can hear him whisper hoarsely, 'We've been compromised. Repeat, B-team is compromised.' Then he turns and smiles broadly at Harry.

'Hey there. Um, who are you?'

Harry, thinking this is an odd way to greet a stranger in a relaxed environment such as this island, introduces himself and his dog. Then, in cocktail party manner, he asks the men their names.

The man who had whispered into his shirt cuff looks uncomfortable. He looks around again, his eyes focus on a plaque on the side of the lighthouse and he blurts out 'My name's J.P. Raddemuller.'

'Oh,' says Harry. 'What does J.P. stand for?'

The man looks stumped, mutters something that sounds like, 'It didn't say,' then smiles and says, 'Oh, nothing. Just J.P.' He gestures to his friend, who, by this time, has corrected his sunglasses so they sit almost squarely on his nose. 'And this is my friend….'

Now it is his friend's turn to feel uncomfortable. He looks around nervously, then up to the top of the lighthouse, then brightens and stares at Harry. 'My name's Woolf. Um, Vuh-er-gin – Virgil. Yes, Virgil Woolf. Um, we're tourists. You?'

'Well,' says Harry. 'Actually, I'm looking for someone. Two people actually, I guess. One was a writer who was a resident at the Arts Centre until quite recently. I guess he twisted his ankle here.'

Both men look at Harry and lick their lips to hide their nervousness.

'And the other is a woman named Sita Simpson, but that's a long story.'

Now the men look at each other in true surprise. Virgil Woolf speaks first.

'Stan, we should get back to the water filtration plant.'

'You're right, Phil,' J.P. says to Virgil. And they both take off in a brisk walk that is really pretending not to be a run. J.P. begins shouting whispered commands into his shirt cuff. 'Positive ID, we got 'em, move in C-team, B-team moving to filtration position, over.'

Harry watches them hustle away. Han thinks about joining them but is ordered back by Harry. No sense in bothering them more than need be, he thinks. Harry notices that J.P. has dropped the measuring tape and he goes over to pick it up. Harry reads the plaque and learns that J.P. Raddemuller was the first lighthouse keeper on the island. He mysteriously disappeared in 1815 and his bones were found some years later, prompting speculation that the lighthouse was haunted. Harry picks up the measuring tape. Han pees on the rockwork just below the plaque. As he does so, the noise of a truck engine intrudes on the quiet and virtually traffic-free island atmosphere. Through the bush breaks a spanking new Hummer, freshly painted with the words 'Water Filtration Plant, C' on the side. Four men jump out of the Hummer. They are dressed like J.P. and Virgil although they wear hiking boots from Roots instead of Italian leather shoes. The man from the passenger side, apparently the group's leader, strides over to Harry.

'Mr Kumar? Come with us, please.' And he hustles Harry into the back seat of the Hummer. Han, not wishing to be abandoned so close to meal time, hops in beside Harry.

((

Harry and Han are in a small room several dozen floors under the Gibraltar Point Water Filtration Plant. The Hummer drove a tight semi-circle, through the gates of the plant, and up to a series of garage doors around back of the plant. One of these doors opened, the Hummer drove through, and as in some spy movie thriller, the entire floor descended on a lift for almost a minute. Judging by the speed with which they appeared to be descending, Harry assumed they were about three floors under the surface of the island. After putting Harry and Han in the back seat, the four men had said nothing to them, nor had Harry uttered a word. He was tired of asking questions because lately the answers he had been getting were too absurd to process. So he sat in the back seat of the Hummer and waited for what was in store for him. When the floor stopped descending, the men exited the vehicle and two of them escorted Harry to this tiny room. Han, being uncharacteristically obedient, heeled with them along the way. This, thought Harry, was a good thing because the men seemed unconcerned with Han's presence and if Han had not hopped into the Hummer and was now not walking alongside, Harry felt the men might have abandoned his dog to the wilderness of the island.

After a few minutes, a gaunt, balding man enters the room. He is followed by a person whose gender Harry cannot quite determine. This person has short, but not buzz-cropped hair, wears a lumberjack shirt and jeans, and wire-rimmed glasses. The balding man speaks.

'Mr Kumar. You know, no doubt, who I am.'

Harry shakes his head. The balding man tilts his head querulously to one side and then speaks in staccato tones to his underling.

'Why does no one ever know who I am? I told you, if they don't know who I am, tell them before I get here so I don't embarrass myself.' He turns back to Harry and smiles. 'I'm sorry. Well, let's just say that I'm the, uh, leader of this particular co-operative operation.'

'The water filtration plant?' asks Harry, still a bit naïve about what might be happening here.

The balding man smiles. 'Uh, no, not exactly, but let us just say for a moment that yes, I am the, uh, director of the "water filtration plant." Do you know what really gets my goat? I mean as director of the water filtration plant? It's when my water gets polluted. You know, when foreign objects invade my water and change the entire character of the water. You see, as director of the "water filtration plant" it is my duty to keep certain elements out – all the while keeping the water in. Do you see?'

Harry doesn't see. He nods.

'Good. Now, I believe you've met my associates?' The balding man nods to his underling who presses a button on the side of the door. After a moment, the door opens and J.P. and Virgil walk in. Virgil is still wearing his sunglasses, which might account for why he bumps into the table and has to back up a step to stand, like J.P., with his hands folded in front of his crotch.

'Oh, yes,' says Harry. 'It's J.P., um, Raddemuller – is that right? – and Virgil Woolf.'

The balding man turns to stare at J.P. and Virgil. He shakes his head sadly. His underling scribbles down a quick note on a pad.

'J.P. and Virgil, is it?' says the balding man despairingly.

'He came upon us in a flash, Director Merrick,' J.P. explains. 'We had to think on our feet for cover names.'

90

'I see. Virgil Woolf.'

Virgil nods, ashamed. 'I thought, well, I looked at the lighthouse and I thought, Director Merrick....'

'Yes, yes, I see. And J.P. whatwasthat?'

'Raddemuller,' Harry interjects. 'Um, J.P. Raddemuller. He was the lighthouse operator until he died mysteriously in 1815.' Virgil, J.P., the balding director, and the underling all stare at Harry. 'Um, it was on the plaque.'

Director Merrick turns his attention to J.P. 'Fast thinking. J fucking P and Virgil fucking Woolf. Very good. Oh, for fuck's sake, tell Mr Kumar who you really are.'

J.P. steps forward. 'Stan Lipinksy, special agent, CSIS.'

Virgil comes forward. 'Philip York, special agent, CIA,' he tells Harry. 'That's Central Intelligence Agency, USA.'

'He knows what the C fucking IA is, you moron,' shouts Director Merrick. Then he looks at Harry. 'Now do you understand what's up, Mr Kumar?'

Harry hasn't the energy even to shake his head.

Director Merrick sighs. 'Okay, I don't know if you're dumb, or just playing dumb, but I'll put our cards on the table and then we'll see what you know, okay? Okay. Remember what I said about water filtration. This is no ordinary water filtration plant, Mr Kumar. Oh, but what I said about keeping certain elements out is very true. We're living in a time of change, Mr Kumar, winds of change. But I believe there are certain things worth fighting for, see. Do you know what certain people, certain dangerous people, want to do on this site, Mr Kumar? Do you? They want to tear it down. That's it, yes, remove it in its entirety. It's a perfectly good "water filtration plant" if you get my drift, has been for years, built from the blood, sweat, and toil of men better than you'll ever know, Mr Kumar. Yes, we built this plant in a rite of passion and virtue on December 6, 1992, and those of us who work here are devoted to it. But they want to take it down, brick by brick, and build in its place another, different plant. See? Oh, sure, they'll tell you they're only rectifying history – what a bloody lie – that they want to restore the "original water filtration plant" to its former glory. Well, you want to know a secret, Mr Kumar? Do you? Truth is, a long time back, far before a time you might remember, it was *us* who had built the original water filtration plant, us, yes, and *they* came along and tore it down and built their own. So, I ask you, aren't we justified in paying them back in kind? We don't want any special treatment, Mr Kumar, just our due. Who are *they*, you wonder?

Well, sometimes so do I. They are the foreign devils, the foreign predators waiting for our one moment of weakness, then *pow*, they move in and take out our plant and build a new one, one that they command, in its place. Do you see? And they have operatives everywhere, Mr Kumar, don't you think they don't. They sneak them in at night, violate our borders, usually at sea but by air as well, and the citizenry of this proud nation don't even know it. Now, do you get it, Mr Kumar?'

Harry finds the energy to shake his head. 'I think so. But if you're worried about foreign powers, that is, I mean, why is the CIA here?'

'Oh, god, man, not those sort of foreigners, no, for chrissake. They're American. This is a joint operation, like I said, and you need your allies. No, there are other foreign operatives we have to watch out for. Like that "writer," the one you say you're looking for. The one from Chilliwack. He – or she – is not really from Chilliwack, you know.'

'I thought he – or she – was from Camrose or Canmore, or maybe Cargil,' says Harry.

'Very good, very good, we may be able to use you yet, Mr Kumar, if that is your real name. Yes, which brings us to the question, why are you looking for this writer?'

Harry takes a deep breath. 'It's hard to explain, really. It has more to do with my missing friend, Sita Simpson. Do you know of her?'

All the government operatives shake their heads. Director Merrick gestures to his underling in a fashion that indicates 'run a check on that name,' and the underling again scribbles a quick note on a pad.

'Oh well,' says Harry. 'It's just that you seem to know everyone else. Anyway, she's gone missing, and I'm going crazy trying to find her. There are all these clues, cryptic ones, like she's been kidnapped but not really, I dunno. And the latest clue brought me here to this Arts Centre. See, I have it here. This. This is what I mean by cryptic. It's signed by this Brasso Pilgrim Junta – now I don't even know if that's a person, a place, an organization....'

'Give me that,' orders Director Merrick. He grabs the piece of paper Harry has just taken out, feverishly reads the scant words on it, holds it to his chest, closes his eyes in bliss and chants, 'Oh, my Junta, my Junta.'

Harry looks bewildered. 'You know this ... this Brasso Junta thing?'

Director Merrick opens his eyes and glares at Harry. 'Oh, no, Mr Kumar. Brasso Pilgrim Junta is no "thing," I tell you. Why, the Junta is ... the answer, the truth. You are truly blessed, Mr Kumar, to be receiving this correspondence directly from the Junta. Truly blessed.'

'Well,' says Harry, 'blessed or not, it didn't seem to do me much good, just keeps leading me on a wild goose chase. See, when I got here, thanks to this Pilgrim Junta ... ah, answer ... and it took me to the Writer, do I find Sita? No. Instead, when I got there the Writer gave me this.' He pulls the printout from his shirt pocket. The Director tears the note from Harry's hand and reads it aloud, deliberately and without emotion.

'*Islands and separations. Islands, separations, and prisons. Prisons are islands of separation. Islands are separated from mainlands as justice is separated from history.*' The Director looks up. 'This is pompous stuff,' he says to Harry. He continues to read: '*Sita is looking for you, too, but how can she find you when you're too busy getting lost? She's not here and never was. Here's the deal. Freo, Lot 150. Think about it. This may provide some answers to these conundrums of separation and islands. Freo. Lot One Hundred Fifty. Routed through the woolly coasts of Sydneysiders. Sita waits.*'

The Director looks at Harry. A new and dangerous expression is spreading across his face. 'Let me get this straight. You actually *saw* the Writer? And he gave you this?'

Harry nods.

'Good *god*,' exclaims the Director, and suddenly the room is abuzz with activity. The csis operative shouts into his shirt sleeve. The cia operative pulls out what appears to be a miniature handgun from a hidden thigh holster. The underling madly presses the door button again. The Director continues yelling, barking orders and obscure commands. 'Alpha Team, mobilize. Beta Team back up. We have a *go* on the centre. Exercise extreme caution and bring in the Delta Repair squadron for cleanup. Co-ordinate time at zero-zero-seven. This is not a drill, go go *go*.'

All the excitement makes Han, who has been sitting quite placidly until now, himself very excited and he begins barking orders of his own kind. The Director yells at both of them, as he rushes out of the room, 'Don't think we won't not be watching you.'

Harry ponders this statement for a moment. Does that mean Director Merrick and his band of merry men *will* be watching Harry, or is he being warned that, whatever he might think, the surveillance, if there ever was any, has been called off? The latter does not make much sense, so Harry assumes Director Merrick meant the former and only accidentally added extra negatives in the statement. At any rate, by the time Harry has finished speculating, the room is empty but for Harry and a barking and salivating Han. Harry thinks he can hear a helicopter in the background. Harry thinks for a moment. Han's barks turn into growls.

'Whaddya say,' Harry says to Han, 'we go for a quick walk?'

water taxi

Harry walks to the door, opens it, and peers outside. There is no sound of life in the immediate vicinity. He motions to Han who scurries from behind him, out the door, and directly to the elevator that brought them down. Harry follows more cautiously, still looking around nervously. He comes to the elevator and pushes the green button on the extruding control panel. The elevator's gears kick in and Harry waits impatiently; Han lifts his leg and pees on the elevator cage. When the elevator arrives, they both get in and Harry looks for a button to press. There are none. Harry had not noticed on their trip down that there are, apparently, no controls in the elevator, only smooth silver walls. The doors close behind them and Harry is suddenly nervous.

'Elevator up?' Harry orders, his voice creaking. Hope that the elevator is voice-controlled vanishes. Han sniffs a corner of the elevator, then sits. Harry looks at Han. Han lies down, preparing for a long wait. Then Harry notices a small cupboard door at chest-level on the side of the elevator. The door is flush with the side of the elevator, and it is almost impossible to make out its definition; for a moment Harry doubts his perception. Upon pressing the door, however, it pops open. Inside, quite ominously, a red phone receiver hangs.

'Of course,' says Harry. 'Great.' But, seeing no other option, Harry picks up the phone. There is no dial or push-button keypad so Harry merely pushes the receiver to his ear and waits. After a couple of moments, a fuzzy voice crackles in his ear.

'Wabba gackey,' says the voice.

'I'm sorry?' says Harry. 'I beg your pardon?'

'Who is this?'

'Um. I'm, uh, calling from – from the water filtration plant.'

'Uh-huh. And you need a water taxi?'

Harry pauses. This could be a trick question. He ponders, then plunges.

'Yes, indeed. There are – two of us – and we have finished our – operation here … for the evening.' Harry grimaces at his inability to sound official and waits for the inevitable denial of service, and most probably the arrival of an armed tactical squad.

'Is this Director Merrick?'

'Um. No. No, it's Special Agent Lipinksy.'

'Lipinksy? Why are you on Director Merrick's private phone?'

'Oh, yes. Ah, special condition, code – red. The Writer was sighted and we had to, um, move. Yes, move. And Director Merrick wanted me to ... order a water taxi ... if it isn't too much trouble.'

There is silence on the other end of the phone. Harry is sure the special agent is trying to determine what sort of weapon to use to kill the incompetent intruder. But he is wrong.

'Look, Lipinsky. Director Merrick gave me explicit instructions. This phone is to be used by him for two express purposes: bringing him back from Church Street after a late-night drunk, or bringing him pizza. He never said anything about no writer or code red.'

'Oh. That means you won't pick me up?'

Silence again.

'Oh, what the hell, it's a slow day. Want me to pick you up at Pier Four?'

Harry thinks back to his afternoon, a distant memory now, when he left by Ferry for Hanlan's Point. Someone said something about tour boats and Pier Four.

'Isn't Pier Four on the Toronto side?'

'Yeah, of course.'

'But I'm at the water filtration plant. Can't you pick me up here?'

'There? I dunno. It's an awful long way. Just meet me at Pier Four.'

'But I have no way of getting to Pier Four. I'm stuck here without access, see?'

'No access? Oh.'

'So, will you come and get me?'

'Where are you again?'

'At the water filtration plant!'

'Oh. That's mighty far away. Why don't you meet me at Centre Island? It's only a fifteen-minute walk.'

The elevator chooses this precise moment to begin its slow ascent to the surface. Harry is worried that, assuming the elevator is not voice-controlled and on a weird delay, someone has called it to the surface.

'Shit. No,' says Harry, 'I can't meet you there. I don't even know if I'll get out of this elevator alive, let alone walk fifteen minutes to some island I don't know how to get to.'

'It's easy. Just follow the road around....'

The elevator is near the surface now.

'Look, I don't have time to – listen, will you come and get me here or not?

The elevator grinds to a stop. The door begins to open.

'Where are you again? Hanlan's Point?'

Harry watches as the door opens to bright sunlight. There is no one there.

'The water … filtration … plant.'

'Oh, well that's mighty far–' the voice is suddenly cut off.

'Hello? Hello?' The phone is dead. Harry and Han walk out into the sunshine and walk the six paces down to the lagoon. Harry can still hear the distant sound of a helicopter, but there is no evidence of any covert operation occurring near the water filtration plant or near the Centre. Harry hasn't the slightest idea what to do when he hears the engine of a small tug rounding the bend in the lagoon. He looks up. It is a brightly-coloured yellow powerboat with the words WATER-TAXY painted on the side in red. The pilot cuts the engine and pulls alongside the dock, bumping into the tires. There is a curious flicker of light from inside the canopy before a figure emerges and lithely leaps onto the deck.

'Hey, Harry,' shouts Athnic. 'Think we best be going, eh?'

reclamation

Harry sits in the gunnel of the boat. He is not exactly sure if that's what it's called, a gunnel, where he now sits, but Athnic has told him so and Harry, not being a seafaring sort, has decided to believe him. What other choice is there? So Harry sits listening to the unnaturally loud sound of the water taxi as it ploughs its way back to the pier on the Toronto side.

Harry wants to turn to Athnic and say he thinks something fishy is going on at the water treatment plant. He also wants to ask his friend what he is doing piloting a water taxi through Toronto harbour when his normal routine is much more land-locked and hotel-based than this. He wants to ask Athnic for, if not the answers to the universe, then at least some of the answers to Harry's life. But Harry does none of this and he realizes that he has no real idea what Athnic is doing here in the first place. Athnic was the one who scurried Harry off to Galiano Island on what turned out to be a whim, an eerily correct whim, but a whim nonetheless. And Athnic was the one who drove Harry straight from the Tsawwassen ferry terminal to the Vancouver International Airport and negotiated his ticket directly from the counter, somehow coming back with a cut-rate price for what should have been a full-rate ticket. And – Harry was quite clear on this – Athnic had said nothing about accompanying Harry and Han on his flight. As a matter of fact, Harry had pleaded with Athnic to take care of Han but Athnic had tossed his don't-worry look over at Harry, the look that told Harry that all was as it should be and everything was pre-arranged and pre-ordained. That look also meant that, no, Athnic would not be taking care of Han, which was why Harry was quite nervous when he took the ticket from Athnic, rolled Han across the airport corridor inside the travel-kennel that Athnic just happened to acquire, and checked in with the surly Air Canada agent. And it is probably not even worthwhile to mention how utterly frustrated Harry was to turn around after his encounter with the ticket agent and find that Athnic had quite disappeared from the terminal.

And yet, here he was, Athnic the water-taxi pilot. But although Harry has the inclination to ask these questions, he doesn't have time for they are at the water taxi terminal at Pier Four and Athnic is tying up before Harry can get to his feet. Han, ever the agile one, leaps to the pier and loses his footing, his hind legs not quite making it to the landing, so he has to scrabble with his front paws to ensure his hind end does not pull the rest of him into the murky and obviously unclean water. After a heated battle with the concrete at dock's side, aided by a particular grimace evidenced only in the back quarter-inch of his lips that indicates, Han-like, a struggle for pawly purchase, he manages to get one hind foot clawed up to the surface and drags himself up. Three children visiting from Germany giggle at Han's antics and point at him, urging their parents to let them visit the crazy dog, but their parents, fortunately, are stoic enough to refuse.

Finally, Harry hesitantly offers his first words since Athnic rescued him from the water treatment plant plight.

'That was a quick trip,' he says.

'Oh, it wouldn't have been a century ago,' retorts Athnic, indicating to Harry that there is quite a story to tell on this one. And so there is. Again, Harry could swear that lights are dancing behind Athnic's eyes, but then decides the sunlight reflecting of the harbour water is playing tricks on him and when he looks at Athnic again, everything is back to normal.

As they make their way to the dockside coffee shop, Athnic enlightens Harry. Did he know, Athnic asks, why Front Street, several blocks up from the harbourfront, might be called Front Street? Harry, of course, doesn't know, and Athnic reminds him that Front Streets in other cities tend to front onto something, usually water, hence the name which is often a shorthand for 'waterfront,' so, technically, Athnic argues, there should be an apostrophe in front of 'front' so that it looks like ''front,' but rarely is that the case. Harry nods. Athnic, at the coffee counter by now, orders two long espressos and water for the dog, and then tells Harry that it's all about reclamation. 'Reclamation,' Harry echoes, knowing Athnic will pick up on that as a request for clarification which, indeed, Athnic does. Everything from Front Street down to Queen's Quay is reclaimed land, Athnic explains, an enormous reclamation project to push the growing city into the harbour, or, more accurately, to push the limits of the city onto a landfill that occupies what used to be not waterfront territory, but pretty much straight water. He starts to explain to Harry about silt buildups and real estate claims and urban planning, until Harry is completely lost, and still Athnic goes on for several minutes explaining how, after all, the trip to Toronto Islands is now a considerable number of metres shorter than it once was. Of course, adds Athnic, what comes around goes around, or something of that order. If the city fathers reclaimed part of the lake, it was of course perfectly natural for the lake to reclaim part of what it had lost, or was to lose, whatever the case may be. And Toronto Island, which, in actual fact, was for the longest time Toronto Peninsula, although it was never really called that, owing to a sandspit that extended along the eastern shoreline and out to touch what is now Ward's Island, was certainly at one time connected to what would become the megapolis of Toronto. But stormy weather of a century ago, perhaps anticipating the desire of realtors and urban dwellers alike to make sand where the waves roll, decided to take a peremptory step, one that fulfilled the desire of the day to dredge an eastern passage into Toronto Harbour through said spit, and washed away that little arm of sand that made Toronto Island a peninsula in actuality but never in anyone's mind. You see, Athnic continues, now happily sipping on his coffee, it was an act of imagination. When York was settled and then became Toronto, the people of the city never really saw the Toronto Peninsula as such, but as an Island, and it came as no surprise or bother that the lake reclaimed its staked out territory, giving way some years later to the indiscretions of bulldozers and landmovers. Reclamation is as reclamation does. Water builds on land as land builds on water and the cycle continualy repeats itself. Do you understand now? Athnic asks Harry.

Harry looks at Athnic, then down at the smiling Han, and while he is totally confused and inarticulate, he is somehow managing to form the words: 'The water filtration plant,' to which Athnic responds, 'Exactly.'

reclamation by physics

It is perhaps important to interrupt at this particular juncture to explain a bit about the politics of reclamation. Now, I'm hardly a physics expert – when someone uses the words, 'time,' 'space,' and 'continuum' in one sentence, why, I can barely keep my eyes open – but it's a physics example that I am about to give, so sharpen those pencils, focus those eyes, and, as they used to say in grade school, put on your thinking cap. First, you have to think back to the, until now, non-recurring motif that introduced this whole story; that is, the boundless yet repetitively useless energy of a hapless dog leaping up one stalagmite as far as he can, falling down to earth, and then repeating said task on the next available stalagmite. Think of what those Dutch sailors might have seen had such an apparition greeted their eyes; instead of what appeared to be the ruins of an ancient city growing out of the desert, they might have proclaimed this land to be inhabited by demon dogs, rabid hounds that preyed on the flesh of living mortals and then ritually celebrated through the day by leaping heathenishly from one pointy rock to another. Think of the stories they would have told, and perhaps then, sailors who arrived in a different century with different histories, might not have been so quick to insist that the land they first set foot on, the land they reclaimed from their seagoing vessel, was *terra nullius*, a vacant lot, a no-strings-attached piece of real estate. Perhaps along with stories about boys, fingers, and dikes, there would be fireside tales told by wrinkly grandmothers to their pink-faced descendants about the Land Where Crazed Canines Lived, and how the invading sailors had to pay obeisance to the Dog God before humbly coming ashore.

Whatever the case, how interesting, is it not, that a butterfly's single wingflap on the other side of the hemisphere might alter history in such an inevitable yet unpredictable fashion that nothing you remember occurring has ever occurred, and further, never even come close to occurring, since a wisp of wind has the power, so they say, to move mountains. It is the wind, after all, and the rain and the sun, one surmises, that created the picturesque Pinnaclesque scenario that Han leaps through, that might have been observed by the Dutch sailors had they arrived four hundred years later or were Han performing his mad dog ritual quad-centuries earlier. Be that as it may, the dog we see at the beginning of this story is running from one stalagmite to another – let's leave it at that for now – hurtling himself as far as inertia will take him up the perpendicular side before gravitational forces contradict his ascent and, after seizing him for one infinitesimal moment so that he neither rises nor falls, push him back to the desert floor at a rate of nine point eight metres per second squared. Now, it might seem untoward to move to an invisible spectrum, but move we must, to that layer of nothingness that is the air, the atmosphere this crazed dog pushes through in his Sisyphusian task of hauling himself up one boulder after another. Yes, he pushes through this air, this atmosphere; he displaces this gaseous substance inasmuch as it must re-order itself somewhat further afield. And true, it being a gaseous substance subject to the whims of prevailing weather conditions and the like, you may argue, it was inevitable that said air mass would eventually move.

But my point, if you bear with me, is that while the atmospheric bits and pieces would, given time and conditions, move around, they do so now wholly because a dog is running amok amongst its molecules, dispersing them at an incredible and frenetic rate. And further to my point, once the canine mass has passed through this air mass, what is left but the potential of a vacuum which, as our high school physics classes again come back to haunt us with, nature abhors. So, that air displaced by the collection of hair, tissue, blood, and numerous other fluids and chemicals that we call dog is, yes, replaced by a whole different combination of molecular collections, air to be sure, but very different air, completely different air if the truth be told, the previous combinations having been rushed out of the immediate vicinity by the leaping dog. So this new air reclaims the space laid bare by the old air, precipitated by the animal wildness.

And, yes, I could go on, tell you about the minute particles that, having endured centuries of erosion, give way in a fraction of an instant under canine claws, some of them coming to rest as they should only inches from the base of the pinnacle, others blowing apart and becoming pieces of dust so small they become invisible to the naked eye and rise with the unnoticeable air current that, as the sun heats the sand, expands upon the conduction of heat and moves the particles far into the ether. Those particles, by their actions, must displace either air or other dust particles that might feel a certain right to be there, having been there first, but such is the way of the world, certainly under the jurisprudence of physics as we know it – and so there are no apologies, no pardon-mes, just a sudden interruption of the universe as air molecules push others out of the way, as dust pieces singularly and collectively monopolize a prime piece of atmospheric space, as rock crumbs tumble down and edge out rock crumbs that have lived there for minutes, hours, perhaps months, and no one stops to think of the loss or the movement or the tremendous energy it takes for reclamation. What's mine is yours, goes another lovely expression, twisted by cynics to read what's yours is mine, all of which ignores the possibility, of course, that both can co-exist but not necessarily at the same time. Oh, time – here we go, I could go on for hours like this, but I think I've drawn a pretty good picture, if I do say so myself, and Athnic is waiting there patiently to tell the rest of the story to Harry, so I shan't delay him any longer. Unless, perhaps, he is already finished. Besides, I have a guest to attend to.

Athnic plans Harry's trip

'And so,' says Athnic, 'there's such contention over the water treatment plant that there's just no telling who's telling the truth and who's lying.'

Harry looks puzzled, but is still wary of asking too many questions, aware how that often translates into too many complex answers. But he is quite curious about what this Director Merrick is doing in the plant, why he and his compatriots built their version of the plant in 1992 on the foundation of the old one, why the space is so hotly contested, and most of all, what any of this has to do with his search for Sita. Then Harry remembers the note from the Writer, now in the hands of Director Merrick.

'Athnic,' says Harry, 'I got another clue about Sita.'

'About time,' says Athnic. 'Well, let's have it.'

'Um – I don't have it anymore. That is, this Merrick fellow took it from me.'

'And what did it say?'

Harry furrows his brow, trying to remember the pertinent details of the note. As a credit union clerk, he is trained to recall numbers, not words.

'Something about islands and separations. Oh, and prisons.'

'That was it?'

'No, there was more. Just give me a second. Islands, prisons, something about Sita looking for me just like I'm looking for her. Then there was this name, Freo, and Lot – Lot 150, that was it. Oh, and it ended with some weird stuff about woolly Sydney coasts, Sydney woollen coasts, something like that.'

Athnic nods slowly. 'Right, then,' he says.

Harry figures he needs a long, hot bath to figure out, not the answers, but the right questions, so he is perfectly content when Athnic suggests they overnight in Toronto.

Athnic is about to say to Harry that he hasn't the slightest idea what to do the next day when he experiences that flash of light that migraine and hangover sufferers alike live in fear of, and just as suddenly the light behind his eyes dims and Athnic calmly nods at Harry.

'We can stay right here at the Westin,' explains Athnic. 'I know some people here.' Harry mumbles an agreement, remembering how the countenances of hoteliers change when Athnic's name is breathed upon them. 'Yes,' says Athnic, 'we shall overnight in Toronto. I'll make some calls and see what we can do about arranging your flight to Australia.'

Harry does not let this sink in because he does not want to let this sink in.

'You'll start off in Sydney, of course,' says Athnic as if all this were self-explanatory. 'Then you'll have to take a short trip down the coast before going across to the west.'

'To the west?' asks Harry, finally breaking his confused silence.

'Yah,' says Athnic. 'Perth.'

The last time Harry heard the city of Perth uttered aloud was when he was playing a game of Risk and someone used Perth as a perch from which to take over Asia. His opponent had amassed considerable armies in Perth and it foretold world domination, Harry remembers, although he is reasonably certain Athnic is not suggesting either he or Harry portend to such massive visions. Athnic misreads Harry's face and tells him not to worry, that he will arrange safe passage back to Vancouver for Han, as Australian quarantine laws are quite strict and will not allow any dog to come through its borders without lounging about for six months at authorized compounds. Were this a normal conversation, and Harry truly doubts he will ever have another normal conversation with Athnic again, Harry might ask how Athnic knows so much about Australian immigration, or would perhaps ask for more details about the country, bordered by ocean on all sides, and what it does and does not let inside its perimeter. But, this being a far thing from a normal conversation, Harry just nods dumbly and thinks a hot bath might be the remedy for what has just transpired, but is unlikely to assist in what is yet to come.

They are at the Westin. Before they have had a chance to hit the revolving door, a bellboy calls out to Athnic. Within moments a flock of hotel service people, from desk clerks to concierges to bellboys to chambermaids, is upon Athnic. A blonde woman in a stretch limo is disgruntled as she watches the doorman resolutely ignore her and heartily greet a not-unattractive-but-certainly-underdressed-for-a-celebrity-looking man, and the starlet has to open her own door. Not having done this before, it takes her a moment to find the door handle, but once she has got this far, a slight smile crosses her face as she wonders in amazement at the extent of her talent. Someday, she thinks to herself, she shall roll down a window, and not just a regular window, but one of those hand rollie thingies, she's not sure what they're called, but some cars have them, where you crank them and the window opens. And her fantasy continues to include a trip to the Nevada desert in an old car with hand-rolled-down windows and an air conditioner that doesn't completely cool down the car and perhaps a gas station in the middle of nowhere. And she is alone except for her driver, and the gas station attendant is a young guy who looks familiar, almost like that likeable fellow over there who is being thronged by hotel staff.

Athnic, indeed, has to hold his hand up to quiet his peers and he says to one of them, finally, 'Hey, Ike, what's the chance of getting a room for tonight?' and by the time his hand has dropped from its request-for-silence gesture, a key has been dropped into it. 'Cool, thanks,' says Athnic. And he, Harry, and Han head up to the honeymoon suite to reflect on the day gone by and to plan for the days ahead.

in servitude

Can I get you anything? Anything at all?

Sita looks up at me placidly. 'You know what I want.'

I can get you luscious fruit from any region of the world. I can get you fine wines if you like, or delicious nectars. I can get you sweet treats beyond the imagination.

'You know what it is that I need.'

If it's apparel that attracts your fancy, I can have seamstresses and tailors design the most splendorous of outfits, gold thread woven into fine fabric. Or shoes, there's the thing, hand-crafted from the softest of leathers. All of this I can give you.

'You know what it is.'

Sita still looks up at me placidly, but there is a firmness in her voice that belies her gentle looks. Damn her. I can never win her over. I have offered her riches and treasures, I have made vicious and uncalled for threats, I have begged for her trust. None of it works. She just sits there, waiting. I tell her about the laws of physics, of its inevitability.

One thing, one being, is bound, in time, to replace another. That crazy dog, displacing bits of sand, bits of matter from one moment in time and space to another, that's all he was doing. Following the law. The natural course of things.

I tell her about great stories from the past, her past and mine, from the ancient past that is so long into history it has achieved the status of myth, legend, religion. I tell her about the island that was displaced in time and name by conquering forces, not once but several times and in succession.

What was Lanka becomes Ceylon – but even that becomes too simple. Lanka, Ilankai Lakbima, Lankadeepa, all of these are one, and that one becomes another one, that is, Ceylon or Ceylan or Seylan or Zeylan. Sinhaladvipa or Ratnadvipa (that's precious stones, not rats) Siri Laka and Lakdiva (that's the island south of India and not the small Lakdiv islands belonging to India). Serendib became Serendip. Oh, but islands are constantly being recreated, reclaimed, if not by the sea then by those who come by sea. I tell her this is just fortunate happenstance perhaps, serendipity. Take one piece of sand and throw it into water, is that an island? Grind that sand down into subatomic particles, is that air?

I tell her all this and still she looks at me with that placid stare.

Well then, I can give you what you're waiting for. A battle, no? But I have to lead that prince of yours away from what was to what will now be. I've dropped him clues, you see, bits of matter like so many grains of sand, so he will follow us, will follow you. I will lead him through island prisons and prison islands and we'll just see if he can really recapture his jewel, his precious. What do you have to say to that?

'You know what.'

Yes, I suppose I do know what Sita wants. She wants things to be different this time. The battle will happen again, the same events will transpire, but what she wants can never be won (or lost) in battle. No, that will happen later, serendipitously or not.

Oz is

Harry has made a new resolution. It is to never be surprised at anything that happens from here on in. He has made such a resolution because, if he did not, he would surely be surprised at pretty much every event that were to occur in the next few days, of this he is certain. So, he will not be surprised, he tells himself, if Han begins to spout off limericks; he will not be surprised if Director Merrick becomes appointed to the Canadian Senate or, for that matter, to the Supreme Court; he will not be surprised if he spends the rest of his life searching for Sita in just about every corner of the known universe, nor will he be surprised that he will remain intent on this task for the rest of his live-long days; and he will not be surprised, he tells himself, if the counter person at Pearson airport has stuck him next to a white supremacist agoraphobe who will repeatedly grab Harry's hand for emotional support during the five-hour flight to Vancouver, only to throw it down in disgust upon realizing he is clasping the brown fingers of a hand belonging to a gentleman of an inferior race.

Fortunately, as Harry makes his way to the seat Athnic has booked for him, Harry notices that there is no swastika-tattooed yahoo in the seat assigned next to him, but an attractive thirty-something woman in a business suit. Harry nods at the woman. The woman smiles and nods back. Harry throws himself into his seat and sighs. In four hours and forty-five minutes, according to the co-pilot, the 767 will touch down in Vancouver. While this is where he lives, Harry will not go home because Athnic, bless his soul, has arranged for a flight leaving less than two hours later for Sydney, via Honolulu. Why Sydney, Harry remembers asking Athnic, when the clues are pointing Harry, according to Athnic, to the other side of the country? But Athnic just smiled at the question, one of his you'll-see-soon-enough smiles, and promised to ensure Han got home safely. So Harry, trying to follow his new resolution, resigns himself to watching the in-flight movie and eating the in-flight meal. He glances at his seat-mate and decides not to initiate any small talk, although he will be polite, if a bit curt, if she engages him in conversation. That seems unlikely, though, Harry surmises, as the woman was now intently involved in a mystery novel. Harry closes his eyes.

'Do you like mysteries?' Harry hears through a semi-doze, some ten minutes after take-off (he assumes since the plane has not yet levelled off but is past the seatbelt sign stage).

'Mysteries?'

'Yes, like mystery novels.'

'Oh, well, umm. No. That is, I don't know. I – no.'

'Oh. Nor do I, really.'

Harry looks over at the woman. He looks down at the mass-market embossed book cover and catches the words 'murder,' 'park,' and 'midnight,' not necessarily in that order, before looking back at the woman.

'Oh this,' she smiles, holding up the book so he can see it better. 'Yes, that's why I was asking. You see, this is the first mystery novel I've ever tried to read, and I find it hard going, you know?'

Harry stares at the woman with what he hopes comes across as polite lack of interest. Clearly the woman reads this as a silence encouraging her to continue.

'I usually read technical manuals,' she says, throwing off a laugh that is halfway between a girlish giggle and a guffaw of derision. 'I write them, actually.'

Harry realizes any further refusal to speak will come across as boorish so, against his better judgment, he responds: 'Oh, really?'

'Oh, yes, yes. Funny, you know, most people think that's a dead-boring job.' She emphasizes the word 'most,' apparently indicating that, in her mind at least, Harry is not one of those people. Perhaps it was the way he said 'oh,' Harry thinks, or 'really,' or perhaps he just doesn't have the right facial muscles to indicate dead-boringness.

'So, what do you do?' asks the woman with earnestness never heard outside of cocktail parties and economy flights.

'I'm a clerk, a teller,' says Harry, 'for a credit union in Vancouver.'

'Oh, really,' says the woman, fairly accurately approximating the tone and timbre that Harry used when responding to her work. Harry does not believe she is similarly interested. 'And that brings you to Toronto?'

'No. No, I was here for – personal reasons.' No sooner has Harry stumbled over his reason for being in Toronto, pausing in that oh-so-mysterious way, that he knows he is in for a long conversation. He sighs again and waits for his seatmate's question.

'I see. So, what sort of personal reasons?'

'I'm searching,' he begins slowly, figuring the story is bound to take them all the way to Vancouver, 'for a friend who went missing five days ago.'

The woman's eyes widen. 'Really?'

'Yes, really. My friend, Sita, disappeared, and we've received, well, some very odd clues as to her whereabouts. I mean, it's like she's been kidnapped, but not really.'

'And the police?'

'The police – well, I haven't told them. I've told some friends and her father, but they tell me the police can't help. And there are these odd notes, you see, and they keep cropping up in the most unusual places, so now I've been to the Gulf Islands, to Toronto Island, and now, after we land in Vancouver I mean, I'll be heading out to Australia, because the last note, the last note said something that made my friend, Athnic, made him think....' Harry stops to reflect on what he has just said.

The woman's eyes have grown bigger still, and the flight attendant is hovering over them asking for drink orders. Harry requests a tomato juice. His companion asks for a double scotch. After they have received their drinks and the woman has downed half of hers in single gulp, furtively checking out the flight attendant's speed to ensure she will have enough time to drink another before dinner, she looks at Harry and motions him to continue.

'Listen, I know this sounds very odd,' he begins, but the woman shakes her head vigorously and swallows the remaining scotch she was swishing about in her mouth.

'No, no, not at all. Now, this is a real-life mystery. This Athnic fellow, that wouldn't be Athnic Long, would it?'

For the rest of the flight, true to his prediction, Harry details all the events of his as yet unfinished search for Sita. The woman interjects only occasionally to encourage him to continue or to punctuate his story with exclamatory comments like, 'How bizarre,' or 'No, really?' or 'Omigod.' She does not utter another complete sentence until they land and begin to collect their belongings. Harry moves out into the aisle, and an impatient young man from two rows back presses in from behind, so Harry's seatmate – they never did introduce themselves – does not really get a chance to say goodbye. But as Harry makes his way toward the exit, he hears her call out after him.

'Good luck, mister. Good luck. It sounds like an epic love story and I hope it all works out for you in the end.'

((

Three hours later, after sitting at a jade bar watching endlessly confusing videos on a series of screens mounted in the vaulted ceiling, Harry is again airborne, now in a 747 just clearing Canadian waters off the Pacific coast. He is thankful, joyous even, that there are few people on this early evening flight and he has the entire row to himself. He has instructions from Athnic to go to the Rooftop Motel in Sydney's Glebe district and wait for his call. Harry still does not know why Athnic wants him to go to the east coast of Australia when his final destination is supposed to be Perth. Still, Athnic must have his reasons, Harry supposes, and he sleeps all the way to Honolulu. They are forced to disembark at the airport, watched intently and herded into a dark and morbid area by gun-toting customs officials, an area that during the day might pass as a waiting lounge. Harry notices a couple across from him dressed in identical neon-purple jackets, reminding him of the fluorescent prison uniforms he has seen on films and television shows depicting prison buses in the southern United States. He does not know why this comes to mind, but it does, and it is an image he cannot shake as the passengers wait for two hours to be transferred onto the Honolulu-Sydney jet. Hair is unkempt, shirts hang out, skin is pallid, eyes are droopy. We should make a break for it, thinks Harry, and the elderly man next to him looks up so sharply from his magazine that Harry wonders if he utters this aloud. He licks his lips to see if they've been used without his knowledge, but no, they are dry and parched, and he is sure he has not spoken.

Still, the thought of prisoners in a vessel lingers, and it stays with him even after they board the Australia-bound plane, and during the entire flight to Sydney, even as he clears customs and walks into the too-bright sunshine of a Sydney morning. This thought is with him even after he departs the cab which has taken him to the Rooftop Motel. He realizes where the motel gets its name as he lugs his suitcases up three flights of stairs to a grimy lobby area where the clerk is visible through a window that has been crudely cut out of a former wall. The clerk is ancient and works diligently at some papers in front of him until Harry clears his throat to announce his arrival.

'What?'

'Um, I have a room booking?'

'What, here?'

'Uh, yes.'

'Today?'

'Yes.'

The clerk looks grumpy and sighs his best tourists-are-welcome-here sigh. He turns the guest book around and shoves it at Harry.

'May as well sign in then. I'm putting you in 207. Here's your key. Come back and pay before you go to sleep or out or whatever.'

'Thanks,' says Harry, signing where indicated and forcing a smile.

He picks up the key and turns to find his room.

'Don't forget to come back and pay right away.'

'Sure,' says Harry, and he brings his luggage down a floor to his room. It is dingy and has an odd smell Harry cannot quite place. The bed sags in the middle and the ceiling fan threatens to fly off at every revolution. None of this prevents Harry from kicking off his shoes, laying his head down on the lumpy pillow, and immediately drifting off without regard to the desk clerk's order to return for immediate payment. He dreams of flying and prisons and Sita. And he does not wake up until dusk is settling in.

((

There are two activities frequently performed by animal companions, specifically designed to wake their human companions from even the deepest slumber. The first is the sound of a cat vomiting, a sound which, were it to be canned and sold, would make for a most excellent alarm clock buzzer. Such is the sound that it not only awakens, but inspires the sleeping soul to leap out of bed to find the offending animal and ensure it is not using an expensive carpet or duvet cover as a makeshift vomitorium. The second is the less aural but more persistent act of a dog licking a sleeping person's face. This tongue-to-cheek activity often starts slowly, a bare touching of animal tongue to human face, but as the sleeping continues the lollingness of the tongue grows to such an extent that, if the sleeper does not rise in short order, huge portions of the human face are slavered upon, leaving copious quantities of dog spit on skin, pillow, and, depending on the output of salivary glands, mattresses as well, leaving future mattress owners to speculate on the origin of such stains. Harry has never owned a cat and so he has never woken to the sound of a feline regurgitating by his forehead, and he is a better man for it. However, he has lived with Han for four years now and if Harry ever has the misfortune of sleeping past 8:12 AM, Han is wont to perform the second act, the incessant licking action dogs are so well known for. And it is this very dog-tongue to human-face contact that awakens Harry at dusk at the Rooftop Motel in Sydney.

'Hmm, stop it, Han,' murmurs Harry. The licking continues. Harry opens one eye and sees Han's tongue just before it licks Harry's eyeball. He closes that eye and opens his other eye to see a poorly-crafted bedside table. In exactly eighteen seconds, Harry goes from wondering what time it is and whether he has enough of it to walk Han before work to realizing that he is in a grungy hotel in a large cosmopolitan centre in the southern hemisphere where Han is certainly not meant to be. Harry sits up in the bed and puts his hand on Han's face. Han licks his hand. Harry is not dreaming. There is a knock on the door. Before he can rise, the door opens with a passkey and the elderly clerk enters, looking more surly than before.

'I told you to pay me right away,' he says, barely looking at Harry. 'That was six hours ago.'

'I'm sorry. I – fell asleep.' Harry looks at Han, looks at the clerk; the clerk looks at Harry, looks at Han. Harry feels a couple of words will do the trick: 'The dog?'

'No dogs allowed,' says the clerk. 'Unless you pay extra. Five dollars. Up front.'

'But the dog – he shouldn't be here....'

'That's right. Not without paying. I'm off shift. Come down and pay me for you and the dog before I leave. I mean it.'

The clerk leaves and doesn't even shut the door. Han continues to lick Harry's hand. Harry begins to think of what may have occurred, but then remembers his promise to not be surprised and thinks that perhaps they should go out for a walk around the Glebe. Harry looks at his dog, closes his eyes and wills his friend home, across island continents and oceans, back to the Vancouver apartment on Main. When Harry opens his eyes, Han looks at him, sticks his nose forward and burps, ever so slightly, announcing his most definite presence. Harry keeps his eyes on Han and reaches for the telephone receiver. After several attempts through unhelpful telephone operators, Harry is connected to Simpson's home.

'Where are you?' asks Sita's father.

'Sydney. I'm in Sydney,' Harry says deliberately.

'Good, good. So, any news on Sita?'

'Simpson,' says Harry, still keeping his eye on Han. 'My dog is here with me.'

'Uh, that's good,' says Simpson. 'Say, don't they have pretty strict quarantine laws down there?'

'Yes,' says Harry, 'yes, apparently they do.'

'Oh,' says Simpson.

'There's something going on here,' says Harry. 'I'm not sure I'm supposed to be here. And I'm absolutely certain my dog is not supposed to be here.'

'But,' says Simpson, 'what about my daughter?'

'What?' says Harry, still caught between reality and something else.

'My daughter. You're there to find Sita.'

'But my dog?'

'Like I said to you before, son, you just have to trust. If your dog's there, well, just trust him.'

'Sure,' says Harry.

'And call me when you get some news,' says Simpson.

'Sure,' says Harry. 'Sure thing.' And he hangs up the phone while watching Han chew on his left front paw.

((

Harry and Han walk all around the Glebe district, although Harry is still not entirely sure that his dog is really with him, and then some, and two hours later they find themselves in a brightly lit part of town with just a mite too much energy. Harry decides it's a good idea to go back to the hotel but, since most of the evening he has been following Han, he is not sure which way to go. He has already promised himself that he will be extra quiet when he re-enters the hotel, since he had the misfortune of meeting the desk clerk's night replacement when he had settled the bill, and the night clerk was even more surly than her predecessor. She had one of those faces that looked like it was perpetually dragging on a cigarette, a cheek-sucking appearance that quite frightened Harry and made Han produce one of his deep-throat growls. So Harry hoped, upon reaching the hotel, he could sneak by the clerk without her noticing, because if he did not he was certain she would make some sort of derogatory comment about him or Han or both. With all this in mind, Harry decides to flag a cab on the assumption that while he may not know which way is home, the taxi driver will certainly be able to find the Rooftop Motel. Harry tells Han to sit behind a lamppost so as not to deter any cab drivers from stopping; Harry figures he can always plead foreign ignorance about rules concerning dogs in cabs, but he has to get them to stop first. Besides, thinks Harry, chances are Han is not really there, and he is oddly comforted and disturbed by this notion.

((

Harry sees a yellow-top in the distance and holds a hand up to signal the driver. He hails and hails and hails. The first cab waves him off, heading, perhaps, for a previously called fare. The second driver spins around the roundabout, drops a gear, and eyes Harry carefully; his lip gives way to a sneer and he guns the engine, harder and louder than would be necessary to propel him out of the roundabout. Harry is left waving vainly and is completely nonplussed that the driver has not stopped. Did he, too, suddenly remember a fare he had, a call to pick up? Or did Harry's appearance strike the fear of god into the driver, fearful for his life perhaps, that Harry might threaten his very livelihood just by being in his cab? All these thoughts trail through Harry's mind as he continues to wave vainly and as the sound of the cab engine recedes. His efforts appear to be of no avail as ten minutes later, Harry is still holding his hailing hand up high and Han is starting to get bored, licking parts of himself to the bemusement of passersby and the embarrassment of Harry. Finally, a third driver slows, appears to accelerate, then hesitates and pulls to the curb. Sunlight glints off the taxi's side window, momentarily blinding Harry. The driver has a cap pulled down over his eyes so Harry wonders how he can see the road, but tourists can't be choosers, and Harry sticks his head into the front.

'Just me and my friend,' he offers, slapping his thigh in a command for Han to leap into the car. Han looks up with boredom, decides he is quite happy on the street, and resumes licking. Harry slaps his thigh again, stinging himself a bit.

'C'mon, Han, c'mon, boy.' Han jumps into the car. Harry, however, does not, as it was not his voice that has just ordered the dog into the cab. Harry looks at the cab driver; a broad smile from underneath the cap beams back at Harry. The driver tips his cap back and looks right at Harry, laughing. 'You too, boy,' Athnic says to Harry. 'Hop in the back.'

((

On the way to the Rooftop Motel, Harry tries to remain calm. Athnic chuckles to himself for several minutes, waiting for Harry's inevitable questions, but Harry refuses to humour him. Finally, Harry speaks.

'So, you didn't call.'

'Pardon?'

'The hotel. You said you'd call at the hotel. And you didn't.'

'I got busy,' responds Athnic. 'Working.'

'Hm. And you have a work visa or what?'

'Nah, well, sort of. Pulling a shift for a friend, works downtown at a four-star. Then I saw you, figured you could use a lift.'

'Couldn't get a cab to stop for me for my life,' says Harry. 'Even hid Han so he couldn't be the reason.'

'But no one stopped.'

'Nope. No one stopped.'

There is silence between the two of them, a familiar silence when they both reflect upon their lot in life and how they are friends despite their histories, their ways in the world. Athnic, always the charmed one, always gregarious, and Harry, the insular one, the introvert who never moves outside. That part they were both content with. But the silence descended whenever they experienced an incident like this. Harry knew, and so did Athnic, that the drivers didn't pull over for him because the night was dark and Harry was dark. And, unspeaking, they both knew that Athnic would have been able to hail down a cab in half the time. Not because he was Athnic, but because he was white. Harry was half-white, but of course, that meant he was also half-brown, and Harry realized that such half-caste realities often meant less than half a chance at getting a cab. And, of course, Harry knew he was in a part of the world he was unfamiliar with, but this very familiar act was enough to make him feel, curious as that may seem, at home. Great, thinks Harry, things are the same all over. Sometimes, of course, it was not so obvious. It might not be a cab driver not pulling over, but it might be in the middle of a cab ride, the way the driver checks Harry out in the rear-view mirror. Or it might be a slight quiver in the voice of a fellow teller when talking to Harry at a coffee break about the present government's immigration policy. Or it might be an attitude neither seen nor heard by Harry, but intuited, an inner feeling obscure enough to make Harry wonder if he's fabricating the whole ordeal, but an inner feeling so strong that he knows he wouldn't have the imagination to fabricate something so awful. The same all over. How comfortable.

'So,' says Harry after the pained silence lasted almost all the ten-minute drive back to the hotel, 'how come we're staying in this dive anyway? You usually have contacts in more high-brow places. Like that friend you're driving for, he works in a four-star, didn't you say?'

Athnic now pulls the car over to the curb in front of the Rooftop.

'True enough,' says Athnic. 'But we're not staying here.' He nods toward the front door of the hotel and there, beaming, is the old woman from the front desk, Harry's luggage by her feet.

'Am I being thrown out because of Han?'

'Oh no, no. I just asked them to get your stuff ready – you're being picked up in, oh, about now.' Athnic points to a black limousine just coming around the corner.

'Picked up? I just got here. And where am I going – Perth?'

'Perth. No, not yet, not quite yet.'

'Then?'

'Wollongong.'

'Wollongong? Why?'

Athnic again points to the limousine, its back window now rolling down. The trunk pops open and the desk clerk, still all smiles and showing remarkable strength for a smoker her age, tosses Harry's bags into the back. She slams the boot, pounds on it twice, waves to the driver, and then heads back into the hotel, pausing only to turn and sneer in Harry's direction. Nice, thinks Harry, although he is not altogether certain if the clerk has a problem with Harry because of race or if she's just naturally surly to everyone – everyone except Athnic. The limousine window is almost fully down now and a black-cuffed hand reaches out, beckoning, clearly to Harry.

'He'll explain,' says Athnic. Harry begins to protest, but Athnic holds up a hand as if to block out a particularly brilliant ray of sun. 'I know, Harry, I know this all seems odd. And you're probably wondering what I'm getting you into now. But you just have to trust me. I'd never let you get hurt, Harry, you know that.'

Athnic reaches back and opens the door so that Han can leap out, race across, and in through the window of the limousine. Harry is confused again. And although he has no idea why, he *does* trust Athnic, however absurd and contrived his friend's actions may seem to be. Perhaps it's because Harry so desperately wants to find Sita. Perhaps it's because Athnic seems to know the game they're playing, even if he won't tell Harry the rules. Or perhaps it's because Harry knows, deep down, that this is the way things are supposed to be. Whatever thoughts about trusts and loyalties that lie within the deep recesses of Harry's mind, however, are interrupted dramatically when Harry hears a muffled scream from inside the limo. Harry follows his dog, choosing to open the door rather than leap through the window.

'See ya in Perth,' Athnic calls out to him, pulling away from the curb. 'Trust me.'

Harry turns, but Athnic is gone. He pulls himself into the car and feels the door shut firmly behind him. Han is happily chewing away at the black cuff worn by the middle-aged man sitting in the back, looking rather alarmed but unhurt. It is Director Merrick.

Sita and Anna Varre

Sita sits in the spherical vessel and studies her travelling companion. She makes a mental note of my physical attributes: left earlobe missing, strange wavy tattoo above the temple, hair that is more silver than grey but more grey than its original jet black, a profile that is at once pretty, smart, and fearsome. She has not heard me speak as yet, but has been privy to my thoughts and she has heard me utter a guttural and loathsome (yet sweet and murmuring) laugh, the same one she recalls from a long time ago – was it through a telephone? – and only occasionally do I look over at her, studying her face, but only in brief, unguarded glances.

When she tires of me, Sita looks around her and tries to determine the nature of the vehicle she is travelling in. It appears to be made of glass, but when she touches its smooth walls, her hand feels like it's touching feathers, or maybe warm water. Her hand almost goes through the material, but is gently pushed back, as if from danger. She knows the vessel is spherical because she can see no corners, but she can see through it from every angle. Yet she is not aware of being encased in a sphere of any kind. And when she looks out she can see not one continuous panorama as she would expect, but a variety of vistas, all of them containing bits of land and water, all of them images of islands in large bodies of water, and all showing people trapped or incarcerated or struggling to get free. She should be that way, too, she thinks, yet she is not struggling, however trapped she might be.

We have been travelling non-stop, never spending more than one night on any single island. Yet Sita is not tired, just a mite bored. She must wonder how that could be, travelling and travelling and travelling and never tiring, never stopping to rest, to see the sights, or at least grab a handful of local colour. Yet this has been our way since she found herself travelling with this odd-looking person in this odd-looking vessel.

Our first stop was close to home, just a quick fly and dive – the strange vessel takes to the air as easily as it submerges, Sita noted with some surprise on that first trip – into the Georgia Strait and onto a small, inhabited island. She had managed, during a brief restroom break, to sneak away and carve her name into a picnic bench with a small pen-knife. But then I was there, urging her back onto/into the bubble (but not before I added the necessary clues beneath her name) and off we went, for what seemed like days, until we found a haven from the stormy weather in the old water filtration plant. No, we had not slept, but I permitted her a brief beach walk in the cool evening air and it was there she had met the man she only referred to as the Writer, a man who walked with a slight limp and whose gaze kept flitting away from her, as if he was totally uninterested in what she had to say, all the while professing his complete dedication to her tale of woe. He would make note of this, he had told her, and send rescuers on the way. On the way, she had asked? Why couldn't he notify the authorities immediately? Because, he told her, they would do nothing, for they would not listen to him, and besides, in the eyes of some authorities he was already a wanted man, for refusing to co-operate in the way they saw fit. And why, he asked her, if she was in such a hurry to get away, did she not simply make good her escape right now? He gestured to the left of her, to the right of her, behind her, and sure enough, Sita could see me nowhere. She had to admit to the Writer, whom I have to admit was unknowingly working on my behest, that she did not know why she could not run away, just that the time was not right. The Writer nodded sagely and I, from my place not to the left or to the right or behind her, but from my place all around her, laughed.

(

And then we were off again in our bubble, this time for a length of time that completely eluded Sita's sensibilities. Was it a day, a week, a month passing over and under and through bodies of water that were sprinkled with bits of land mass, over and under and through forests and moss and earth that was always, always completely surrounded by water? And everywhere she went, I, her companion-captor, must have seemed dissatisfied. No, not here, not here, were my muttered words entering Sita's brain directly without passing through eardrums. And we would be off again. Here we stopped and Sita could make out the faint silhouettes of kangaroos hopping toward the horizon; here she could make out smaller such creatures, surrounded by strangely-clad people with cameras and scuba equipment; here she could see the ghosts and shadows of men long since dead, all within the confines of a thick, cold limestone structure; here she sees herself and her companion and our strange craft floating above a single tree atop a single hill, and then a draft precipitated by a hovering helicopter blows them further away and the chopper jigs for pieces of the tree. Yes, she must think to herself, this is all a dream, a strange and awful dream, and then she finds herself in the depths of a sulphurous pool, oddly comforted but saddened all the same.

At times during this interminable sojourn, I might disappear for hours on end; Sita would wake from her fitful slumber and find herself alone and with no idea how I had left or where I had gone. Truth be known, I was laying out more clues, putting together more messages, for if this battle was to be fought in a different setting, I had to make meticulous plans and make them well-known to my adversary. Sita should have made her break then, you would think, and so did she, although she never seemed to find her way clear of that bubble-vessel, or perhaps she never wanted to. Try as she might, she would always find herself up against yet another level of density preventing her escape. In time, Sita must have realized that she would have to sit and wait, although for what she knew not. It did occur to her on occasion that she was supposed to wait for Harry, but this thought was so unappealing, that she was to be trapped here like a fairy-tale princess with no other recourse than to wait for her man (or in this case, her friend Harry) to come and rescue her helpless and hapless self, that she told me she quickly abolished the thought from her active mind. The thought persisted, however, and tended to recur when she was tired, irritating her all the more. She was never one to let men have their unsavoury way, whether it was in the matter of sex or privilege, and she knew she had alienated many a man along the way, although she knew that none were worth salvaging. Still, she told me this thought irked her and she would have been pleased not to entertain it at all.

Perhaps she still thinks I am planning an epic battle in which I will vanquish Harry. Little does she know. Yes, there will be an epic battle, and yes, one will be a vanquished, but none of that is the point. It's what happens in the battle's aftermath that matters most. I would tell her this, tell her to trust me, but I don't believe it would make a spot of difference. Not a spot.

Harry and Merrick go for a drive

Harry stares at Director Merrick, trying not to show fear or alarm. He is, however, furious that Athnic would betray him this way, although in the back of his mind he keeps thinking of Simpson's insistence that Harry trust his friend. Trust indeed. Director Merrick smiles sweetly, the sort of smile affected by those who think they are on television. Or by those vain, elderly sorts who have had a third facelift. Or by those who have power and know they have power and want others to know they have power. Han licks Director Merrick's hand, startling him out of his pasty smile a few moments earlier than he would have dropped it on his own.

'So, Mr Kumar. You remember me, I presume?'

'Yes. Mr Merrick, director of the water filtration plant on Toronto Island.'

'Why, yes,' Merrick says, chuckling. 'Yes, of course, the water filtration plant.'

Harry swallows hard and decides to be bold. 'So, you're doing research on water filtration techniques down under, is that what brings you here?'

Director Merrick frowns. 'Did you know, Mr Kumar, that there are three ways of killing a man in the back seat of a car without even using your arms?'

Harry shakes his head. Merrick continues.

'No, I don't suppose you would. Well, Mr Kumar, just so we know who's boss around here, who's asking the questions, hmm?'

Harry turns toward the front of the vehicle and decides to ask no more questions.

'Did you really think you could escape me that easily, Mr Kumar? Did you?' Director Merrick smiles and produces the piece of paper Harry received from the Writer. He reads the bottom section: '*Freo. Lot One Hundred Fifty. Routed through the woolly coasts of Sydneysiders. Sita waits.*'

The limousine winds its way through Sydney's major thoroughfares toward what Harry ascertains are its outskirts. Finally, a good twenty minutes into their journey when the cityscape is giving way to a sparser suburban sprawl, Merrick speaks again.

'You know, of course, where we're going, perhaps?'

Harry sits stonefaced, unsure of what to say.

'Well, I'll tell you. We're going to find your Sita Simpson.'

Harry turns to Merrick, alarmed. 'You know where she is? Do you?'

Merrick laughs. 'I see. That gets your interest, doesn't it? Yes. Well.

Perhaps we can work to mutual satisfaction. I might help you to find your girlfriend and you will help reunite me with Brasso Pilgrim Junta. My junta.' Merrick smiles blissfully.

'She's not my girlfriend,' says Harry.

'What?'

'Sita. She's not my girlfriend.'

'Oh, I see,' says Merrick. 'Whatever you say.'

'But she's not.'

'Yet you feel compelled to travel the world to rescue her, is that it, rescue this woman you feel nothing for?'

'I didn't say I felt nothing. I said she wasn't my girlfriend. Which she isn't.'

'Right. Whatever you say.'

'Anyway, who the hell is this Brasso Pilgrim Junta? And what does this have to do with Sita? And what does Athnic have to do with all this? And why do you need my help, since I'm clearly blundering my way across the world without a clue about why I'm doing anything?'

Merrick sighs. 'Remember our pact, Mr Kumar? I ask the questions. And by the way, if I use my hands, there are forty-seven ways to kill a man in the back seat of a limousine. Comprendé?'

Harry is despondent and his body shows it. He is no closer to finding Sita, at least not that he can tell, he is trapped on the outskirts of Sydney in the back seat of a limousine with a certifiable madman who Han seems to be quite fond of, and his good friend has adopted this nasty habit of appearing out of nowhere to impishly guide Harry to his next ridiculous assignation.

'We're going to Wollongong,' Merrick says, as if that should explain everything. 'A seaside visit.'

Harry thinks on this. Woolley coasts of Sydneysiders. Wollongong. Somehow this Wollongong was to lead to Sita.

'Did you know,' says Merrick, 'that British prisoners were once shipped to these shores? Oh yes, it's common knowledge, I suppose, Australia the penal colony. But did you know, Mr Kumar, that after a while the Sydneysiders had enough of the convict imports? No more, they said, no room at the inn. So what do you suppose the British prison export industry did about that, hm, Mr Kumar? Sent them, the convicts, to the other coast, that's what they did. Perth, to be exact. So, do you know where you and I are heading after Wollongong, Mr Kumar. Hmm? Can you guess?'

'Perth?' asks Harry.

'Perth. Very good, Mr Kumar. Perth.'

how Varre Anna

So, okay, time for a recap. Start with one pinnacle-crazed dog, a start we haven't actually got to yet, but be patient, for we shall arrive. Move onto the sorely unexciting history and details of the life of one Harry Kumar and watch how that might mobilize into a catalytic moment when he meets this Sita Simpson. Then, poof, she's gone and it's up to Harry and his global peripateticisms to find her, thus beginning an island quest that takes him to Galiano Island, Toronto Island, the island continent of Australia, and soon to an island-off-an-island on the continent's west coast, and yes, finally to yet another South Pacific island where all will come clear. Can you feel the gusto of the travel narrative, truly bringing vigour into tired old sedentary bones? Why, this is one big vacation, what with international airports, hotels, limousines, the whole shebang. All to culminate with a romantic pirouette off the front porch, Harry and Sita in each other's arms, together forever, lost in love, chaste to all but each other, stage-screen kissing as if there were no tomorrow or at least no scheduled showings after tonight, and all live happily ever now in this short life we call today. Ah, but those voices are irksome, aren't they, the questions about all these messy and inexplicable characters? What does Director Merrick have invested in this quest, for instance, and what are all his concerns about rebuilding and protecting and secret servicing? Who or what is this Brasso Pilgrim Junta – Merrick's long lost love, perhaps, or a particularly faithless ipo that has absconded with all his pension? Or might this Junta be a movement, one that demands cult-like adoration from its followers, of which the dashing and admirable Director Merrick is one? And what might we make of this Athnic Long fellow, the senior concierge at the Quality Inn in downtown Vancouver who appears to make few appearances at that establishment but appears flittingly and at times a little too conveniently, to salvage the perpetually-lost Harry? Well, a concierge is, after all, the sort to provide directions (but whether that makes him a Director is another matter, as is the question of whether Director Merrick would then qualify as a senior concierge, or would have to pass a hospitality-service test first, an exam with which one might expect he would have considerable trouble), but to actually go so far out of the way as to become an actual guide, why that's downright beyond the call of duty and responsibility, wouldn't you say? Oh yes, and lest we forget, there's always Han, loyal, obedient, and apparently equally peripatetic as his human companion, though one would imagine a canine would encounter considerably more resistance in obtaining air passage by himself, owing to a certain lack of credit rating and vocal skills, although this latter ability will be addressed shortly if you are patient enough.

Okay, I'll let you in on a secret: Han was not home snoozing away and dreaming of not-so-fleet-footed rabbits the day that Harry met Sita. Quite the contrary. Han was in a very discreet way responsible for their fated meeting, though I've given away enough and will not, I promise, revisit the issue, so on this you're now on your own.

And finally, there's me, my role. You might see me as a guest narrator, someone who pops in and out to help the story on its way, although truth be told, the story more or less tells itself and my role, if I have any to play, is really just to provide the occasional interlude, an interruptive update now and then. Consider me a news anchor, breaking in on your favourite television show to tell you about disasters around the world, or at least disasters that might have an economic effect on you, interrupting your pleasant soap opera starring Harry and Athnic and Sita and Han and Merrick and the assorted cast of extras. I will tell you this, however, that I do know something special about the Brasso Pilgrim Junta that I have not yet let on. We are close, BPJ and I, so close sometimes that it's hard – oh, but there I go again, revealing more than I should, not at all a good girl, and I'm sure someone's mother used to say, 'Anna, get some clothes on right now,' if the girl's name was Anna which, in the context of this narrative, is entirely possible. But this choral break, so to speak, is almost over and it's time to get back to the two lonesome characters in the back seat of the limousine which, by the way, is arrogantly left-hand drive, obviously imported from North America to the down-under, right-hand drive world of Australia, and this particular feature is something our hero is just about to notice.

international license to drive

As Harry looks out the window, he notices the landscape has changed from urban to decidedly rural, a dense forested scape of hills and valleys and, off in the distance, sea. Green hilltops as far as the horizon, then a deep blue. Then, figures Harry, at least this part of Merrick's story is accurate. If not for all the goings-on, thinks Harry, this would be a rather relaxing escape. Such thoughts are quickly shattered, however, as the limo begins to negotiate a roundabout and is greeted with a chorus of blaring horns and screeching brakes.

'Driver,' yells Merrick. 'What's going on?'

The driver, who Harry has yet to see because of the smokescreen glass dividing the left-hand driver's seat from the rest of the car, shouts back hoarsely: 'Bloody wrong-sided drivers goddammit-to-shit.'

Merrick is silent for a minute as the limousine careens around vehicles that have angrily halted to allow the limo to drift past them.

'And that would mean you tried to do the roundabout from the wrong way, would it?'

'It's not my bloody fault,' yells the driver, wrenching the wheel to negotiate a path around a honking Volvo facing him on the roundabout. 'I'm used to driving on the right and because we imported this goddamn car from goddamn Detroit, the wheel's on the wrong side for these approaches, goddammit.'

'I see,' says Merrick. 'And the police car behind us, do you think he will be pleasant enough to understand I have a moron for a driver?'

Harry turns around and, true enough, the flashing lights of a police car are signalling the driver over. The driver utters more expletives and, having now left the roundabout, on a straightaway, pulls the car over to the right shoulder, once again crossing lines of traffic and eliciting angry horns and yells from left-side drivers who have just been cut off.

'Oh, nice move,' says Director Merrick, his lip curling.

'Yes, Director,' says the driver in exactly the same tone as he has been uttering expletives, leaving Harry to believe the driver was substituting, in his head, two other words for the ones he has just vocalized.

'I'll handle this,' says Merrick. He rolls down the window and thrusts a wad of identification papers at the police officer who has just made his way to the car. The officer appears startled and does not take the papers from the black-cuffed hand offered from the back seat.

'I need to talk to the driver,' he says tersely. This he does, eventually asking the driver to get out of the car. The police officer is not overly polite as he makes this request. By this time Merrick has leapt from the car and is directing rather irate invective at the officer. Harry sits still and catches a few choice words. Merrick explains he has duties of international importance and that while he does not exactly possess diplomatic immunity, he's close enough to it to warrant the officer's consideration. The officer, in turn, suggests they should have left their American car on the other side of the pond and hired a perfectly efficient right-hand drive if they couldn't find a driver who could figure out the rules of the road in Australia. Merrick, mistakenly pulling rank, insists on seeing the officer's superior. The grinning officer agrees, pokes his head inside the limo, pats Han on the head and nods to Harry.

'Can you drive?'

'Yes,' says Harry.

'Well, I'm taking your friends in to chat with my superiors. Their request, you understand. So you'll be all right on your own?'

'Fine,' says Harry, saluting his respect so as not to be arrested himself.

Harry exits the car to move to the driver's seat. Merrick is yelling directions at Harry as the officer none-too-politely pushes him into the back seat of the police car. The driver, smiling slightly, follows obediently. Harry does not catch much of what Merrick says, but he does hear the name of a hotel uttered before Merrick disappears into the car. Harry sits down in the driver's seat and pulls down the sun visor, exposing a piece of CIA stationery on which are written full details for a luxury suite at the Novotel Hotel. Sounds nice, thinks Harry. He starts up the limo, carefully manoeuvres it to the left side of the road, drives forward and resolves to stop at the next petrol station for directions.

Anna's sonnet and soliloquy

Random acts and everything at stake,
And if I lose again, is that the end?
Verbose I be, but this vow I do make:
Alone forever or with her, my friend.

Not yet, howe'er will I meet my demise
At islands or at prisons in between.
To tell the truth, I'll cut them down to size:
Harry and Han, in one sulph'rous scene.

'Enough,' you say, 'enough of cryptic clues!
Director Merrick, Athnic, what's their game?
Enlighten us or else give up your ruse.'
My friends, you see, I must protect my name.

Of this I am quite certain and aware,
Now this I claim or I'm not Anna Varre!

☾

Oh yes, step by step, line by line, we draw ever closer. I've been reciting my poetry to Sita from the day we left and I do believe I'm getting better. I still need to work on that romantic stuff – battle cries and apostrophes are more my level – but I think I might be winning her over. Not that she's given me any signs. Quite the contrary, actually, in that she goes for days ignoring me, but I am not that easily dissuaded. I try to keep her up to date on the progress being made in the great Quest for Sita – progress, I should add, that would be going nowhere if it weren't for me. I am constantly visiting these fools, leading them around by the noses like the pigs they are. Some of them, that true patriot Merrick, for instance, truly believe they're on my side – or would, if they knew who I was – but even *they* need some obvious misdirection; others, yes, Harry, Athnic and that lot, don't really know why they're hithering to and fro as they are, just *that* they are, and I figure it's my job to keep them going at a steady pace. Which brings me to that asinine dog. Why, if he's not scrabbling up pinnacles as if they were banyan trees, he's materializing and dematerializing all over the place. He's causing trouble, that one, and I'll have to keep my eye on him, even though he's relatively clueless about all the goings-on in the world. He reminds me of those three dogs sitting in a row, see no evil, etcetera. See, hear, speak. Speech, now there's a fine idea. Just give me a minute.

Harry makes some friends

Several men – are they Greek? Italian? – are playing chess in downtown Wollongong square, on a board that's mapped out onto the courtyard, each man rubbing a cheek, looking across at his opponent. The chess pieces are gargantuan, the pawns two feet tall, bishops, knights, rooks another foot higher, and kings and queens coming to chest level on the men. They move pieces by hugging and lifting, or kicking them forward, and captures mean a double gesture of removing the opponent's piece and then returning to move their own onto the captured square. Smoking, thinking, biding. Harry watches the men watching the chessmen. Animations and animated motions. Harry watches and wonders if he is more of a Greek man in downtown Wollongong or a plastic chessman in downtown Wollongong. The animator or the animated. He shoulder-checks to ensure there is no deified hand making his move. He is not entirely sure he doesn't see such a hand on his shoulder. He takes a step forward, then hesitates, retraces, and moves in a southerly direction.

He stops at a street-level coffee vendor, orders a flat white, a delightful discovery for someone used to plain espresso or franchised cappuccino, and reflects. A trip to the ocean is necessary, he tells himself, then wonders if someone else was doing the telling to himself, and shakes his head.

When he found the luxurious Novotel, Harry checked in and took his bags up to the designated suite. The concierge looked at Han doubtfully, but Harry had only to mention that his friend Athnic would be joining them shortly and the concierge became all sweetness and light. Indeed, after Harry had collected his thoughts for a moment, the concierge had even come to the suite and kindly suggested that he would take Han out for a beach run, freeing Harry to wander into shops and the like if he wished. Normally, Harry would not have let his dog into the hands of a stranger, but since his entire life was now strange itself, Harry figured this could not hurt. After the concierge left with Han, Harry decided a walk downtown was indeed in order.

Thinking he might run into the concierge and Han, Harry begins the trek down to the ocean, but gets lost along the way. He starts heading toward the place where he saw the break in the buildings, but, lost in thought, ends up doing a circle and is in downtown Wollongong again. Night is falling and the darkness makes it harder for Harry to determine where, exactly, he is lost. Around the corner is a bright blue neon sign advertising some sort of club. Harry, not much of a drinker, figures an

Australian beer, of which he has consumed surprisingly few since arriving from Sydney several days ago, would go down nicely right about now. Harry is not prepared for the blast of industrial music as he steps into the club. It is, after all, early evening and there are notably few people drinking in the bar. However, rather than turn away and leave, embarrassing himself as the fourteen sets of eyes belonging to patrons in the bar have all swivelled in his direction and are now in the process of staring through him, Harry figures one beer couldn't hurt. He bellies up to the bar. He orders a beer. The bartender looks at him quizzically and asks him to repeat himself. Harry does so; the bartender continues looking at him quizzically, unable to match the accent to the face, but, being a bartender, realizes that if he serves a customer up with a beer he can't go too far wrong, and this he does, to his and Harry's satisfaction. Harry lays down a five-dollar note since he cannot for the life of him hear what the bartender tells him is the cost of the drink, and Harry does not check the change the bartender returns to him, assuming all must be fine.

In the corner, the dimmest corner of the bar, is a man who goes by the name of Chick. He is twelve stone, naked, close to thirteen when fully garbed with a solid silver belt buckle and several strands of gold that might pass as decorative chainlink fencing were they not strung about Chick's neck – what there is of Chick's neck, that is, because to any casual observer in the bar, in whatever state of inebriation they may be in, Chick is quite neckless. His chin and cheekbones seem to rise directly from his shoulders or, more accurately, from a place a good several centimetres below his shoulders, almost like a pumpkin on a fencepost, a pumpkin which has been there for a long time and is starting to sag a bit from internal rotting. Which, while none would say this to his face, is not an inaccurate description of Chick himself. Chick comes to this very bar every evening after work and on Saturday afternoons at two. He leaves every evening, including those Saturdays, at closing time, whatever that may be, depending on the amount of beer being served to the clientele. Chick is what you might call a regular here. And, being a regular, Chick does not like irregular goings-on in his bar. Which is why, when Harry walks in, Chick's are one of fourteen sets of eyes that swivel to the door, and while other sets linger on Harry for considerable lengths of time, only Chick's remain on Harry all the while Harry orders his beer, pays for it, and takes his first sip. Chick sees a man he does not know walking into his bar, having a beer, and looking around as if he owned the place. So, not being one who likes irregularity or accommodates it well, particularly considering his profession as prison guard at the local remand centre who watches his inmates get away with a lot of shit Chick is pow-erless to stop – especially now that he has amassed three warnings for use of excessive force – he decides to make an overture to this dark stranger.

Chick rises, a considerable feat after thirteen glasses of beer, and the beer in the most current glass, filled to such a proportion as to form a concave meniscus, owing to Chick's habit of filling up a new glass with dregs from the old one and, as the evening wears on, the meniscus fre-quently reaches breaking point – and at this moment, the beer in the most current glass slops over the side and onto Chick's shoes, something the rising man does not notice, fixed as he is on Harry at the bar. Spilling beer all the while, he approaches Harry and stands before him, to his left, waiting for Harry to notice him. This Harry does, but only after casually surveying the dance floor which should be empty at this time, and would be, were not two teenagers in the throes of love dancing a slow waltz step to the industrial beat. Harry thinks this odd, then notices a large man off to his side. Harry turns to this man, who turns out to be an inordinately huge and balding man with no apparent neck. Harry looks at Chick. Chick looks at a slightly blurry Harry. Chick opens his mouth as if to speak, but nothing comes out. Harry takes this opportu-nity to have another sip of beer to moisten his rapidly drying lips. Harry even has the time to swallow before words actually come out of Chick's mouth. As the large man speaks, Harry notices, Chick slops beer from his amply full glass onto Harry's feet, but Harry thinks it inopportune to mention this offense at such a time.

'So,' says Chick. 'You're a–'

Harry does not quite hear the last word that Chick utters and, against his better judgement, leans into Chick to hear him repeat him-self. This Chick does, spilling more beer down the side of his glass onto Harry's trouser leg, and into the side of Harry's left boot. Again, Harry hears only, 'You're a–' but again misses the last word. Harry stares at Chick and Chick stares at Harry. Harry slips momentarily into a child-hood memory, sparked, no doubt, by the extraordinarily large gentle-man in front of him.

((

The curry factor: *harry harry smells like curry*. My name's not Harry, he would tell his fellow urchins, but Hari, really, although my father did always call me Harry, said it would make things easier, but my mother was always insistent to drop that extra *r*, to *i*-ify the *y*, make Hari out of

Harry. So it's Hari, pronounced a little bit more like hurry than Harry, which is sometimes pronounced hairy. The urchins would stare at him. This made things decidedly easier they would nod to each other, *hurry hurry smells like curry*, scans rather well, don't you think? Hurry Harry, curry carry, it's all the same thing. So it is all the more surprising when, now thirty years later, a world apart, Harry hears those voices behind him, Hey, hey, so you're a curry, are ya? Here too? Masala as world mix. Moving transnationally, how wonderful, the turmeric curmeric smells of coriander and cumin. So, you're a curry, are you?

That is the question Chick asks Harry.

Curry? Am I a curry? No longer just the smell, nor the adjectival curry-head, no, now the very foodstuff takes him over, wraps him up in a banana leaf of flavour. Me, curry? Yah, you're a curry? Indeed.

Chick looks at Harry inquisitively. Harry begins to respond by assuring the large gentleman that he really does not know what he is talking about. Chick does not like nor does he trust Harry's accent. Not broad enough for kurri, not strong enough for American, not recognizable to his trained ear as any Asian accent he is familiar with. Who is this strange man with a strange accent?

'You're not kurri?'

Harry stares blandly, not blankly, but blandly, without flavour and certainly without curry. Harry stares at Chick and Chick stares at Harry. A continental impasse. 'Right,' says Chick, as if he has ascertained the truth of the matter when actually nothing could be further from the truth. 'Right, have a good day.' And off he turns on his heel, gesturing as if to tip his hat were he wearing one, but instead he just spills some more beer, this time into Harry's right boot. Good day and he is off, back to his corner, strangely satisfied with this encounter, although he has forgotten it by the time he sets himself down at his table and only an odd feeling of déjà vu prevents Chick from rising once again when he notices a strange, dark man in his bar.

What a strange place, thinks Harry. He takes another sip of beer and looks back to the dance floor. The teenaged couple are finished dancing and are moving in his direction. Boyfriend notices Harry first and smiles broadly; Girlfriend, too, grins and they both come up to him. Boyfriend continues to smile and it is Girlfriend who speaks first.

'How ya going?' Girlfriend asks, nodding congenially.

'Yeah, how ya goin'?' echoes Boyfriend, adding a soft but manly chuck at Harry's shoulder.

'So, ya from Sydney?' asks Girlfriend.

'Ya from Sydney?' is Boyfriend's contribution.

'Um, no,' admits Harry. 'Not Sydney. Canada, actually.'

Girlfriend and Boyfriend stare at Harry dumbly.

'Canada? Yah?'

Boyfriend does not repeat this, just mouths it in surprise.

Girlfriend looks at Boyfriend and explains. 'He says he's from Canada.'

Suddenly Boyfriend is animated and speaks his first unrepeated words. 'I coulda swore he was a kurri.'

'Yeah,' says Girlfriend, picking up on Boyfriend's dialogic switch. 'Thought he was kurri.'

'You certainly look kurri,' says Boyfriend. He smiles at Girlfriend and as if explaining, says, 'We're kurri, y'know, though ya might not know it ta look at us.'

'Yah,' says Girlfriend. 'We're kurri.'

Harry looks exasperated.

'Look,' he finally breaks in, 'I'm clearly not getting something. Maybe it's the music, but, what is this "curry"?'

'Naw, not curry, like the food,' says Girlfriend, snuggling up to Boyfriend. 'Kurri, like aboriginal.'

'Yah, we're kurri people down here,' explains Boyfriend, 'but if you go up to Queensland, the aboriginals call themselves "murri," just in case ya ever go.'

'Oh,' says Harry. 'I'll remember that.'

'Hm,' says Girlfriend, tugging Boyfriend back to the dance floor. 'He sure looks kurri, doesn't he?'

Boyfriend nods and is about to let himself be led back to the dance floor when he turns for one final question.

'So, what brings ya to Wollongong?'

'Um, I'm looking for someone. A friend of mine is, has been, well, I think she's being held against her will.'

'Ah, right. That would be in Derby then?' asks Boyfriend.

'Derby?'

'Yah,' interjects Girlfriend. 'Port Hedland detention centre up in Derby.'

'Yah,' says Boyfriend, 'if your friend tried to get into Australia, that's where they'd stick her. Or maybe Curtin or Woomera.'

'Yah,' says Girlfriend. 'Used to be the refugees weren't put in places like that. Used to be I had friends who would take 'em fishing and everything until they was processed.'

'Used to be,' says Boyfriend. 'Now they stick 'em in camps. Bad places, them, cramped quarters, leads to riots and such.'

'The Australian government does this?' asks Harry.

'Nah, that's the funny part,' says Girlfriend. 'Used ta be managed by Australian immigration. But got too many refugees coming in, so they hired an American prison firm.'

'Never asked us, though,' says Boyfriend, and he begins to laugh.

''Course, they never asked us the first time they brought in convicts either!' says Girlfriend, and she too begins to laugh, now pulling Boyfriend back onto the dance floor.

'See ya,' says Boyfriend.

'See ya,' says Girlfriend.

'Yes,' says Harry, mulling over refugees being treated like convicts in multinational prison complexes. 'See ya.'

Harry decides to knock back the rest of his beer and try to find the ocean. Kurri, Curry, Murri. Way too confusing.

☾

By the time Harry gets back to the Novotel, after a short evening stroll along the beach, Athnic and Han are sitting on the kingsized bed watching television.

'Where's Merrick?' asks Harry, though he really doesn't care to know. He had actually played with the idea of not going to the Novotel, of finding his way back to Sydney instead, but he realized if he was ever going to find Sita he would have to play by the rules, whatever the rules were. Still, he was glad to see Athnic there.

'Cops called,' says Athnic. 'Seems Merrick got impatient, took a swipe at the senior officer on duty. They're trying to figure out whether to charge him or give him over to national security for deportation. Go figure.'

'Hm. So, Athnic, I guess it's up to me to ask this. What's next?'

'We wait,' says Athnic. 'Merrick said we'd get a message by seven PM and it's now,' looking at his watch quickly, 'seven-ten.'

The phone rings. Harry and Athnic both look at it. Athnic gestures to Harry and Harry picks it up. A computer voice on the other end of the line says, 'Good evening Harry Kumar room twelve-oh-eight you have new information on channel fifty-seven,' and hangs up.

'What'd it say?' asks Athnic.

Harry doesn't respond, but picks up the remote and switches to channel 57, the one normally reserved for automated checkout. A beam of light emits from the television screen and Harry can swear it is directed right at Athnic's face, bouncing off his eyes and back at the television, creating a fuzzy text fills the screen, slowly coming into focus: Freo Lot 150.

'That's the same message,' whines Harry. 'The same message the Writer from Toronto Island gave me.'

'Wait for it,' says Athnic, 'wait and watch.' Both men and dog stare intently at the screen. Harry thinks it starts to fade out of focus again. The letters are plasticky as they re-mold themselves, smaller, into more detail, more serify. 'There,' says Athnic, jubilant, 'that's what we're waiting for.'

Harry reads the now-shimmering text: *In a freo structure built by unfree labour is where you will find a residue of she that will lead you to the She in question.*

'Now what the hell does that mean?'

But Athnic has already grabbed the remote control and is flipping back to a sports channel featuring surfers. With his free hand he lifts the telephone receiver and dials the front desk, never letting his eyes leave the television screen.

'Carol,' he says into the receiver, 'Athnic. I'm great, thanks. Say, Carol, can you go into my room account, twelve-oh-eight, and print off the latest input message? Yah, thanks. My friend Harry will pick it up. You're a trooper. Bye.' He hangs up and, eyes flickering every so slightly and still focussed intently on the surfer channel, Athnic says aloud, apparently to Harry, 'That's why we're heading out west.'

'West?'

'Western Australia. Fremantle. Freo.'

'To this Lot 150?'

'Well, that's where we'll start,' says Athnic, as if that explains it all. 'Relax, Harry, chill out for a moment.'

'But what about Sita?'

'Relax. We'll find her no prob. We leave tomorrow at two.' And Athnic, much to Harry's frustration, turns back to the television without further explanation.

Han, a parked car, and a passing Australian cattle dog

Harry, Athnic, and Han do indeed leave at two the next afternoon, fortunate to get bumped into business class owing to the none-too-extraordinary fact that the woman at the air ticket counter took a liking to Athnic. Han was rather displeased to be once again kennelled into the cargo hold, but proceeded to fall asleep rather quickly and stayed that way for most of the flight.

When they land in Perth, Athnic tells Harry to rent a car while he checks into accommodations, and by the time Harry is in the driver's seat, Athnic shows up with directions as to where to drop him off.

'You mean,' says Harry, 'you're not coming with us?'

'Oh no, I'll meet you there. But, you see, there's this friend of mine who works in Northbridge–'

'Athnic! We're here to find Sita.'

'Yes, and we will, Harry, trust me. Here,' and he hands Harry a piece of paper. 'Drop me off in Northbridge and meet me tonight at this hotel.'

Harry sighs, takes the paper, and navigates the car out from the airport to where Athnic needs to be dropped off. Once Athnic leaves the rental car, Han takes the liberty of hopping into the front seat so as to get a better view of western Australia. Harry looks at Han; Han looks at Harry.

'Okay, boy,' says Harry. 'Which way to Fremantle?' and Han barks once, helpfully, and looks out the front window.

((

Harry parks the rental car on the wrong side of the road. Like Director Merrick's driver, he is not used to driving on the left and it shows, most particularly when he goes into roundabouts at breakneck slowness and when he parks. It should seem perfectly obvious to him that he should park the car on the same side of the street as all the others are parked, but instinct takes over and he swerves, somewhat panic-driven, to the wrong side of the street, especially if he has to parallel park, which he can only do on the right-hand side of the street. He parks in front of an old Italian coffee shop right in the heart of Cappuccino Strip in Fremantle. He has not a clue what he is doing here in the heart of Cappuccino Strip in downtown Freo, and he is even more clueless as to how Han has managed to join him, despite Australia having some of the world's fiercest quarantine laws for canines.

'We don't have rabies here – and we don't want it,' was what the immigration official told him when he had inquired, more out of vague interest than actual intent, at Sydney International Airport. Six month quarantine for any fur-bearing animal companion. Visiting rights once a week. When Harry inquired about the conditions of the quarantine, again out of mere curiosity, the immigration official rolled his eyes, ordered Harry to wait at the counter, disappeared behind a large green door, and then re-emerged several minutes later with a sheet of crumpled paper. This he thrust at Harry and waved him on. Harry read the sheet:

> Animal to be kept in a secluded area thirty-five kilometres west of Sydney. The Eastern Creek Quarantine Station keeps dogs in kennels constructed of brick and mesh with galvanised mesh enclosures. The majority of kennels are six metres long by one-point-four metres wide and contain enclosed sleeping quarters which are one-point-five by one-point-five metres. Each kennel contains a trampoline for sleeping. A sprinkler system provides evaporative cooling during the summer months.

Harry began to turn back to the immigration official, who was already scrutinizing a beige passport from a very short woman. He was going to ask why the kennels were equipped with trampolines, but upon seeing the grumpy expression on the face of the immigration official, thought better of it and made his way to the exit. He read more of the sheet:

> Bedding and soft toys which travel in the crate with your pet will be destroyed on arrival. It is very difficult for AQIS staff to clean these soiled items. If you wish to send bedding for your pet's stay in quarantine it should be attached to the outside of the crate. Alternatively bedding and toys can be sourced in Australia and sent to the quarantine station. No bean bags are allowed into the station.

Harry looked around, wondering if it was worth asking anyone why bean bags were being excluded, but seeing no one official, he stashed the sheet of paper in his front jeans pocket and left the airport.

But then, here was Han, travelling along in the passenger side of the rental car (and, like Harry, always going to the wrong side, that is, driver's, to be let in while Harry fossicked for keys at the passenger side, creating curious stares from numerous passersby, some of whom undoubtedly believed that this dog would drive, that this strange foreign-looking man would take the passenger side) getting immense amounts of hair on the cloth seats and hanging his head out the window, seriously sniffing out kangaroos which he knew were there though he had yet to actually encounter one. And, now that Harry had parked, there was Han in an intolerably hot car, waiting for Harry who went into the Italian coffee bar to ask something of the waiter, something which was taking Harry enough time that Han decided to cool down by sitting on the floor of the passenger side. Han panted. He was hot and he wasn't used to the particularly quality of air and light that was peculiar to the southern coast of western Australia. Han noted with some satisfaction that Harry had rolled down the driver's side window and both back windows were slightly open, so a pleasant if warm breeze passed through the Honda. After several minutes, Harry had still not appeared and, despite the open windows, Han was starting to feel nauseous. Perhaps he was a bit car sick as well. They had driven a stop-and-start game from the airport, and Han was a bit travel weary. When he was a pup, Han had enjoyed more attention from Harry who would give him a bit of Gravol whenever they went on longer trips. But, with age comes a type of reliance on what simply is, and Harry no longer medicated his dog, particularly not now when he wasn't absolutely sure what Han was doing there or how he had arrived.

Han perked up a bit, though, when he thought he could smell an Australian cattle dog not too far away. This, he thought, might be a distant relative, and it would be rude not to say hello. But, being cattle dogs and all, it would be equally rude, and somewhat poodle-ish, to announce one's intentions too far ahead of time. Han allowed his black nose to rise to seat level, just so he could ascertain the correct distance the cattle dog might be, and when he should leap out the window and bark his fool head off. Smelled like twenty paces. Better give it a count of twenty-two paces, just to ensure a timely arrival. Best get to the window just as dog and companion pass by, for a too-early announcement was quite a waste. The human companion would not be startled adequately, nor would the cattle dog be caught off guard. Too bad he was feeling slightly off, or he would be enjoying this more. Fifteen paces now. Twelve. Haunches tighten. Timing was everything, Han tried to teach Harry. Timing was better than the event itself. Eight, seven. Harry rarely listened to Han about temporal issues, seemed far too preoccupied with human timekeeping, which generally meant running around trying to be someplace 'on time' and fearing 'lateness' as if it was a piece of pork chop that some mongrel had gotten to before you. Human time quite confused Han. Four, three. Han readied himself, steadied himself. His stomach growled uncomfortably, which Han usefully converted into a throaty growl-warning of his own volition. One pace away. Now. Han leaped furiously at the passenger side window. As he did so, he caught a peripheral glimpse of the open driver's side window and recalled that only three of the car's four windows were actually open and the one he was hurtling his body toward was not one of these. Plus, the sudden movement had truly upset his already upset stomach and he could feel the few morsels of mushroom omelette, part of a breakfast that Harry had so generously shared with him that morning when they dropped Athnic off, starting to search their way up his esophagus, but everything was set to go now and Han truly didn't have the language to suggest that this, or anything for that matter, was too late.

The young woman walking the elderly cattle dog along Cappuccino Strip in downtown Fremantle was lost in thought as she recalled an old girlfriend who had suddenly popped into her mind. This girlfriend, she recalled, had suddenly popped into her life three years ago and then, just as suddenly, had popped out eight months later, so it was entirely illogical for her to be thinking of said girlfriend now, for no apparent reason, and it was this thought that caused a quizzical frown to cross her face. The frown turned to momentary fright when the wrong-way-parked Honda she was walking by lurched in her direction, and out of the corner of her eye she caught sight of a dog not unlike her own smashing its face against the closed window while simultaneously uttering a cross between a howl, a bark, and a screech. She had not time to turn to see what was happening, but her ever-alert though aging Fritz swung around to catch the sight of Han slamming into the window while vomiting copiously into the glass frame, so that, to the untrained eye, it would look like Han's head had exploded into a profusion of partially digested mushroom omelette; though, of course, all this did for Fritz was to bring back images of puppyhood and, had it not been so hot and had Fritz's tongue not already been hanging out in a sustained pant which was his regular behaviour at this time of year in downtown Freo, Fritz might have licked his lips expectantly in the distant memory of regurgitated dinner from his now long deceased mother. However, the young woman, in a mild panic and in a rush, tugged at Fritz's collar and led him away before the last sounds of Han's howl were echoed by the splash of dog vomit on the side window.

Harry chose approximately this moment to exit the coffee shop, smiling, as he had received just the information he required, and then groaning loud enough to attract the attention of the coffee-shop patrons as he saw his dog flatten his nose against the side of the car window while projecting a considerable portion of his breakfast straight onto the smooth and highly reflective, for light as well as solid, surface. Harry sighed. Han, looking through a somewhat smeared window, smiled. And he woofed a brief acknowledgment of Harry's return.

the Esplanade Hotel

'Well, Han,' says Harry, hopping into the Honda and surveying the dog's damage to the rental vehicle. 'Looks like we're going to stay a few days. Maybe enough time to clean up the window. And the car seat.' Han looks up at him happily. Harry starts up the car and whips down a street near Cappuccino Strip and follows it to the end. In front of them is a large green park, perfect, thinks Harry, for Han's morning ablutions. Beyond that are a series of waterfront restaurants that the coffee barista has told Harry about, a good place to eat if you like fish and being by the water, a pleasant change from town. Harry nods, satisfied, and swings the car around to park beside the impressive structure on Marine Terrace. This is the Esplanade Hotel, the place where Athnic is to meet them. It is expensive, the barista has told him, the most expensive hotel in town, a four-star accommodation that vies for five-star status, but owing to its location and the local lack of full amenities, it's a dream far off. And while Harry would normally stay at more modest digs, this is not a normal trip and nothing he had done so far felt in the least bit normal, so Harry feels perfectly happy walking up to the front desk – with his dog, no less – and demanding a room that can accommodate the two of them.

The clerk begins to protest Han's presence, but once Harry mentions Athnic's name, the clerk is all smiles. And, since it *is* off-season and since the room Harry insists on *happens* to be a smoking room, the clerk checks them into the executive suite on the third floor. The clerk seems anxious to get the paperwork done, and the reason becomes obvious, for once Harry's credit card clears, the clerk begins to pepper him with questions about Athnic Long. How is he doing these days, is he still a concierge, has he refused promotion up and out of the hotel lobby business? Harry answers all these questions the best he can, and finally excuses himself and Han when a bellboy arrives to take Harry's bag to the room.

He nods at Harry and introduces himself as James.

'James Henty. If I can do anything, anything at all, to make your stay more comfortable, please don't hesitate to call on me.' He pauses as they wait for the lift. Once the door opens and they are safely inside, he once again turns to Harry. 'I understand you know Athnic Long. Is that true?'

'Yes,' admits Harry. 'As a matter of fact, he's one of my closest friends.'

James the bellboy looks at Harry with wide-eyed admiration.

'Athnic Long. That name's a veritable legend around here. I've never met the man, you understand, but I know all about him. He's said to be able to take the grumpiest customer and turn him around so's that same grump will make sure his entire corporation's hotel bookings are done through Athnic's employer. And he makes a good tip out of it, I believe. Oh, sir, I'm not hinting, please. As a matter of fact, it would be an insult to take a tip from a friend of Athnic Long. No, I won't hear of it. But would you tell me, sir, if it's true that Athnic once managed to arrange for rooms for the entire London symphony when their bookings were lost?'

'I really wouldn't know,' says Harry. 'He's my friend, but we rarely talk about work, really.'

James Henty looks a bit disappointed, but is still clearly thrilled to be in the company of One Who Knows Athnic Long.

'Would you …' begins James, '… would you tell Athnic Long about me? I mean, if it's not an imposition. Would you?'

'Um, sure. What do you want me to tell him?'

'Oh, tell him that he's my idol. No, wait, tell him that I was the most impressive bellboy you ever encountered. No, don't say that. Oh, my.'

They are now at Harry's room, have entered, and James continues to talk as he steadfastly refuses Harry's offer of a tip.

'Tell Athnic that James Henty, bellboy, is named after the very first owner of the Esplanade Hotel. That's right, sir, the original J. Henty came to Swan River from England with his two brothers, back in 1829 it was, and the first thing he did was purchase this land, right beneath us here, Fremantle Town Lot 150. That he did. He didn't do much with the land, though. Got married a couple of years later and then took off for Tasmania a couple years after that. I wasn't really named after him, you know, it just happens that my parents, the Hentys, called me James, and I just happened to end up working here. But it makes for a fascinating story, don't you think? I think Athnic would be pleased with this coincidence, since he's a master of turning coincidences into a positive experience, isn't he? Oh, tell him I'm very knowledgeable, too, just as he is. Well, probably not as well-versed as he is, but good, you know. For instance, I can tell hotel clients that my namesake sold Lot 150 to Captain Daniel Scott, who put up some wool stores on this property. But when the governor, Charles Fitzgerald, approached him with his prisoner housing problem – this was 1850 – Captain Scott stepped up and offered his stores as a makeshift prison. That's right, Mr Kumar, this hotel is built on the land that was, for all intents and purposes, Fremantle's first prison, not counting the Roundhouse, of course. Anyway, Captain Scott left the property to his children, and it was eventually sold by his daughter, Mary Ann Gale, in 1878. It wasn't really used very much as a prison, by the way, just a temporary makeshift variety, really. Anyway, the property changed hands several times until William and Martha Meadly decided to turn it into a hotel. That was 1895, '96 by the time the Esplanade Hotel actually opened. Bought out, though, by the Swan Brewery in 1902 – common practice, back then, for breweries to buy up hotel property since that's where folks got their beer. See, you buy a hotel and then only let it sell your beer. They called it "tying trade." A captive audience, no? Well, Mr Kumar, I should leave you to rest. Please tell Athnic I said hello. Well, like I said, he doesn't know me, so, well, just say you met me.'

Harry nods, although he is thinking about the only detail in James Henty's whole monologue that piqued his interest, that the Esplanade Hotel was built on Lot 150. That, thinks Harry, is why Athnic arranged to meet here.

Bellboy James is on his way out, still refusing a tip, when he suddenly spins on his heel.

'Oh, Mr Kumar, just some recent history. The last renovation of the Esplanade was 1996. Twenty million dollars of improvements, can you believe that? We have a fitness centre, two heated swimming pools, a sauna, three spas, two fully licensed restaurants, a lobby gift shop and a total of 259 rooms.'

'Two-fifty-nine? Really. The hotel brochure said two-fifty-eight.'

Bellboy James looks at Harry quizzically, amazed that anyone would pick out that subtle, yet important, difference.

'Are you sure it's two-fifty-nine?' asks Harry.

'Well, yes sir, as a matter of fact I am. Yes, 258 is the figure that circulates and, truth be known, it's the figure we're told to mention in our orientation. You see, the two hundred and fifty-ninth room is one that never gets opened.'

'Never opened? Why?'

'Well, it's a long story, Mr Kumar.'

'Listen, James, I need to see that room. Never mind the story, just take me to the room.'

'Oh, Mr Kumar, I'm afraid I can't do that. Quite literally, it would cost me my job.'

'You won't take me there?'

James shakes his head sadly. At this impasse, James and Harry both turn to the sound of a gentleman clearing his throat directly outside the door. Han lurches out the door and runs to the figure, jumping up and whimpering excitedly.

'Well, if you won't take him, will you take me?'

'Athnic,' Harry exclaims.

'Arf-arf-arf,' Han exclaims.

'Athnic Long!' James the bellboy exclaims, and he leans against the door frame for support, overcome as he his by the presence of greatness.

((

Athnic Long and Harry Kumar sit in a lounge of the Esplanade Hotel lobby. Athnic has just returned from the mysterious room 259 of the hotel, once James Henty recovered enough from meeting his idol – neither Harry nor Han were invited for the room tour, James being afraid of losing his employment by such a transgression. Han keeps staring at Athnic, waiting for the next peanut to fall his way. Athnic looks placid and content.

'So, when are you going to tell me what this is all about, Athnic? What was so special about that room?'

'Well, it's a long story,' says Athnic, munching on peanuts and throwing a couple Han's way.

'Excuse me, Mr Long?' The bartender is at their table carrying two very full beer glasses. 'This is compliments of the front desk for you and your friend.'

'Thank you,' says Athnic, as if the bartender has performed a service he was expecting all along, which, of course, Athnic being Athnic, is true.

'The room,' says Athnic, tossing another two peanuts to Han, who, confused by the double treats, misses both of them, 'was what they call the Born to Party Jacuzzi suite.' Athnic looks at Harry who obviously doesn't know the jargon. Athnic looks at Han who obviously wants another peanut. 'Most hotels have 'em – it's a top of the top, cream of the crop, super-deluxe regal suite.'

'And it has a jacuzzi?'

'Well, actually, no. I mean some of them do, in other hotels, but this one, well no, but we still refer to them as Born to Party Jacuzzi suites. It's just the name that's stuck.'

'And these rooms are never advertised? I mean, they keep them a big secret?'

'Well now, that's the funny thing. Most hotels are quite proud of their Born to Party Jacuzzi suites – they're the rooms, after all, where they can boast celebrities have stayed and all. So, no, they're not usually secretive. Except in this case.'

'And?' Harry is becoming impatient. So is Han, but he just wants another peanut.

'And in this case there was an incident in that room about ten years back. A murder-suicide that caused quite a scandal. Seems a local politician and his lover conspired to tear down a town monument and build a rather xenophobic statue in its place. Apparently this was part of a plot to lock down the country to any and all immigration. Anyway, the scheme was discovered, the townsfolk rebelled, and the politician and his lover hanged themselves in that very room.'

'So much for a Born to Party Jacuzzi suite,' says Harry morbidly.

'Indeed,' says Athnic.

a visit to Fremantle Prison

The following morning, Harry sits on his bed with Han. On one side of them is a pile of tourist maps and brochures; on the other, the clue that Athnic had printed off from the Wollongong hotel message system: *In a freo structure built by unfree labour is where you will find a residue of she that will lead you to the She in question.* Harry studies the note for what must be the twentieth time and then rustles through the tourist brochures until he finds the one he is searching for. He holds it up to Han and smiles.

'Let's go for a walk,' Harry suggests, and Han does nothing to deter that idea. The two of them head off through the restaurant, an Italian bistro that was sold some years back and is still operated by the Aga Khan Foundation, into the Esplanade green and then make their way past the waterfront restaurants. In the distance, Harry can see a round, sandy structure on the water's edge. They approach it along the water and it is a massive structure indeed. When they finally get up the stone steps to the base of the structure, a tourist sign tells them that this is the Roundhouse, built in 1830. It has the appearance, thinks Harry, of an obese lighthouse. He follows Han through an area that is described as strictly off-limits and looks out onto the Indian Ocean. In the distance he sees a ship and wonders, in passing, if any of the ship's mates see him.

If this were June 2, 1850, he might have been spotted through the keen eye of a sailor on the vessel *Scindian* anchored off the coast of Fremantle. She carried seventy-five convicts and fifty pensioner guards, the latter of whom were accompanied by their families. The problem, however, was how to house these men, as the only existing prison complex, the Roundhouse, built twenty years earlier, contained only seven cells, each capable of holding three prisoners. And the Roundhouse already had a no vacancy sign posted out front since it was overflowing with far more than the suggested twenty-one prisoners. The logical solution, then, was to build another prison complex, which was started pretty much immediately at a site on which, by the end of the next century, would stand a four-star hotel demanding considerably more cash for a single night's stay than a convict would earn in his lifetime. And the prison would likely still exist where the Hotel Esplanade now stands, but for England's not-in-my-backyard approach to its criminalized element. By the time the inmates and passengers of the *Scindian* were still contemplating their future homesteads, England sent another nine hundred convicts to join their fellows in

Western Australia. By this time, you see, the Sydneysiders of New South Wales and the Tasmanian immigrants had already placed an embargo on future shipments of convicts on the grounds that they had received more than they could reasonably handle. So, Western Australia it was. By 1852, the ragtag bunch began building what would be their own place of incarceration. Three years later, they moved into their unfinished dwelling, watching the final construction finish in 1859. By the latter part of the century, the conditions in the prison were so appalling that the building was condemned, but owing to poor communication and the fact that there really wasn't any big push to build yet another expensive prison complex, the condemnation orders were belayed. By some ninety years actually, and it wasn't until a heatwave-induced riot in 1988 that officials seriously undertook a review of the prison. On November 8, 1991 the last prisoners were transferred from Fremantle Prison. Seventy-seven days later, the prison re-opened as a tourist site.

Harry and Han make their way to the other side of the Roundhouse and down the steps to where they discover a huge tunnel under the structure. It is completely boarded up, a sign suggesting this was done for safety reasons, and that the tunnel still runs the length of the town, originally built by convicts as a transport for fresh water from here to the site of the Fremantle Prison. Harry peers inside the darkness of the tunnel and wonders how many people actually walked through this place, perhaps as far as the prison itself. Harry looks down at Han.

'We're going to visit a prison,' Harry says to Han.

Harry and Han are standing at the front gates of the imposing Fremantle Prison. An enormous iron grill hangs ominously over the five-metre wide archway that functions as the entrance to this prison-cum-tourist-destination. Harry takes a deep breath.

'Here we are, Han.'

Han looks up at Harry, opens his mouth to loll out his tongue in agreement, then wanders off to lift his leg against the visitor information sign. Harry can't help but notice that one of the points of information suggests strongly that dogs are not welcome in this prison. He is studying this particular point when a burly gentleman with a crew cut comes up to Harry.

'There's no dogs allowed, sir,' says the burly gentleman. He reminds Harry a bit of his encounter with that other burly gentleman in the Wollongong bar.

'Oh,' says Harry. He looks around hopefully for a spot in the shade. 'Is there a good place I can tie him up?'

The burly gentleman looks around, then looks at Han. He smiles and Han, in his canine way, smiles back. The burly gentleman nods at Harry.

'Tell you what. I can take care of him while you're inside. It's not busy and I like dogs.'

Harry gets a worried look on his face, mostly because when the burly gentleman says, 'and I like dogs,' his hand reaches down to pat Han on the snout. Harry often pats Han on the snout, but is very aware that Han must know someone, at least sniffingly well, before he will let anyone touch him on the snout. Otherwise....

'Actually,' Harry begins, but has no need to finish his sentence owing to the direct action taken by Han.

'Oh, *jeez,*' cries out the burly gentleman, quickly withdrawing his hand from Han's mouth. 'Ooh. Ouch.'

'Sorry,' says Harry formulaically, 'I don't understand. He's never done that before.'

The burly gentleman rubs his hand and, as do most folks after their first rough encounter with Han, says, 'No worries. My fault really.'

Then he looks down at the smiling dog, looks through the gates at the paltry number of visitors inside, and gestures to Harry. 'Tell you what, it's really not that busy. Why don't you take him on in. Just pick up after him, see?'

'Oh, certainly,' says Harry agreeably. And he and Han walk under the enormous steel grate that threatens passers-under guillotine-like.

The bored gate attendant who takes Harry's five dollars informs him that he has just missed the tour, but he will have no trouble catching up with the group if he hurries toward the workshop areas and number one gunpost. Harry and Han stroll off in the direction that the attendant points. He pulls out the crumpled note from his pocket and reads aloud the cryptic instructions:

> *In a freo structure built by unfree labour is where you will find a residue of she that will lead you to the She in question.*

Harry once again thinks about the faint signature from the earlier clue from Galiano Island. Brasso Pilgrim Junta. Once again he wonders if this is a name, an organization, a joke? Brasso Pilgrim Junta. Whatever it might mean is lost on Harry. So here he is, in the Freo Prison, which must be the structure alluded to in the cryptic note. Fremantle Prison was built by convicts. He has read that in the guidebooks. And, as Athnic pointed out, local residents call Fremantle 'Freo.' He must be in the right place. Only problem now is where to look? Inspired, Harry offers the scrap of paper to Han on the way-off chance that his dog might sniff out the solution. It is something Harry has only seen work successfully on *Lassie* and like-dog television re-runs, but he is truly desperate and, after all, what does he have to lose? Han sniffs the paper. He licks it. He takes it from Harry's hand and begins, obediently he thinks, to give it a pre-swallow chew. In frustration, Harry snatches the paper from Han's jaws. Han looks up guiltily at Harry, at his odd-tasting, reneged-upon treat. He licks his lips. Harry looks down at his dog and shakes his head at Han's uncanine ineptitude. What would you do, Harry wonders, if the house was on fire? Would you bark me awake or would you sleep through the inferno? What a dog. He actually mutters this last statement, instigating much tail-wagging on Han's behalf.

Harry and Han walk together towards the number one gunpost. They see the tour group huddled around the boot workshop, but Harry is not interested in listening in. He has work to do and he hurries Han along. Directly ahead of them is the old Women's Prison wing. It's inaccessible from the prison compound, however, since, upon decommission, that section of the prison was immediately remodeled and rented out for private businesses. So Harry and Han turn to the right and head toward the main cell block. They walk past Four Division, then on to Three Division. It is at this point that Han stops, sniffs the air expectantly, and runs back the way they had come, past the main cell block to what a signpost tells Harry is New Division. Han barks three times in quick succession.

'What is it, boy?' Harry actually says this aloud, sounding far more like the boy in the *Lassie* films than he can bear. 'Um. What's up, Han?'

Han repeats his three-bark signal and, if he were a pointer, would be pointing directly at a particular cell. However, not being a pointer, but a heeler with a long ancestral line of working cattle dogs, Han proceeds to try to round up the cells he is barking toward. Of course, being inanimate and foundation-laden objects, the cells are resistant to being rounded up, causing Han some amount of frustration before he finally runs up to a particular cell. He barks and barks and barks, then scratches pathetically at the steel door with his right paw.

'Well, well, well. How much is that doggie in the cellblock, ha ha ha.' This comes from a woman's booming voice directly behind Harry. Startled, Harry turns to see a very small woman, no more than four-foot-six and certainly less than ninety pounds. Harry wonders where such a petite person gets such a commanding voice. Han looks at the woman and bares his teeth, as good-naturedly as a dog of his ilk will permit of a stranger.

'I'm sorry,' Harry stammers. 'We got lost, I guess, separated from the group.'

'No worries,' assures the little woman. 'Yer dog found the special cell all right.'

'What's that?'

'Take a look.' She stands on tiptoe and peers in through what Harry has learned, from various signposts around the cellblock, is called a Judas hole. She stands down off her tiptoe position, allowing Harry the opportunity to look in as well. 'Well, notice anything different?' Harry has noticed that the tiny woman has a mole on her left temple in the shape of a tilde. And that her left earlobe is all but missing.

But he makes no comment on this and when he looks in through the Judas hole, Harry sees a square cell without any furnishings. On the side wall are the washed-down remnants of what might have been a painting of an ochre snake. Way back in the far corner is a small white square object with a bright red ribbon placed on top of it.

'Different? Different from what?'

'The other men's cells, that's what. See, the standard man's cell is one-point-two by two-point-one metres. This one's one-point-four by two-point-four. Tell ya anything?'

Harry looks at the woman mutely.

'It's a woman's cell. In the men's cell block. They don't tell you that on the regular tour. Don't figure they even know about it. But me, I did my research. Ya can tell, too, 'cause there's a regular bed in there. Men's cells only had hammocks.'

Hammocks. Harry thinks back to the sheet of paper about quarantine regulations and recalls the dogs slept on trampolines. Regular beds seem unpopular in the Australian incarceration scene, he thinks.

'Why is there a woman's cell in the men's block?' Harry is curious, about both the strange bit of information and the strange conveyor of this information.

'Martha's,' says the woman. 'It was Martha's.'

Harry waits for the explanation. Clearly this diminutive woman is enjoying her narration, so Harry figures if he keeps quiet and looks attentive, he will eventually get the whole story.

'Martha Rendell. Only woman to walk the thirteen steps to the gallows here at Fremantle Prison. October 6, 1909. Willful murder; took out her employer. He was also rumoured to be her lover, y'know.'

Harry shrugs, gestures the woman to continue.

'Oh, yes, a lively one that Martha, from all accounts. I know what you're thinking. This isn't death row. Death row was down there a ways in cells thirteen ta eighteen. So why wasn't Martha in there? Well that's the story, in't? Truth is, Martha was in cell fifteen for two weeks, but then they up and moved her. Why? Well, she was a sexy one that Martha, apparently so, and she put some sorta spell on the warden, as they say. And he used ta visit her in this revamped, and very private space, I might add, ev'ry evening at midnight. Yessir. That's what they say. He'd wait in his office and then, under some pretext of trouble on the cellblock floor, he would march out of his office and right down here, ostensibly to investigate, or so they say. He'd slide open this Judas hole and look in on her, just watch her for ages on end, is the story. And then after watching her and after being fully satisfied that she knew he was watching her, he'd have the guard open up the door and he'd slip inside. The warden had some mortar on both sides kicked out, widened the space on the pretense that a woman, even one on death row, deserved the same as her lady inmates, see. Truth is, at least the way I see it, the warden wanted a bit more space for his love nest. Hey, are you sure you're interested in this?'

'Yes,' blurts out Harry. 'Oh, yes, this is exactly what I came here for. Isn't it, Han?' Han looks up at the mention of his name, then returns to licking himself in such a way that Harry averts his eyes.

'Well then, on the Wednesday mornin', as per usual for the deathwatch, Martha's woken up at five AM, taken for a shower, and given this special dress that's got tapes instead of buttons. Don't know why. They did this, apparently, with all the condemned prisoners. Guess it was easier to disrobe them after death, I dunno. Anyway, at six she was taken into the holding cell where she was asked if she wanted to see a clergyman. "Nope," says Martha, "just want to see my one true love. Bring me the warden," she says, much to the shock of the deathwatch screws who weren't privy to this knowledge as were the boys on Three Division, you understand. But this being her final hour and all, they comply, get the warden, who, by all accounts is hiding in his office bawling his eyes out. But they drag him down and get him into Martha's last room. There she is sitting with her tea and toast, the traditional final meal, with a dirty mug of cheap brandy which was also traditionally administered, if the condemned so desired, for a last flight of fancy before flying from the gallows. Martha looks at the warden, I don't know what his name was actually, and he looks at Martha and damned if he doesn't break down into a whole line of new tears. "How could you do this to me, Martha," he cries, and no one, least of all Martha, has any idea what he's talking about. Then it dawns on her. Here she is, the condemned woman, about to meet her maker, and the warden is accusing her of leaving him. Him! Like this was her choice. Can you believe that? Well, so what does she do? Takes a swig of brandy, that's what, swallows, then downs the cup and holds the brandy in her mouth. She stands up, proud Martha, and walks steadily over to the weak-kneed warden, and she clasps the back of his head and pulls it toward her and damned if she doesn't plant a big fat kiss right on the warden's lips, expelling her brandy into his mouth. Well, he looks like he's gonna choke or cry or spit it all back up, or all three things at once, and she takes one step, two steps back, and begins laughing and laughing and laughing. "You never did trust me!" she says. "You never could find that trust!" That's what she says, yes she does. Yes she does. And then it's one minute to eight and the boys come for her and try to strap her up with hobbles on her ankles, but she was having none of that, "I'll be in hell soon, lads," she says, "No bother showing up with ankle bracelets," and what with her display with the warden, who's now quivering like a little kitten, they let her walk her own way up those thirteen steps. The hangman had travelled all the way in from Kalgoorlie, snuck him in through the women's entrance as was the habit, and he tied the knot and did the deed without so much as looking Martha in the eye. She swung that morning, she did.'

'And the warden?' Harry asks, now quite intrigued with this story. 'What happened to the warden?'

'Ha, well, that's a story indeed. Couldn't bring himself to watch the hanging. But when they went back to the holding cell, they couldn't find him there either. After a bit of a search, they finally tracked him down late that evening to this here cell, his and Martha's private love nest. See, they hadn't checked in here earlier, 'cause the cell had been padlocked from the outside. Still, no one knows how he got in 'cause the attendant swore up and down there wasn't no warden inside when he padlocked the door.'

Harry is so engrossed in the story that he does not notice the small woman pull out a key from her hip pocket and swiftly turn it in the lock of the cell. So when she says 'padlocked the door' she accentuates the end of her story by swinging the door of Martha's cell wide open.

'G'wan in, if you like,' she says. 'Take a look.'

Harry walks into the cell. He traces his fingers along the snake design – it looks to him not unlike the aboriginal art he has seen on

Market Street – and looks around the bare cell. He approaches the white object in the corner. It turns out to be a square envelope. The red ribbon is familiar, he thinks, as he picks it up. He sees the neat lettering on the envelope at the same time that he notices the red ribbon is indeed familiar, for it is the same length and breadth of ribbon Harry has seen once before, at Sita's place, hanging in her spare room, looped through a gold medal she won for a 200-metre race during a university track meet. And at the same time as he notices the neat lettering, clearly in Sita's hand, spelling out his own name, and that the ribbon is indeed Sita's, Harry hears the cell door slam shut behind him.

mongrel racinations

Time for what they call a long shot in cinematography. Or perhaps, in fictional terms, moving from limited to full omniscience. In either case, here's the scene. Harry Kumar, on a quest for his lady love (who is neither his lady nor his love, as I've tried to iterate over and over again, but narrative habits die hard), is now stuck within the walls of a decommissioned prison in Western Australia. But, more than stuck, he is quite literally imprisoned, locked behind the cell door that ninety years ago swung open to take Martha Rendell to the gallows. She was the only woman ever executed at Fremantle Prison and while many of the history books find this noteworthy, none appear to mention the torrid affair she had with the warden at the time. Perhaps this is because such an affair never happened. Perhaps it was too scandalous to mention. Perhaps, instead, Miss Martha had an even more scandalous affair with one of the many men who preceded her to the hangman's noose, men with names like Ah Chi, Sin Cho Chi, Chow Fong, Yong Quong, Lyn Nye, Mahomet Goulam, Jumma Kahn, Peter Perez, Pedro de la Cruz, Stelious Psichitsas, Sabara Rokka, Ah Hook, Mahomet Mianoor, Pablo Marquez, Iwachi Oki. They all met their state-sponsored end within the two decades preceding Martha Rendell's eternal necktie event. (Yes, of course, chances are she never had the opportunity to even meet these men, segregated as she was by gender and twenty years, but stranger encounters have happened.)

Perhaps, even, Miss Martha had the gall and the tenaciousness to take more than one lover, perhaps the warden as well as one of these fated prisoners. And maybe that is why the warden, a civil and gracious man, with the power and the will to indefinitely stay any execution, decided not to do so with his fair Martha, for she had been with another man, and not just any man, but a savage Chinese man, or Greek, or Spanish, maybe even a dreaded Mohammedan. How could he, then, a man with a clean conscience and a white heart, stay an execution of a woman he loved, but of a woman so tarnished so as to deserve the eight-foot drop with weights around her feet, if not for the crime she was sentenced to die for, then the crime of cuckoldry, cheating on the honest warden, and perhaps the greater sin, that of miscegenation? For what can come of such ill-conceived unions? Brown-skinned children that don't quite fit the tonal preferences of either parent (just ask Harry if you don't believe me, or ask Sita if you can find her). Why, you might as well mate human and beast and see what you can do with a creature boasting the head of a monkey and the body of a man, or the mind of a human and the body of a dog. The possibilities are endless – and frightening. All these are possibilities. But the possibility Harry is forced to contemplate right now, as he sits in the dark and damp cell that once housed Martha Rendell, is whether he shall ever emerge from this place.

Han to the rescue

Outside Harry can hear Han whimpering softly, not in despair, but in a slight form of anxiety that he cannot see his comrade Harry. And, besides that, Han is becoming quite famished, not having anything in his stomach since the fateful moment that Australian cattle dog crossed his path the day before. For a moment, Han thought the friendly and thoughtful woman would hand him a morsel or two, but upon closing the cell door she did the most unlikely thing and vanished, poof, into thin air. Were Han human, this would have been the source of extreme disturbance, and would have led to ghostly questions about who this woman might have been. Was she the spectre of Martha Rendell herself, Han might have asked, or was she the matron of the women's cell block, herself rebuffed by the playboy warden once he had cast his eyes on the condemned murderess? Or maybe she was a simple tour guide prone to performing magic tricks in the market on the weekend for a few extra laughs and dollars. However, Han, not being human, had none of these questions pass through his canine lobes. The small woman was, most simply, there and taking up space and then, after closing the door, she was not there. Han was used to humans coming and going so this was really not that extraordinary.

For Harry, however, this was an entirely other matter. Who was that woman? he kept asking himself. Not a ghost-believer, and not witnessing the little woman disappearing in a flash as did Han, Harry assumed she was just some ill-willed tour guide operator who tricked him into the cell as punishment for straying from his tour herd, and she or someone would be bound to come back for him sooner or later. It was, however, now somewhat later and the afternoon light, what little of it was available through the cell window, was giving way to dusk. After shouting some and pounding on the door to no response, Harry has set himself down in the far corner of the cell and finally opens the square envelope that was addressed to him in Sita's hand. Inside, however, is no further message, only an odd conglomerate of objects that reminds Harry of those childhood games where pictures were presented so as to hint at a word, like the drawing of a ship's anchor plus the letter 'a' plus another drawing of a measuring scale would be a clue to 'anchor's away,' or some such silly saying. Of course, in this envelope are no drawings of anchors or weigh-scales. Instead, what Harry finds is this: a yellowing advertisement clipped from what appeared to be an American newspaper from some years back as attested to by its aged composition and archaic typography, which, Harry recalls from his younger days of delightfully scrolling through microfilm of 1940s newspapers, happily promoting a plumbing business called 'Roto-Rooter'; a photograph depicting a young lamb in the foreground and sheep as far as the eye could see along rolling hills of green in the background; and a photocopied coupon that entitled the bearer and a guest to enjoy the revitalizing effects of some place called the Polynesian Spa, a place depicted in a line drawing as a series of A-framed buildings amidst a pall of brimstone-like smoke. All these images and fragments have a meaning, Harry is certain, but it will be difficult for him to do anything with them while locked up in Martha Rendell's cell. And to top it off, he has to pee and he is getting hungry.

Fortunately for Harry, Han, too, has to pee, which he does at great length, and within Harry's earshot, against a metal pole just outside Martha's cell. And Han is now quite hungry, it being some two hours since the tiny stranger slammed the door shut on poor Harry. Han isn't particularly fond of being within smelling distance of Harry but out of his sightline, so he paces around a bit and finds, hidden by a table sporting yet more information about the prison, a drainage pipe that he can just squeeze into. This he scrunches his body through because Harry's smell is emanating from the drainage pipe with particularly encouraging strength and, sure enough, after a ten-foot crawl, Han finds himself nose to a bricked-up wall through which some light shines and, more importantly, Harry's smell permeates. Han woofs slightly.

Inside the cell, his back to the wall, Harry can hear as well as feel, as a slight tousle of breath on his back, the bark of his very own Han.

'*Han!*' exclaims Harry.

'Woof,' retorts Han, exhaling more warm dog breath on Harry's back.

'Han!' repeats Harry and he spins around to peer at what appears to be a solid brick wall but, after some relatively easy manipulating, turns out to be a pile of bricks unmortared and hence quite moveable. After pulling out three of the loose bricks, Han pokes his nose through and begins to negotiate the rest of his body through the opening that clearly cannot accommodate the full width of his body. Fortunately, the bricks around his neck fall back and Han is through, gleefully licking Harry's face while looking about the cell for any sign of food that might lie therein.

'You're truly a magnificent dog,' remarks Harry, once again thinking about various Lassie rescues. He investigates the opening through which Han has come and notices with some regret that the ingress large enough for a dog is not an exit sufficient for Harry's body. That is, the drainage pipe is too small, although the bricks shove wide enough apart for Harry to enter the small, yet cavernous space, that leads to said pipe. Han barks at Harry, whom he can now see only from the rear, and Harry appears magnificently headless and shoulderless as he investigates the hole in the cell wall. The bark, which was a well-intentioned note encouraging Harry to source out some food for Han, has a different effect, causing Harry not only to look up and see an ancient and rusted ladder leading to some dark place above but to believe that his dog's bark was somehow translatable to, 'Look up, Harry, look way up.' Harry sees the ladder, produces an awe-inspired groan, and repeats his earlier magnificent dog comment.

Harry climbs up the ladder, a short eight-runger, followed by Han, who is surprisingly spry when it comes to vertical climbing. They ascend towards a spot of light above them, but when they reach it, Harry is disappointed to find that it is only reflected light from a space in the ceiling. He looks down the crawl space where the light is coming through. It must be a couple of hundred feet to where the light is coming from, and the crawlspace is only eighteen inches high. Harry sighs. Han, however, is quite loving this adventure, and when he sees Harry look down the crawlspace, Han scrambles over Harry's back and thrusts himself into the tunnel. Han, of course, can almost run down the crawlspace if he hunkers down a bit. For Harry, this will be somewhat more arduous. He looks back down the ladder and decides it better to accept the ills he knows not of, the road less travelled, all that sort of nonsense, and he lifts himself into the crawlspace. Edging along on elbows and knees, Harry gets about half way when he has to stop to rest. Han, meanwhile, has been to the end and back fourteen times and is distressed that Harry is taking his own sweet time.

On his fifteenth trip back, however, Han brings a gift, a small hand-bound book covered in red cloth. Harry can just barely make out that it is a book, owing to the severe lack of light, but once he has progressed another fifty feet, the light from the end of the tunnel is enough for him to read the title page. It is a diary belonging to one Owen Hooper. The first entry is 1969; the last is dated 2 AM, July 7, 1972. He recalls the tour guide, as he and Han passed by, saying something about an escape by Hooper. He flips through the last few pages, recounting Hooper's narrative about how, as prison radio operator, he was able to pull together enough parts for this daring escape. Harry realizes he is crawling along the very same ceiling space the three men used in 1972, although his entrance to this tunnel was somewhat less ingenious than that of the escapees. They had rigged up an elaborate trap door system through the concrete ceilings, which, upon its discovery, was resealed by the prison authorities. Harry's avenue had been a service vent; apparently, it had been unused for pretty much the entire life of the prison, except, speculates Harry, perhaps by the prison warden in his trysts with Martha Rendell. Han barks at Harry to hurry. Harry finds out that the men crawled along this ceiling tunnel then, using Cooper's electronic skills, tapped into the prison telephone system, sending a false alarm to the guard tower at no. 2 to watch out for suspicious activity at the other end of the prison. Harry continues to crawl toward the light, figuring he can read the rest of the journal when he exits. As he nears the light, however, a telephone starts to ring. He speeds his progress, not sure why or how a telephone might be ringing at this specific time or place, and, by the twenty-third ring, Harry has reached its source. There is no receiver and no obvious microphone, just a clapper and a button. Harry takes a chance and pushes the button. The voice of the strangely short woman emerges.

'About time there, Kumar! You can stand up now, you know.'

Harry looks above him. The woman is right. There is a hole in the asbestos above him, part of the escape route that the prison authorities never bothered, surprisingly, to fix. He stands.

'You made it this far, Kumar, but the boys in '72 had a makeshift ladder that could get them o'er to Knutsford Street. That's more than ten feet, Kumar.'

Harry listens to this in a daze. He can't recall ever telling the strange woman his name, and yet there she is, using it in a most insulting and commanding manner.

'But I have left you an option there, Kumar. Go on, climb up on the roof. That's it.'

Harry does as he is ordered and finds himself in reasonably bright sunshine. The voice is right – the wall is over ten feet away and Harry is not sure he can jump that far, not if failing to do so means falling a full storey down.

'Know what yer thinking, Kumar. "Can I make it?" Well, Kumar, ya gotta ask yourself a question. Do you feel lucky? Well, do ya, Kumar?' The voice cackles away at this commentary. 'Well, today might be your lucky day, Kumar. Take a look to your right. That's it, right there.'

Harry looks down and sees an old trampoline covered in dog hair. It is positioned on an angle so that, he surmises, a good bounce will propel him over the wall and onto what he has been told will be Knutsford

Street. What the hell, he figures. In for a penny. He grips Owen's journal under one arm, takes five steps back and then three giant strides toward the trampoline. He lands on it with two feet and feels himself propelled toward the wall. Too well propelled. His feet skip off the top of the wall and he trips over and down, landing four feet below on the roof of a blue Volkswagen. He is momentarily out of breath, but Han is on top of him, reviving him with wet kisses and dog breath. Harry turns his head to the street side.

The strange little woman is face to face with him, laughing as she puts away her mobile phone.

Harry lies there and watches as she cackles and then strides up the street. He is too tired to pursue her or even to ask any questions.

Twenty feet up from Harry, the woman turns and speaks one last time.

'Take a look at the final page of that journal, Kumar. That will be all.'

Harry looks skyward. Who was that woman? he thinks to himself. Han's face appears in front of his. But, instead of panting more dog breath at Harry when he opens his mouth, Han speaks, clearly and with only a trace of an Australian accent: 'Her? That was Anna Varre.'

Rottnest Island: a story

In sixteen hundred ninety-six,
De Vlamingh sailed the river Styx
And found not hell across his bow
But rats galore, he named it so.

(

Okay, so nobody ever called Anna Varre a poet. Ah, but I do have a demon wit, no? So here we are, Harry and I, we have had our first confrontation, face to face. It was Sita's recommendation, really, that to remake history we had to remake the story itself. And since setting is so much part of how the story goes, I figured, why not an island in the South Pacific, a considerable way away from the original playing out of our original encounter. Which story, you may be wondering? Well, suffice it to say, a story far away from birthplaces like Ayodyha, what with its raised and razed holy structures, far from castles and palaces in Lanka, far from places where myths are too close to reality and truth is too far from anyone's grasp. That's why I've brought you here. And so, a brief story about where Harry is about to be headed:

Captain Willem de Vlamingh was a Dutch sailor out looking for action. That, and several other Dutch ships that had, over the course of exploratory years, gone off course and been surmised shipwrecked. It was up to de Vlamingh and others like him to catch up with these sunken sisters and try to make some sense of why Holland kept sending out one unseaworthy ship after another. But this isn't really about de Vlamingh, only inasmuch as he was the first European to landfall at the little island off what would sometime later be known as Fremantle. From his anchored position offshore, de Vlamingh could see hundreds, thousands, of creatures frollicking over the island rocks.

'Rotts,' he said to his first mate.

'Rotts,' agreed the first mate. Their first landfall in weeks and it was covered by dirty, slimy, filthy rats. Of course, they weren't actually rats, weren't rodents of any kind, but a type of marsupial not to be found anywhere else in the world – the quokka – but the Dutch weren't to know this from such a far off vantage point. So, the name stuck and a very pleasant island off the coast where the Swan River met the Indian Ocean was to be forever named after rats.

A century and a half later, another captain, a Briton this time, James

Stirling, was megalomaking his way around the west coast of Australia when he hit upon an idea. The main problem with trying to settle an uninhabited terrain, a *terra nullius*, was that its original inhabitants considered themselves to be, well, inhabitants, and thought the adventurous invaders were somewhat remiss in their refusal to acknowledge the hometown crowd. Add to that a couple of interesting features. The visiting boating crowd were having a heyday decimating the kangaroo population, something the Nyoongar people thought was a bit of a travesty since these kangaroos had to last a long time if they were to feed the people in this uninhabited land. Fortunately, however, these yacht clubbers weren't all one-way, or so the Nyoongar thought, since while the sun-deprived foreigners did a handy job of knocking off enormous numbers of kangaroos, they also brought replacement animals for a sense of variety. A bit slower and less of a hunting challenge than the kangaroos, these pigs and sheep proved to be an easy target for the keen-eyed hunting Nyoongar. Imagine their surprise when the boat people more or less flipped out when the Nyoongar simply took a few head of sheep and a couple of pigs when the white-skinned ones were dropping the kangaroo like they were going out of style. Imagine the Nyoongar's further surprise when they found out that if they continued to pick up a bit of extra rations here and there, the boat folk would come to them, grab the hunter who had been successful, and put him up, for no apparent reason, in a stone building with no windows.

Enter James Stirling again, who in addition to being a keen explorer, was something of an urban designer, and he fancied that there was a problem with locking up the aboriginal folks in the same place as the newly arriving convicts and the newly processed criminal element in western Australia. For one thing, the aboriginal prisoners wouldn't do the convict labour requested of them and ended up dying in fairly inefficient numbers. So in 1838 Stirling came up with an idea: put all the aboriginal prisoners in one place, some place where they couldn't leave very easily, but don't lock them up in case they up and died on you. Rottnest Island, of course, came to mind. Stirling floated this idea around; it was picked up very favourably by the establishment, and in August of that year Constable Lawrence Welch was called into Governor Hutt's office.

'Look here, Constable,' said Hutt, 'you've been doing a bang-up job here in Freo, a bang-up job.'

'Why, thank you,' said the modest Welch, 'you're too kind.'

'No, really,' insisted Hutt. 'I think a promotion is in order. Don't you?'

'Why, a promotion, sir, the thought hadn't crossed my mind. Thank you, sir.'

'Yes, let's say your new title is, oh, Superintendent of the Government Establishment, Rottnest.'

'Rottnest, sir? You mean that island way out yonder?'

'Yes, Superintendent, that's exactly what I mean.'

'But, begging your pardon sir, there's nothing out there.'

'Ah, dear Superintendent, that's where you're wrong. You will be out there. Oh, be a good fellow and take these rotten fellows along with you, will you?' Hutt handed his new superintendent a roster of six names: Buoyeen, Mollydobbin, Tyoocan, Goordap, Helia, and Cogat. 'Oh, and while you're out there, Welch, have the boys build some buildings and what-not, would you? There's a good chap.'

So, Superintendent of the Government Establishment (Rottnest) Welch sailed across to Rottnest with his aboriginal prisoners. The aboriginals did not understand English. Superintendent Welch did not understand the Nyoongar language nor any aboriginal language or dialect. Unfortunately for him, the six prisoners did.

'What are you in for?' Mollydobbin asked his colleagues on the boat trip over.

'The boat people call it "theft,"' said Tyoocan.

'Same for me,' said Goordap.

'Really?' said Mollydobbin. 'Me too. Go figure. What d'ya suppose this "theft" thing is all about?'

'Well,' said Cogat. 'I only used a bit of butter churned by that old fella on the hill and they grabbed me and put me here. So this "theft" must be about using condiments improperly?'

The others agreed that Cogat's crime was certainly not one. How can you commit crimes around food? they argued. Food was food.

'What about you?' Mollydobbin asked Buoyeen.

'Ah,' said Buoyeen. 'Well this whitefella wouldn't show me this very cool knife he had. I woulda given it back, really, just that these folks can be so damned possessive.'

'So, what you do?' asked Helia, the only one who hadn't spoken so far.

'Thwocked him on the head,' said Buoyeen, laughing. 'Got to look at the knife. But they didn't hit me up with theft, just some thing they called a "salt."' Preoccupied with foodstuffs, these newcomers, they all agreed.

The question goes to Helia.

'Well, pretty much the same thing. Except I wasn't trying to look at anything these whitefellas have, just minding my business, eating a bit of crayfish, when this arrogant young whitefella comes up and starts berating me for something or other. Have a feeling it had something to do with this concept the whitefellas have cooked up about possessing food. I mean, ya can no more own food than a woman, hey? Now, I've picked crayfish out of that bay for years, and this whitefella is saying, I think, that I have to go away and stay away. Didn't rightly understand him, although I tried to say I'd be happy to engage him right and fair once I'd finished eating.'

'And?' Mollydobbin was quite fascinated with this story.

'And so the fella thwocks me on the shoulder. I tell him to stop it, that I don't want to hurt him, so what does he do, thwocks me on the other shoulder. Well, me, I had just finished the big claw of the crayfish, so I stands up and points it at him, and the bugger, he thwocks me on the head. I see he needs fixing, so I fixes him. Crayfish claws, now they can go through a man's throat real fast, but not quite as fast as they take you away for such an action.'

'Ha. You killed a whitefella?' says Buoyeen.

'Yeah. Killed a whitefella. And the joke of it is they let me live. I liked killin' that whitefella, you know, and if I has half a chance….' and Helia gestures towards Welch, who is having some difficulty manoeuvring the boat to an appropriate docking point on Rottnest Island. All the aboriginal men laugh and Welch looks back at them, disapprovingly. This makes them laugh harder.

After they get off the boat, Welch starts to use some sort of strange sign language. After a few minutes of this, Buoyeen tells the others that he thinks Welch wants them to collect rocks so as to build some sort of shelter.

'Why don't he build it?' asks Tyoocan petulantly.

'Ah,' says Buoyeen, 'you know them whitefellas, especially the finely dressed ones. They never do any hard work themselves. Lookit, they even bring over some of their own, tie 'em up in irons, and make them work for no reason.'

'So,' asks Goordap, 'are we going to do this?'

'Let's get a crayfish,' suggests Helia.

'Nah, let's humour him,' says Buoyeen.

'Can we do him in with a crayfish later?' asks Helia.

'Sure,' says Buoyeen, 'why not.'

But the six aboriginal prisoners do not kill Welch. Neither, however, do they finish the dwelling that Welch had ordered them to do, and they completely balk at his wishes to collect salt, although they happily go out and fish, since they figure they have to eat. But after three days of this routine, they decide it's time to leave.

'We have to go now,' Buoyeen says to Welch.

'What?' answers Welch.

'He still doesn't understand us,' explains Tyoocan.

'Yeah, I know,' says Buoyeen. 'Just thought I'd do him the courtesy.'

'Let's get a crayfish shell, what do you say?' suggests Helia.

'Maybe later,' Mollydobbin and Cogat chime in together, and then giggle at their timing.

'Okay, let's go,' says Goordap. And the six prisoners head down to the beach where the boat is docked.

'Hey, what are you doing?' Welch calls out after them. Even if they understood his gibberish, they would not feel obliged to respond. 'Stop. I'm Superintendent of the Government Establishment (Rottnest) James Welch, goddammit.'

Helia turns to deliver a gesture that requires no translation. Welch is dumbstruck. He searches for his weapon, but by the time he finds it, the six erstwhile sailors are twenty yards out. He fires a shot a them, but never being a good aim, he knows his chances of recapturing his prisoners are hopeless. And, they have the only boat.

A resourceful sort, Welch begins immediately to find a way to signal the good folks at Fremantle that they are about to be invaded by a throng of savages. A signal fire. That's it.

On High Street, a businessman and a banker are discussing the economy of Fremantle when the former sees the smoke rising above Rottnest Island.

'I say,' says the businessman, 'what is that in aid of?'

The banker, who has been in Fremantle a full two years longer than the businessman, turns to see the smoke and matter-of-factly reassures the businessman. 'Ah, you see, that's a signal that whales are off the coast there. The whalers will be heading out and taking one or two I should think. Will keep us in whale oil for the winter, eh?'

And both men laugh. It is only after three consecutive days of desperate smoke signals from Rottnest Island that Governor Hutt decides to send a boat over to investigate. The investigators find Welch, tired and hungry – the prisoners took all the supplies and the Superintendent had no idea how to catch fish – and rescue him from his island prison.

Rottnest Island will remain a prison for aboriginal offenders and protestors until the first years of the twentieth century, although the last prisoners will remain until the 1930s. By the early 1880s a boy's reformatory will be built to complement the men's prison. And in 1883, sixty of one-hundred-and-seventy aboriginal prisoners will die of influenza. Then, into the latter part of the twentieth century and into the heady days of the twenty-first, Rottnest will be a prime tourist site for Western Australians and interstate and foreign visitors alike.

Harry on two wheels

It is to Rottnest Island that Harry, one-hundred-and-sixty-odd years later, speeds to on the superfast Rottnest Express. For thirty-eight dollars, he is told, he will be transported to the island in twenty-five minutes, and returned safely the same day. Just before he left, James the bellboy slipped him a colour photocopy of a piece of art called *Rottnest Island* by Sally Morgan. It depicts happy smiling faces of tourists on the surface of Rottnest. They wave to their friends in boats, their cameras swinging gaily from their necks. They wear Hawaiian beachware and straw hats. They occupy the top one-fifth of the painting. The bottom four-fifths depicts the archaeological layers of the island, the bodies and bodies and bodies of aboriginal prisoners now buried there. Harry stares at the reproduction of this painting, then looks up at his fellow travellers. One or two of them actually wear Hawaiian-style shirts. Of all the tourists on deck, only a few are not sporting cameras. And in the midst of this all, on this island of history, Harry thinks, he might find Sita Simpson.

((

Harry disembarks from the Rottnest Express and strolls at such a pace that other eager tourists quickly slip past him and into the fray of the adventure. Harry finds a bench and sits down, taking in his surroundings before reaching into his windbreaker and pulling out Owen Hooper's journal. He has stared and stared at the last page of the journal, as he was instructed to do, for almost two days. Four words, that's all there were, and words not inscribed with ink as were the other pages, but in a dirty sepia. At first, Harry thought these were words painted in blood, but then realized what he was looking at were marks made by singeing the paper with broad strokes, probably from a cigarette. Four words burned into the paper, four words which at first made no sense to Harry. It was only at the end of the first day, after touching those burnt letters and imagining he could smell the paper as it turned from white to yellowy-brown, that he went down to the front desk with his question. He hesitated since he didn't actually know how the desk clerk would respond to his request, and so it was fortuitous that, as he stood there uncomfortably, Bellboy James sidled up to him with an 'Is there something I can do for you, Mr Kumar?' Yes, he told James, yes indeed, he needed to know what these words could possibly mean, these four words that read, in nicotiney colours, *where the quokkas are*. Of course,

James smiled, for what Fremantlite would not be able to tell a tourist where he might find the quokkas. On Rottnest Island, sir, Bellboy James offered. On Rottnest Island. James then looks over at Han and suggests to Harry that Rottnest Island is no place for dogs, too crowded with people and bicycles. Without too much prodding, Harry is convinced to leave Han in James's capable hands for the afteroon. And so Harry, after staring at those words for yet another day, made his way, dogless for a change, to Rottnest Island where he now sits on a bench, again looking at those words.

'Bird tour, mister?'

Harry looks up, his face a question mark.

'Bird tour?' It is the voice of a red-haired boy, about fourteen years old, whose face, to Harry, is strikingly familiar. 'You looks like you might want a bird tour. Most tourists goes for bike tours but you, sir, you looks like you'd be a bird person.'

Harry stares, then shakes his head. He has to figure out how to find Sita, not go on some ornithological junket.

'You sure, sir? I can shows you coastal birds, the pied cormorant, osprey, crested tern, rock parrot....'

'No, no. Thank you,' says Harry. 'I really can't.'

'Pied oystercatcher, silver gulls, fairy tern, reef heron....'

'I'm actually looking for someone, so–'

'Or then there's the red-necked stint, the ruddy turnstone, grey-tailed tattler, western warbler, singing honey-eater, disappearing simpson, Australian gannet, great skua, and the wedge-tailed shearwater–'

'Stop,' says Harry. 'The disappearing simpson?'

'What's that, sir?'

'Disappearing simpson. What's that, you just said, disappearing simpson.'

'Why, sir, don't knows what you're referring to. I can shows you a sacred kingfisher, or a curlew sandpiper, but don't knows nothing about a disappointing simpster.'

'Disappearing simpson, and yes, you do know something or you wouldn't have said anything. What does that mean? Who are you? What do you know about Sita?'

'Sir?'

'Sita Simpson, goddammit, where is she?'

'Sir, I knows where to find the laughing turtledove and fan-tailed cuckoo, but I don't thinks that's going to help you. I'll just be moving along.'

168

'No, no. Wait. Yes, I want to see those birds. Take me to those birds. How much?'

'Uh. Twenty dollars?'

'Fine. Twenty dollars. Where do we start?'

'Well, that's ups to you. We could start at The Basin, or Thomson Bay, or Quokka Stop–'

'That's it!' shouts Harry, quite agitated and looking frantic enough to trouble the young guide. 'Quokka Stop. We'll start there. Let's go.'

'Yes, sir. Yes, sir, let's go.'

(

Harry is thinking three things as the young guide, who tells Harry his name is Alexander, leads him by bicycle to the place known as Quokka Stop. First, Harry is thinking that, considering the derisive attitude Alexander displayed toward tourists and bike tours, he is more than a little surprised that Alexander is taking Harry by bicycle to the site where he hopes against hope that he will find Sita. And not just any bicycle, thinks Harry. No, these bicycles are unencumbered by multiple gears or, as Harry will find out shortly, adequate brakes, and were he not to know better, Harry would surmise that these bicycles were military surplus, were the military to actually use bicycles for any covert purposes.

The second thing Harry is thinking is that he never was any good at riding bicycles. When he got his first one at age ten, a full two years later than the last of his friends to win a parent's trust and allow for a transition from three wheels to two, he was, as one might understand, a wobbly mess. Harry would dump his bike when he rode over the curb. He would dump his bike when he made a left turn. He would dump his bike when he was just standing there, straddling the frame like he watched his friends do, except when they did it, they ended up riding away, into the sunset or into the smoggy streets or into somewhere exciting, and they did not end up doing a silly little hop-hop-hop before throwing themselves away from the bike frame which seemed, thought Harry in all his ten-year-old earnestness, out to get him. As the years wore on, Harry improved none. When his friends were popping wheelies, Harry was dumping his bike. When his friends devised a ramp over a gully down the alley and leaped their bikes across in stunning perfection, landing hard on rear wheels but rarely tipping over, Harry was dumping his bike as he watched the daredevils perform. And when they got older still and his friends would spin out in front of the very girlish girls of the neighbourhood, the ones that all the boys talked about knowingly even though few of them actually knew the girls well enough to say hello, although well enough to spit gravel at them from the rear tire of their chopped up and banana-seated road warriors, Harry was picking grass out of his teeth after attempting a pretty straight-forward left turn. And still today, his first time on a bike in almost fifteen years and thus with good reason to be a bit off-balance, Harry is just waiting for the first time he will fail to negotiate a left turn and probably ruin the bike and Alexander's business all in one fell dump.

And yet in the recesses of Harry's mind, a third thing lurks, and that is the growing familiarity he feels for Alexander's face. He has met the boy and he has met him recently. Or maybe he hasn't met this boy, but he has met a boy that looks quite like him. Or perhaps, thinks Harry, coming up to an ominously left-leaning jog in the road, perhaps the boy just has one of those familiar faces, one that people respond to like they respond to Athnic's face, for instance. The road is definitely veering to the left and Harry takes this opportunity to test out, for the first time, the hand brake which, he immediately realizes, is pretty much an aesthetic device on this bike, completely unattached as it is to any cabling. And at the precise moment Harry realizes he is heading brakeless and full tilt into what now appears to be a hairpin left turn, the young Alexander turns his head slightly and utters what Harry hears as 'cocklert,' though it is not the nonsensical phrase that concerns Harry, but the fact that – as Alexander turns his head back to Harry to issue the warning that is actually 'quokka alert,' referring to the tiny marsupial which has miraculously escaped death thanks to the skillful riding of the four-teen-year-old but has now leaped suicidally into the path of Harry's bike – Harry notices that Alexander brandishes a tattoo in the shape of a tilde just above his left temple and that it is strikingly noticeable above an ear that is missing its entire lobe.

((

When Harry drives a car, which he does infrequently, he is constantly in fear of cats, squirrels, and other small animals running out in front of him and once, indeed, he did squish a black squirrel even while he had almost rolled the vehicle in an attempt to save the rodent's life. At that time, how-ever, while he might have snuffed out a life, he didn't even feel a tiny bump as his borrowed vehicle thundered forward, the little tufts of squir-rel hair swiftly falling away from the front left radial. This time, however, the bicycle that he has just acquired from Alexander has had tremendous air pressure pumped into the front tire, perhaps as compensation, in someone's twisted mind, for a lack of brakes, and Harry does not only feel like he has hit a six-inch curb as his front tire treads across the squealing quokka, but the tire itself, in extreme self-sacrifice, blows apart under over a hundred and twenty pounds of pressure, throwing the accident-prone animal a good thirty yards into the bushes which, as luck would have it, is remarkably close to his family and home, and Harry finds himself floating over the front wheel of the bicycle, noting as he passes over that once boldly emblazoned letters on the shiny handlebars have rubbed off from years of handgripping to reveal only the initial *b* followed by the word PILGRIM and then the letter *j*, something Harry finds worthy of note even as he pulls off one of the handlebar grips and hangs on to it right through the entire episode, watches as the horizon flips from bottom to top of his visual screen: the result of a remarkable somersault that sees Harry do a perfect flip and end up looking at the unnaturally blue sky while a laugh that is unmistakably Anna Varre's circles around his head.

(

Harry closes his eyes. When he opens them he can see nothing but blue sky and finds that he is oddly comfortable in his reclining position. He closes his eyes again. He opens them and filling the frame is the face of Alexander, smiling a fool's grin. The impish boy points to his left temple and pretends to tug at his absent left earlobe. The voice of Anna Varre comes from his lips.

'If you want her, come and get her,
Don't regret you ever met her,
Find her by the lone Totara
Or my name's not Anna Varre.'

Alexander or Anna or whoever it is whose face fills up Harry's vision bursts into peals of laughter at the conclusion of the nonsense rhyme, faux tugs at the missing earlobe once again, then points skyward, moving away so that Harry can see a small propeller plane pulling one of those advertising signs promoting an upcoming concert by U2. Harry turns his head to find Alexander, but of course he – or is it Anna? – is gone. He turns his head the other way and his vision is again filled up, this time with the canine visage of a happy Han.

'Way cool,' says Han.

'Am I bleeding?' asks Harry, which is his way of avoiding asking the question as to how Han has come to Rottnest Island to find his companion.

171

'I thought you might need my help,' says Han, ignoring Harry's verbal query and answering, instead, the unstated one.

'Could have used you earlier,' says Harry, pushing himself up onto his elbows.

'Came any earlier,' says Han, throwing a darting tongue out to Harry's chin, 'you woulda missed the clues.'

'Of course. Right,' says Harry, now sitting up and turning his head this way and that to check for crushed vertebrae.

'You'll be okay,' assures Han. 'Let's head back to the Esplanade. Athnic's waiting for more info.'

'Right,' says Harry. And he is careful not to even try to think about avoiding thinking about the next question.

'That's a convoluted thought,' says Han, and then rushes off to frighten a bold quokka who has just emerged from the bushes, a bit shaken, but eager to find out what's going on in the world he almost left in such a hurry.

Harry, you're not in
Kansas anymore

It is physically impossible for dogs to talk. Ask any good biologist. Has to do with vocal chords, their voicebox, jaws, stuff like that, they'll say. Dogs can't talk. Except in fairy tales and storybooks for children and science fiction and fantasy novels and in movies about New York summers and, in short, any place humans make them talk. Like that old joke about the man who tries to convince people his dog can talk by asking him questions like, 'Hey boy, what does sandpaper feel like?' and the dog goes, 'ruff, ruff,' and everyone laughs. At least, they're supposed to. But other than that, dogs can't talk. Except when humans make them talk. That in itself is part of the problem. Biologists are only human and only humans make dogs talk, but biologists make sure we all know that dogs can't possibly talk. Therefore, we can arrive at only two possible syllogistic outcomes: biologists aren't human, or dogs can talk.

((

Samuel Churchill always wanted to fly. From when he was a very young child looking up at the designs made by contrails across a deep blue New Zealand sky, he wanted to fly. Samuel was the child of a seamstress from the North Island city of Hamilton and a navy officer from the outskirts of the Rhode Island city of Providence. His parents had met during World War II when his mother was visiting an aunt in Papakura and his father, in New Zealand on leave, got lost on an Auckland city bus and ended up travelling an hour away from the city centre. He wasn't concerned about being lost because he was on leave and had nowhere to go for the next four days, but when he reached the bus terminal in Papakura, he decided he should get off and stretch his legs. He walked into the small shopping district and bought himself a meat pie. He was eating the meat pie when he saw the most beautiful woman in the world pass by. With his mouth full of meat pie he ran up to her and told her she was the most beautiful woman in the world.

Samuel's mother stared at the attractive military man and smiled and somehow she knew that this was not just another line, but that the American had truly fallen in love with her. She told Samuel's father that he should write her a poem about her beauty. She was only joking, but Samuel's father swallowed the mouthful of meat pie and began reciting made-up poetry so truly awful that Samuel's mother doubled over laughter. Okay, she said, I'll marry you. Samuel's father looked crestfallen and said that while she was certainly the most beautiful woman in the world, he was very young and not ready for marriage. This, too, was so funny to Samuel's mother that she made a leap of faith and said, okay, I'll sleep with you. That very night, in a cheap downtown hotel in Auckland, they made love for the first time and immediately thereafter Samuel's father said he had changed his mind. About me being the most beautiful woman in the world? asked Samuel's mother. No, about marriage, he said, and gallantly went down on one knee and begged Samuel's mother's hand in matrimony. She kissed him on the forehead, laughed and said no, at least not right now, maybe once the Allies had trounced the Axis powers, and then she held him close to her belly and rocked him gently until the morning came.

This was the story Samuel's mother told her son so many times as he grew up in their little house in Hamilton that Samuel sometimes felt he could remember it, as if a zygote could have memory tucked away in a single portion of a cell. Samuel's mother and father had four blissful days together and Samuel's father went off to fight in the war, promising to return. He was killed in a torpedo attack in the South Pacific and Samuel's father's best friend wrote to Samuel's mother to say his friend had really loved her, talked about her all the time, talked about moving to New Zealand to marry her and live with her. And for some reason, every time Samuel would hear this story, he would dream about flying.

Fortunately for Samuel, although in his twenties he became a moderately unsuccessful businessman and remained that way for three entire decades, on his fifty-fourth birthday he decided to invest all his life savings in a long-shot dot-com business venture promoting a line of voice recognition software. Fortuitously, the software was sold to a major Hong Kong bank and sales to almost all other national and international banks (although smaller banks and credit unions opted for a cheaper and much less effective copycat software package) quickly followed, each one anxious not to be left behind, and the company posted a sixty-five hundred percent gain before eventually selling off controlling interests to a subsidiary of one of the more powerful international banks. Eighteen months later, Samuel was a multi-millionaire and he quit his contracting business, took flying lessons, and bought himself a private jet.

((

When Harry returns to the Esplanade, he is deep in discussion with Han.

They walk into the lobby and stop in front of the elevators.

'I feel like I'm not in control of my life,' says Harry morosely.

'Hm. And what makes you feel that way?' asks Han in his best $85-an-hour therapist voice.

'Well, you for one. You, Athnic, Director Merrick, and this Anna Varre character. You all seem so ... so unpredictable.'

'And this lack of predictability troubles you?' asks Han. He looks ponderous, as if he were making a mental note that this counselling stuff was a snap and he should hang out a shingle and make some real money once they get back home.

'Hell, yes,' says Harry. 'Look at you. You're a dog. My dog. And I'm having a conversation with you.' Harry punctuates this by pressing the elevator up button.

'Many people talk to their animal companions,' insists Han.

'But you're talking back. I mean, I hear you formulate complete sentences and cogent thoughts.'

'Why, thank you,' says Han. 'But why does this feel unnatural?'

'Because you don't have a damn voicebox, that's why,' shouts Harry, raising the eyebrows at the reception desk of a German couple who don't approve of people yelling at animals.

'I do, too. How else do you think I bark? Think that's some sort of digital recording I carry stuffed behind my collar?'

The elevator arrives and the two enter.

'No, I mean ... you know what I mean. You don't have a human voicebox. You aren't supposed to be able to enunciate human sounds. And besides, you never talked before we got to Australia.'

'Perhaps there was never any need.'

'What?'

Han pauses to snap at a passing fly. To his surprise, he catches it and is forced to save face by eating his prey.

'Yuk. Where was I? Oh, yeah. What sort of animal companion would I be if I didn't help you out when you most needed it? Flies taste gross, you know.'

The elevator doors open on the second floor and Harry and Han exit and walk to their room. Athnic is just coming out.

'Hey guys, how was Rottnest?'

'You wouldn't believe it if I told you,' says Harry, looking down at Han. 'Or maybe you would.'

'Sure, try me.'

'Okay: "If you want her, come and get her, Don't regret you ever met

her, Find her by the lone Totara, Or my name's not Anna Varre."
Followed by a sky-advertisement for a rock band.'

'Hmm,' says Athnic, flipping open a pair of sunglasses and putting them on, even though the hallway is so dimly lit Harry has to strain to see Athnic's face. 'A rock band? Wasn't U2 by any chance?'

Harry sighs. 'Okay, so how do you know and what does it mean?'

'Means we're going to Auckland, right, Athnic?' asks Han, peeved that the two humans appear to be ignoring him.

'Exactly, Han,' says Athnic. 'But first, let's go pick up the car. We're going for a drive north.'

((

The smell of dog vomit in the car has largely dissipated, so the three-hour drive north is not as disgusting as Harry thought it might be. Athnic does not, as promised, tell Harry why they are going north when their directions are clearly to head south and east toward New Zealand. But Han is clearly getting more and more excited the closer they get to their destination which, Athnic finally relents to share with his friend, is a geological oddity called the Pinnacles. Limestone formations, he tells Harry. Look like giant phalluses. Is that why we're going to see them? asks Harry. No, says Athnic, we're going there because Han needs to practice climbing. I see, says Harry, but of course he doesn't truly see until they stop the vehicle in the midst of the sandy expanse from which the Pinnacles appear to grow, and Han, in utter desperation, leaps out of Harry's open window, leaving nasty claw-marks on Harry's chest, and immediately begins an insanely rigorous routine of running from one pinnacle to the next, using pure canine muscle and raw inertia to drive himself up as far as he can, sometimes attaining five feet, sometimes seven, and on occasion even managing to scramble up to the peaks of some of the shorter pinnacles, balancing there precariously on four feet bunched together before tumbling off and beginning the task again.

'What's got into Han?' asks Harry.

'He's doing this for you,' says Athnic.

'I don't get it. I don't get any of this,' admits Harry.

'Listen to me, Harry. Listen to me very carefully. This is for your own good. And for Sita's.' Harry does not think he has ever heard Athnic sound this serious before. He nods slowly. 'You have to remember this moment, Harry. Watch Han closely, watch his every move, his every rippling muscle, every single step he takes to ascend these little peaks. Are you watching, Harry? Are you?'

This is too much for Harry, but he is drawn by the spectacle of Han and by the urgent tones of Athnic. He gets out of the car and begins to watch Han. Intently. Taking in every movement, watching every muscle ripple, committing to memory each step the dog takes on the way to, up, and sometimes over, the limestone formations.

'Now, Harry, listen to me. Han is not really here, Harry, do you understand? You must imagine that he is not really here. Watch him closely, Harry, and remember that he is not here, he was never here.'

'But he is here,' Harry objects.

'Yes,' says Athnic. 'But he is not, too.'

As Harry watches, something fascinating happens. Han begins to disappear, not all together, but in little blips. To Harry, this is like watching an old print of a film that has been spliced and respliced, so that characters move across the screen, suddenly disappear, then reappear after moments of invisibility at exactly the place they would have been had they not dematerialized. But that was film. This was – this was something else. When Han disappeared, his tracks would remain, Harry noted; his pawprints would appear in the sand with no physical body to make them. The sound of long nails, the same ones that had just so recently imprinted their impressions on Harry's chest, he could hear scraping on rock as the dog climbed, invisibly, the various pinnacles. And the oddest thing of all was that sometimes when Han reappeared, he looked like a primate, some creature caught between human and ape, before returning to the shape of Harry's animal companion at one moment, and then flitting into invisibility the next.

Harry watches all this intently and despite himself, thinks he is beginning to understand. Without turning to face Athnic, still watching as Han moves in and out of physicality, Harry speaks.

'We have to go now, don't we Athnic?'

'Yes,' says Athnic. 'It's time to go.'

'And when we get to where we're going?'

'Yes,' says Athnic. 'Han will be there before us.'

bubble, bubble,
toil and trouble

Through the translucence we can see Han bouncing off of stony pillars like a mad dog. Sita, who has taken on a decidedly morose tone over the past few days, actually smiles, at first in recognition of Han, and then in disbelief at his activities. Our bubble lowers to the ground and touches down softly. Sita presses her fingers to the wall as if to reach out to Han.

He doesn't know you're here, you know. He's otherwise preoccupied.

'Then why bring me here?' Her smile starts to fade.

Well, that's the problem, isn't it? You seem to think I'm in total control. Well I'm not. Yes, I knew the silly dog would be here, but I had no idea we'd be here as observers.

'Han!' Sita calls out to the dog. 'Hey boy, hey.'

He can't hear you. I told you, he's preoccupied.

'Han! *Han!*'

The dog, three-quarters of the way up a twelve-foot pinnacle, turns, drops, bumps his chin on the ground and looks directly up at our bubble.

'Yo, Sita!'

'Han? You're talking!'

'Yah, no biggie. Hey, we're looking for you.'

'Who is? Harry?'

Han tries to bark a positive response, but the sound he emits surprises everyone, himself included.

'What was that?' asks Sita.

That's the sound a monkey makes when he's excited.

'Way cool,' says Han to himself. Then, to Sita: 'I could hear Anna Varre speak but her lips didn't move.'

'The novelty wears off,' says Sita. 'Han, how do I know this isn't some trick?'

'Trick?' asks Han, taking another leap at a four-foot pinnacle, grabbing its head by his tail and swinging nonchalantly back and forth.

'Yes, how do I know this isn't one of Anna Varre's illusions? You have to admit, you talking and acting simian is a bit much.'

'True,' says Han, scratching under his right armpit with his left paw, something else dogs are not known to do. 'Tell ya what. I'll go visit with Harry and bring you back a little something to prove it's him and me and all that, okay?'

'What will you bring?'

'Aha, a surprise, that's what, but I guarantee it will make you believe.'

'Um, yes, I guess,' says Sita.

'That okay with you?' Han looks in my direction.

Sure, that's the way the story goes, isn't it?

'Right,' says Han, and he scurries up another rock formation, his front paws gripping and grasping so that he more or less pulls himself up, steadying himself with a now-powerful tail. 'So, like, later.'

'Sure,' says Sita.

Sure. And I thought I'd be able to make this story different. But if displacement is always met with replacement – if those itsy bitsy crushed-into-near-oblivion semi-grains of sand are only moved about for a bit and end up settling just where they started out – well then, what sort of chance does that give me? I admit this new strategy, this replaying of old stories in new places, wasn't all that well thought out. I admit that even the best laid plans of mice and men can be monkeyed with. I admit that I thought it would be a lark to have Han along for the ride, if only he could perform my bidding, give voice to my plans. But he messed with me, didn't he? He put those paws in places they've been before and he figured he liked things the way they were. Trust him to replay the past – doggie see, doggie do.

bright white flight

Harry and Athnic drive toward the ocean. Athnic appears to be looking for some landmark and, indeed, as soon as they pass a fairly innocuous-looking signpost, Athnic taps Harry's shoulder furiously.

'Here, here. Turn in here.' Harry pulls the vehicle into the lookout which turns out to be a majestic view of the Indian Ocean in pre-twilight. He parks the car and they both get out and head through the tall grass toward the beach.

'Quite impressive,' says Harry, looking at the sun as it sets into the ocean.

'Certainly is,' says Athnic, but he is looking south, not west, down an incredibly narrow, long, and flat asphalt road that separates the long grass from the beach. Athnic's gaze is fixed on a bright white object about a mile away.

'Geez, what's that?' asks Harry.

Athnic smiles. 'Well, unless I miss my guess, it's a 1976 Aerospatiale Corvette SN-601, three-seat cockpit, six-passenger, executive configuration.'

'And you can tell that from here,' notes Harry wryly, realizing that once again his friend has spun an intricate plan and will only just now let him in on even the barest details.

'Yup. It's Sam's plane. Let's go.' And Athnic leads Harry along the mile-long asphalt road. On the way he explains that Sam will be flying them to Auckland where they will search for Sita at the site known as Maungakiekie or One-Tree Hill. Harry asks if that was what the clue was about, the lone Totara, and Athnic tells him yes, in a way, although the tree atop the hill was a Monterey pine. Used to be a Totara tree there, planted around four hundred years ago to commemorate the birth of Koroki, son of a chief of the Ngati Awa tribe, but that was chopped down in 1876. European workers were on lookout duty on the hill, the highest point in Auckland, he explains, and due to a miscommunication their supplies never made it to them. Disgruntled, they cut down the Totara Ahua, the Totara that stands alone. So there's no tree there? asks Harry. Not exactly, says Athnic. One John Campbell immediately saw to it that some sort of restoration took place. He planted a fresh grove of puriris to replace it, adding some *pinus insignis* for their protection. So, the site is covered in a grove of puriris? Harry asks hopefully. Nope, says Athnic. The puriris up and died, but the pine trees lived on happily. At least one of them did, or perhaps neither did, but whatever the case, a single Monterey pine became a permanent resident of One-Tree Hill. So, there's a pine tree up there? pleads Harry. Well, not exactly, says Athnic. But by this time they are almost upon the executive jet plane and Sam Churchill jumps out of the cockpit and greets Athnic heartily. I'll explain it on the way, says Athnic.

'Hey, Athnic. How ya going!' shouts Sam.

'Good, good,' says Athnic. 'Hey, Sam. This is my friend Harry. He's the one we have to get to Auckland.'

'No worries,' says Sam. 'Happy to take you home to godzone.' He gestures toward the plane. 'Let's go.'

'Is this legal?' asks Harry, noting that they are hardly on a designated airstrip.

'Nope,' says Sam.

'Nope,' says Athnic.

'Okay,' says Harry. 'Just wondering.'

Inside of two minutes, Sam and Harry are strapped into the cockpit, Athnic's buckled into the executive seating so he can grab some shut-eye, the engines fire up, and the Corvette is speeding along the asphalt in the same direction Harry and Athnic have just walked from. They lift off just as the sun melts into the ocean and Harry catches a glint of sunlight off the top of their rented car which they have now, apparently, abandoned. Sam banks the jet sharply and they turn directly toward the sun before turning a full circle and heading off toward New Zealand.

One-Tree Hill

Sam, in addition to being a multi-millionaire pilot, is a bit of a history buff and he quite generously fills Harry in on the details that Athnic has left out. Over the course of the six-hour flight through darkness, Sam regales Harry with stories about New Zealand history. Harry's interest is particularly piqued when Sam gets to the part about One-Tree Hill.

'So is there a tree there now?' Harry interrupts Sam in the middle of a European-settling-of-what-is-now-Auckland lesson.

'Ah, no,' says Sam. 'Didn't Athnic tell ya?' Harry rolls his eyes. 'Yeah, I guess he's like that sometimes. You know, I first met Athnic when I was scuba diving up by Cairns. He was doing some sort of strange exchange thing with one of the hotels there, the place where I was staying, and we struck up quite the friendship. Amazing fellow, that one.'

'He certainly is. And about the tree?'

'Oh, yes, the tree. They helicoptered that baby out in pieces in October of 2000.'

'Helicoptered?'

'Oh yes, no doubt. Cut it into pieces, then flew it out. See, it's a windy road up there, woulda had to cut it into kindling if they were to drive it out. And there's people that wanted it preserved for posterity or some such thing. Me, I think they should sell it off in little pieces like they did with the Berlin Wall, ha.'

'Why did they cut it down?'

'Had to, on account of the chainsaw attacks.'

'Someone attacked the tree with a chainsaw.'

'Oh, yeah, not once, but twice.'

'For some reason?' asks Harry, hopeful that he is seeing some sense to this story.

'Could say that. Did Athnic tell you about the Totara being chopped down—'

'In 1876. Yes, he did tell me about that.'

'Well, there ya go. So in October of '94 the police were summoned by a frantic caller saying there was this crazy guy who had leapt over the wrought-iron barrier and was making like a lumberjack on the old pine. That would be Mike Smith, Maori activist. They arrested him, but he won on appeal on account of Rangatiratanga.'

'And that would be?'

'Goes back to the Treaty of Waitangi – well, before, really, but the issue is around the treaty. Rangatiratanga is like absolute sovereignty. And that's what the Maori signed in 1840. But the English translation, now that's where the trouble started, because it doesn't exactly say the same thing, more or less suggests the Maori gave up control when they signed.'

'I think I'm getting lost.'

'Yeah, aren't we all. Say, does that look like Tasmania down there? Ah, just kidding you.'

'So what happened to the tree after 1994?'

'Kind of a death watch. Folks said without the chainsaw attack the tree, woulda been a hundred twenty-five years old, would have lasted another ten, twelve years. Claimed the chainsaw whacked that number in half. But then in the spring of '99 – that would be your autumn – a family of four decided to have an outing up there on Maungakiekie and leaped over the protective guarding. Well, you can figure the rest. Cops came, busted the Maori family, charged them with being unlawfully in a closed yard, can ya believe it?'

'And then they cut it down?'

'Yup. See, it's all about who gets to sit where and with whom. That one European pine was put up after the Pakeha took out the Maori tree. Then they decided to protect the pine by surrounding it with bars. Guess that's what they call protective custody. And everyone, Pakeha and Maori, has an opinion about what belongs up there, what belonged up there, what never and always belongs, you see?'

'Not at all,' admits Harry, though the truth is this is all starting to become a bit clearer. Not that he has any idea why he and Sita and Athnic are involved with all these stories of prisons and prisoners of various ilk.

'Say, we've still a few hours to go, why don't you get yourself a bit of sleep? Those exec quarters back there where Athnic is are pretty fine. This Corvette used to be owned by a prince, did you know that? Go on, get some sleep.'

Harry, suddenly realizing how tired he is, does as he is told.

☾

Harry's mother slept fitfully when she slept at all for as long as Harry could remember. She enjoyed sleeping, she would tell her son, as long as it was blissfully, peacefully absent of any intrusion. But constantly intruding, sticking their waifish noses where they didn't belong, were her dreams.

'What dreams may come,' she would sigh as she lay awake in her bed in the early hours of the morning, having just awoken from night-time visions full of colour, romance, danger, and excitement. Not that they were always, or even usually, unpleasant dreams. Quite the contrary, she would tell her husband and son at breakfast conversations. She dreamt of white horses galloping along sandy beaches through pristine surf, of bungee jumping off the Asoka pillar, of being courted by the most handsome and sanguine of gentlemen, of being ruler, courtesan, commandant, and commando. No, her dreams were not the order of nightmares, but were so full of excitement that she just got no rest.

'Imagine,' she would tell her son as he played with his porridge, 'that you ran to school every day and then the first class you had was phys-ed and you began the class by running. Imagine how tired you would be. Well, that's how it is with me, isn't it? A full night of busy-busy dreams leads me to a full day of busy-busy chores. And no rest in between. No rest for the wicked.'

Harry's mother, who had spent all of six months in India shortly after the marriage, retained from that experience an Indian-English patter and a penchant for wearing a salwar kameez for any occasion, habits that confounded and greatly disturbed her husband who, after all, had married this woman for her very englishness.

Fortunately for Harry, while he may have absorbed his mother's ability to live in between places, for the most part he did not inherit his mother's enhanced night visions. He had vivid dreams, but only occasionally. However, unlike his mother, who claimed she was always aware of how dream-state her dreams were, Harry found that his more vivid dreams encroached so much on reality that they seemed far more real than his daily life at the credit union. He knew it was clichéd to think so, but he truly did feel, and he had long conversations with Sita about this, that his waking life was in some ways much more false and hard to believe in than the occasional dreams he had that were so very life-like.

It is such a dream that Harry is now having after settling into a luxurious grey leather executive seat directly across from Athnic. He could get used to travelling in such extravagance, he tells himself just before he slips off into a sleep that is somewhat reminiscent of his mother's restless nights. In this dream, Harry reclines in a luxurious grey leather executive seat trying to fall asleep when Han materializes in the seat next to him.

'Han!' exclaims Harry.

'Yo, Harry,' replies Han.

'What happened? I mean, what happened at the Pinnacles? You kept zapping in and out of visibility.'

'I was searching for Sita.'

'But in the Pinnacles. Why? We had no clues.'

'Sometimes you just have to search in places where there are no clues,' Han states matter-of-factly. 'Sita might have been there – it's a place of time and space, sand and structures-that-are-not-quite-sand-yet, and to tell the truth, I think I made some headway.'

'Meaning?'

'Meaning she showed up and we had a little chat.'

'You found her?' Harry begins to rise out of his seat.

'Well, *she* found me.'

'Where is she? How do we get to her? Is she okay? What happened to her, did she say? When did–?'

Han bares his teeth and unleashes an enormous jungle screech to quell Harry's ridiculous barrage of questions.

'That's better,' says Han, grinning and flicking, rather than wagging, his tail back and forth. 'Now before getting ahead of ourselves, it's time for a lesson in numerology.'

'A lesson in numerology?'

'You'd get somewhere,' says Han panting slightly, 'if you did some deep thinking and quiet listening instead of just repeating everything I said.'

This curt canine comment has the desired effect and Harry sits obediently, waiting for his animal companion to speak.

Han opens his snout, but no sounds emerge, and Harry, forgetting completely that this is a dream, is amazed at how the numbers float out of Han's snout and appear like so many smoke rings in front of him:

> *Part 2, 1991 Resource Management Act*
> *Article 2, Treaty of Waitangi, 1840*
> *2 years jail / $200,000 fine*
> *2 cuts*
> *2nd chainsaw attack, September 14, 1999*
> *2-3 years: life expectancy of tree after 2nd chainsaw attack*
> *U2, band who wrote 'One Tree Hill' song in memorial*
> *to Maori road crew member killed while working for*
> *the band*

'That's two,' says Han.

Harry stares at the serify twos hanging in the air, slowly dissolving in the vibratory air of the jet. 'Two,' he mouths to himself.

> *280 mm deep cut in tree's northern side*
> *88% of trunk's circumference severed*
> *30 cm deep, two-thirds around the trunk*

44-year-old woman
46-year-old man
15-year-old girl
20-year-old woman
charged/convicted of criminal damage

Once again, Harry watches as the numbers float about Han's head, white translucent smoke, tangible yet untouchable. He tries to memorize the details before they once again give way to the Corvette's vibrations and dissipate.

1600: Totara Ahua
1840: site given its Pakeha name by
   Dr John Logan Campbell, 'father of Auckland'
1876: Pakeha and Maori in lone trees on hilltops
1912: John Campbell dies at age 95 buried on the Hill

Han lolls his tongue out and seems to smile. Harry looks at the numbers of history, and through the contained spaces of the eights and zeros and sixes and nines and fours, Harry sees newsreels playing out the histories: men and trees on a lookout over an ocean city, documents signed and interpreted and reinterpreted, all in vivid colour in those spaces in between.

Han takes a deep breath and expels a final number:

5000

'Five thousand?' Harry asks aloud. 'What is five thousand?'

'The number of pounds,' Han explains, 'Campbell ordered his trustees not to exceed in erecting a monument "dedicated to the Maori Race"; he also ordered "that such monument shall take the form of an obelisk." And then he said, or at least this is what his epigraph on One-Tree Hill says, *"si monumentum requiris circumspice."*'

Harry's Latin is not just rusty – it's downright non-existent, but he does hazard a guess: 'If you require a monument, look at your foreskin?'

'Not quite,' says Han. 'If a memorial is required, look around you.'

And as he says this, Harry is at the top of One-Tree Hill. It is past midnight and a man with a mission leaps the fence and the night air is cut by the brazen sound of a chainsaw engine. Sawdust flies and is lit by the moonlight and while Harry watches, police arrive and subdue the assailant. Then it is daylight and the tree, a huge bandage around its trunk, commands the hilltop. Han is there, bounding over the roots, leaping, leaping, leaping up into the branches, barking and yelping, swinging by his tail, desperately searching for something, someone. He does not heed Harry's calls, gets all the more excited, and begins climbing higher and higher into the tree's twisted branches. Harry calls louder and louder but all he hears is a dog yelping excitedly and the sound of an electric guitar and cheering audience.

Abruptly, the sounds stop, the scene changes, and a family of two adults, a couple perhaps, a young woman, and a teenage girl are at the tree. They, too, carry a chainsaw and they too begin to cut into the bark and they too are stopped and subdued by arriving police. And then they are also gone and the bark-cutting buzz of chainsaw is replaced by the air-cutting whir of helicopter, and now official-looking people are using official-looking chainsaws to officially cut the pine into pieces. Each one is elaborately tied into a winch set-up and flown into the distance. Harry watches as the tree revolts against the aging process and becomes smaller and smaller until there is only a sapling where the huge pine once stood and then that too is gone.

Finally, Harry is alone on the hill under a moonlit sky and in his hand is the Sita-ring. It feels solid blue and Harry is surprised that he can feel a colour and he realizes he is crying because he cannot find Sita and then Han is by his side, not speaking, but Harry can see huge white letters escaping Han's mouth, *I can find her*, and Harry is giving Han the Sita-ring, take it to her, take it to her and then come back and then take me to her. And Harry is crying inconsolably, tears falling off his cheeks and landing on his chin and neck and chest. He hears the landing gear of a jet drop from its belly and he feels wheels touching down, and the sound of brakes and windflaps is all around him. He opens his eyes and is staring straight into Athnic's face.

'Welcome to Aotearoa,' says Athnic.

'Where's Han?' asks Harry.

'Funniest thing,' says Athnic. 'You woke up an hour ago, leapt to your feet and called out to him. He wasn't on the plane, of course, but you held out that blue dogtoy of yours—'

'The Sita-ring.'

'Yes, and then the ring disappeared just like Han was disappearing in the Pinnacles and then you just lay down again.'

'I had a dream, Athnic. Odd, complex, but I think it had something to do with that message from Sita at the prison, the Polynesian Spa advertisement.'

'Probably did,' says Athnic. 'Which is why we have to get moving.'

'To that One-Tree Hill you were talking about?'

'Nope,' says Athnic. 'We have to go to Rotorua.'

Rotorua

Dogs are physiologically unable to talk, but what they can do, and do exceedingly well, is walk around proudly with an object of desire in their mouths. Doesn't matter what it is, be it bone, stick, or rubber toy, there's hardly a dog that doesn't exhibit extreme pride when prancing about with a favourite object firmly clenched in its jaws. Perhaps it's instinctual behaviour, something to do with the hunt, or maybe it's a type of puppy-play, grown-up dogs being infantilized by their human companions to such a degree that they can hardly flip over and sleep with their paws in the air, as is fully natural, without people crowing about how neotenously cute the animal is; or perhaps that stick/bone/toy-holding activity is a form of latent capitalism, a form of saying I've-got-something-you-don't-and-I'll-bite-your-fool-head-off-if-you-try-to-take-it-from-me. Whatever the case, dogs, even ones that don't talk, will exhibit this behaviour, which is quite useful, really, since it gives their human companions something to think about when out walking.

On this particular day, at this particular moment, if you were to drive in a southeasterly direction from Hamilton along the Number 1 and then push further east by slicing off and taking the Number 5, and if you were indeed to travel far enough to cross the boundary of Waikato and into the Bay of Plenty, you might just travel far enough to note a fair bit of thermal activity, smoke rising from the ground, reminiscent of Blakeian notions of hell, perhaps, and if you were to go this far, along the lakeside drive around Lake Rotorua, you would chance upon the Number 30 which would lead to the ignominiously-named Hell's Gate. You might note to yourself that there is nothing particularly hellish about this place, other than it may bring to mind European artistic notions of what hell is supposed to be like, with its fire and its brimstone and its bubbling pots of mud and what-not, and you might even say hellishness is really not a solipsistic Sartrian 'everybody else,' but particular somebody-elses who have a nasty habit of living, but not let-living, of knocking down the creations that others have built just to feel good themselves, of proclaiming self-righteousness and hence relegating others to a secondary status, now that might be what you or any other sane person might call hell, not this landscape where steam escapes from the pores of the earth, giving up heat, which is far from the cold pits of the hell you or I might imagine.

Nevertheless, if on this particular day and at this particular moment you were to stop at this touristic intervention on the road to Whakatane, you might well see a curious sight: a dog, padding along the path and emerging from the mist like a hound from hell, although his frightening and slavering visage will seem not quite so off-putting as he will be carrying a bright blue rubber pull-toy. (It's hard to see a dog carrying a pull-toy as a terrifying thing, but then it's hard to see the inviting warmth of steam and rock pools as a hellish design, wouldn't you say?) And if this dog were to see you, he would ignore you and pad along his way – a dog with a mission – and you would be quite within your rights to be peeved at him if you were to call, 'Hey boy, bring it here,' and be steadfastly ignored. But if you were to follow him around the salt-softened water of Sulphur Lake, to catch a glimpse of him as he drifted in and out of the mist as he passed Kakahi Falls, you might see him hesitate at the brink of the boiling pool named after Hurutini – so named, as the story goes, because this woman suicided by diving into the pool, but then again, how much faith can you put in stories when they are there to lure you in, good tourist that you are, and how tourist-grabbing would it be if Hurutini actually named the pool herself, without flinging herself inside? – hesitate and then, with one big dog breath, close his eyes and dive into the bubbling waters, even as you might implore him to stop, desist, come back little puppy, for you shall scald yourself into oblivion, but it would be too late since the stupid mutt would have already done the deed and you stare after him, long after the last tell-tale ripples had subsided, wondering what possessed the crazy canine to do himself in like that.

But it would be a shame you could not follow Han into that steampit, for what you would see would amaze you, amazes even me and I am already there.

Han dives in, dives down down down, deep down, deeper still, so deep he thinks he will not make it far enough, but still he dives and finally, a string of light, a sound of voice, and he knows that he has found her. Han takes a breath, a deep one, and in comes fresh air and not sulphurous water, and he opens the eyes he had closed upon his initial dive and before him he sees a waterscape of untold luxury, a beautiful sunny day, with the tell-tale wisps of rising steam that George Bernard Shaw saw when he said, 'I wish I'd never seen the place' (to which one might respond the place might have wished it had never seen George Bernard Shaw), and in the middle of the brilliant sheen of water Han sees a tiny island, a lily-pad of an island, and there she is, sitting lonely but unperturbed, humming softly to herself a tune she remembers from her childhood, something her father used to sing to her when he came home from work, thinking she was asleep, a strange and jocular tune about labouring for an indecent wage.

Han sees Sita and is overjoyed.

He rushes to her, tail wagging, entire back end wagging, full body wagging, and he would bark his excitement if his mouth were not so full of rubber ring.

'You've found me, Han,' says Sita.

'I looked hard,' admits Han. 'But I finally found you.'

'And Harry, did you bring Harry along for the journey?' she asks, her eyes laughing.

'Oh, yes,' says Han. 'Yes, indeed. He sent me to you with this.' Han drops the Sita-ring at her feet.

'Then it must be you,' she says to Han. 'To tell the truth, I was having doubts. So many visions, so many beings appearing from the mists, it's hard to tell who's friend and who's foe.'

'But I'm your friend,' says Han. 'I always was and always will be.'

Sita picks up the Sita-ring. 'I know that now,' she says. 'I know that now.'

Han's whole body begins to shake with excitement once again. He dives into the water and swims circles around Sita. He finds a stick and begins ripping it to shreds. He rolls around and then playfully tugs at Sita's arm. 'Let's go, let's go,' he says.

☾

Oh, this is all too much, all this schmaltzy reunion stuff. I can't bear it any more. I have to intervene. I step up and show myself. Sita, strong one that she is, doesn't flinch, but Han does a bit of a cartwheel when he sees me. Of course, this whole scene, Han's determination, my appearance, Sita's stoicism, all of this is past tense, so I wonder why I even play along with this charade. Stories are meant to change, just as dogs are meant to talk, but sometimes stories change in such subtle ways that they tell the same old saga.

I do what I have to do. This is a memory from the distant and repressed past, the way my hand reaches out and clasps Han's tail. My hand is hot with demonic fury – smoke begins to rise from my palm, his fur, smoke that is the history of our lives lived together.

'Go, then!' I shout at Han in my real voice, not the silly telepathic one I've been using. He pulls away from me, the flames now leaping from his nether regions, hardly perturbing him.

'Go on, you know you have to!'

Han runs through my little kingdom, spreading flames everywhere. He is laughing and screeching and carrying on as he burns everything around us.

'Go get Harry and bring him here. Tell him Anna's waiting, ha, that'll get his blood going. It's been told like this before, and even though I'm telling it now, go go go.'

Han barks, tries to form some words, but they just sound like wolf pups mewling. He turns to lick Sita on the wrist while his tail flings flames every which way. She touches his head fondly and gestures with the Sita-ring for him to leave this place. Han barks, does a dance, passes fire to a few more of the nice sticks that I have so neatly stacked, and off he goes into the water. *Swim, dog, swim away. The battle's not over until she's gone. And even then, even then, I might still win.*

if you want peace,
prepare for war

'So, it comes down to this?'

I adjust my breastplate, pull it snug. My shoulder armour comes next and it laces with fine gold thread to the shield covering my chest.

'You can pretend to ignore me, but I know you're listening. You will do battle over me, is that it? Here in this place, you'll fight again?'

I wear no face gear. My visage is enough to frighten most enemies into submission, and while that's not to be expected this time, I'm just used to going into battle with my face uncovered.

'And what about me? Don't I have a say in this matter? Isn't this all about me?'

My legs are another matter. I adorn them with ornate, gold-plated armour in several pieces, plates for my shins, rounded pieces for the knees, thick coverings for my thighs, all linked together to allow at least some freedom of movement. My arms I leave mostly bare, although thick pewter bracelets and armlets offer some covering but little protection. I need to keep my arms unencumbered, however, so I can wield my arsenal: double-headed axes, swords half as wide as me and twice as tall, scythes that can split fine hairs, chains for throwing and wrenching and strangling.

'You can't win, you know. You can never win. You can change your name, your battlefield, but you can't change the story. It will happen again as it happened before.'

How little you know about me! Don't you see, it doesn't matter who wins the battle. That's not what this is about. That's not what it was ever about. I can cut off the hero's head and he can cut off the villain's; conquerors can build monuments on the remains of a conquered people's bones and the vanquished can wait five centuries before exacting revenge; dogs can turn into monkeys and ordinary men can turn into gods; a mere hotel concierge can become world-wise beyond compare and espionage agents can trip over their own shoelaces; credit union managers can attempt to be masters of all they survey and migrants can find themselves with nothing to look upon except four stone walls; water can take back the land and the land can liquefy itself; juntas can be formed out of hatred, and love, yes love and trust can be borne out of conflict. All this I know, and all this is the story already told. Don't you see? I don't want to win a silly battle. I just want things to run backwards for a while, for effect to precede cause, for seas to pour into glacial streams, for people to start acting humane. Is that so hard to understand?

Sita is silent. I have ranted and she, surprisingly, has listened.

'I think I see,' she finally says.

She walks toward me, carefully skirting the pile of sticks I had so meticulously ordered and which now lie smouldering. My kingdom is razed and she walks toward me unperturbed. She lays a coffee-coloured hand on my oak-bark shoulder. Her other hand caresses my creased cheek. If I did not know better, I would say that when I close my eyes I can feel softened lips buss my flame-blistered forehead. I feel tears coming.

'I understand,' she says, and the words wrap themselves around my face and enter into both ears simultaneously, past cochlea and stirrup, vibrating drum with delicious resonance.

'I understand.'

Harry goes to Rotorua

Harry is sitting between Sam and Athnic at a three-table Indian restaurant and take-out in Papakura. He is doing a good job of explaining his dream to Athnic in more detail, and Athnic, in turn, is doing a remarkably poor job of explaining why they did not need to go to One-Tree Hill and why he knows their next stop will be Rotorua. Sam nods all the way through the discussion and then leaps to his feet and clears his throat.

'Right,' he says. 'Looks like my work is done. Would love to help further, but I fly an executive jet, not a fighter plane. Going to go visit my mother. Thanks for the meal, Harry. I wish you well. I'll send you a present from home.'

'And thank you, Sam, for the transport here. Athnic chooses his friends well.'

Sam smiles at Harry, at Athnic, touches his forefinger to his forehead and heads out the door. 'See you around, Athnic,' he calls over his shoulder. Sam is forced to turn sideways as he leaves, for another gentleman seeks entrance to the restaurant as Sam seeks to exit. They brush shoulders. The man walking through the doorway wears an expensive pinstriped suit, Italian leather shoes, and reflective sunglasses. He looks to his left, then to his right. If Harry and Athnic could see his eyes through mirrored shades, they would realize the man now looks directly at them and now strides to their table. He leans into the table and puts his hands on his hips.

'Aha,' says Director Merrick.

'Hello,' says Harry.

'Hi,' says Athnic.

'Thought you'd lost me, didya?' Merrick says, hands still firmly planted on hips.

'Didn't actually think much about it at all, Director,' says Harry truthfully.

'How was the deportation hearing?' asks Athnic earnestly.

'Did you know,' Merrick begins, keeping one hand on his hip while removing his sunglasses with the other, 'that there are thirty-six ways to kill a man, even an armed guard, on a fourteen-hour pan-oceanic flight?'

'You killed someone?' asks Athnic in disbelief.

'Well, no, unfortunately all but two of those methods require I not have my wrists bound by those silly plastic handcuffs. And the other two require more legroom than they give you on those chartered deportation flights. So, he got off scot-free. But that's not the point.'

'And the point is?' asks Harry.

'The point is I'm back. I'm back and I've linked up with all the worldwide chapters of Brasso Pilgrim Junta. Together we are strong, united, and we shall never move backward.'

'Um,' asks Athnic. 'Did you come all this way just to tell us that?'

'Don't flatter yourself,' says Merrick, now removing the remaining hand from his hip and jabbing a finger at Athnic. 'You were meant to help me, to be my ally. You failed, and miserably at that, so I've come to tell you that you are no longer welcome at any Brasso Pilgrim Junta events – no parties, no celebrations, no planning sessions, no secret meetings, no nothing. Got it?'

Harry looks at Athnic. 'You worked with this Brasso Pilgrim Junta?'

'No,' says Athnic to Harry. 'But I don't think that's the point.'

'Exactly,' says Merrick. 'You were never part of the Junta and now, thanks to your incompetence, you never will be.'

'Okay,' says Harry, 'enough is enough. What the hell is this Brasso Pilgrim Junta? And don't go off telling me it's not a what or a who or whatever. Just tell me. All right?'

Merrick sizes Harry up, perhaps deliberating on how many ways there are to kill a man in an Indian restaurant, but then sighs and answers.

'The Junta – the junta is nothing short of a movement. We are here to preserve the truth. We are here to protect ourselves and our lands. We are here to keep things from changing. Ever. That is the everlasting motto of Brasso Pilgrim Junta.'

'I see,' says Harry.

'I see,' says Athnic.

'No,' says Merrick. 'You don't see at all. Goodbye.' And he turns on his heel and strides out of the restaurant.

Harry and Athnic watch Director Merrick leave.

'Do you suppose we'll miss him?' asks Athnic.

'I don't suppose he'll ever really be gone,' says Harry.

Harry looks across at his friend. Harry has no earthly reason, he thinks, to trust this man who has led him to islands all over the world with a secrecy and arrogance befitting one of Director Merrick's crew. But every time Athnic has acted, Harry feels it has led them one step closer to Sita.

'I told you, just trust him,' was what Simpson kept telling Harry every time he called Sita's father to report on their latest findings. As Harry got more anxious, Simpson appeared to get that much calmer.

'Why should I trust him?' Harry had asked Simpson when he called from the Auckland airport. 'This guy is crazy.'

'Yes,' Simpson had said. 'He probably is. But, and I learned this long ago, Harry, that the crazier your friends, the better they are for you.'

'What sort of advice is that?' Harry had asked.

'Believe it or not,' Simpson had replied, 'the best advice you're going to get.' He had paused and then repeated his standard phrase. 'Trust him, Harry. You've got to trust him. You've got to trust.'

Trust, trust, trust. Harry looks across at his friend and recalls the actions of the last several hours. Here was Harry, an ordinary guy with a purely ordinary life, and yet a scant few hours ago there he was with his friend, landing in a private jet in Auckland in search of a lost comrade. And no ordinary international arrival it was. Indeed, Athnic was extraordinary when he commandeered the military vehicle, a splashy new Toyota Rav4, that had greeted the Corvette's unannounced arrival at Auckland's international airport. He was extraordinary in that he had not used stern language or manipulation to commandeer the 16-valve double-overhead cam, 4 × 4 vehicle, but had simply smiled at the gruff Samoan officer who demanded to know who the hell they were landing a private jet on a commercial strip. Harry had listened to the officer rant on about indiscretions and illegalities, and Harry had been quite taken aback when the officer uttered an epithet so familiar to Harry from his youth that it brought back familiar palpitations and cold sweats. Harry could have sworn the officer had muttered about how 'you pakis' thought they could get away with anything, although the officer had glared directly at Athnic as he spoke. (It wasn't until later that evening that Athnic explained the interaction – the officer was, indeed, address-ing Athnic, but not with the derogative 'paki' but the descriptive 'pake-ha,' a Maori word, Athnic explained, referring to the Europeans who came to settle in Aotearoa.) Athnic had smiled an extraordinary smile and then leaned in and whispered something in the ear of the gruff officer. In the next few extraordinary minutes, the gruff officer was smil-ing and laughing with Athnic, insisting Athnic and his friends borrow the suv – complete with power moon-roof and variable-valve timing with intelligence – for as long as they needed it. A brand spanking new Rav4 and Athnic had it on loan. Extraordinary. And it had not ended there. If anything, the royal treatment Athnic was used to receiving was enhanced since they landed in New Zealand. But as he became even more admired, Athnic became less forthcoming with Harry than he had been before, if this were at all possible. And yet, the person who was arguably the closest to Sita, her own father, kept telling Harry to trust Athnic, no matter how unforthcoming he might seem. What did Simpson know that Harry did not, Harry wondered. If only he knew.

welcome to my lair

Hello, Harry. Welcome to the story. What's that? Oh yes, you've already been participating, and very adeptly I must say. No, no, no intrusion at all, quite the opposite actually. What's that the evil villains of comicbook and cheesy film and TV are fond of saying? 'Welcome, superhero. We've been expecting you,' followed by a sinister laugh. So, welcome, Harry Kumar, of course I've been expecting you. We've all been expecting you. What did you expect, that you would arrive unexpected? But I forget my manners (isn't that also what evil villains say before seducing the super-hero into a diabolical death trap?), forgive me, m'lord. Allow me to introduce you to the characters in the play. Sita, of course you know, although you haven't had the pleasure of her company, as have I, for the last couple of weeks, but more on that later. Han, well you know Han, we all know Han, don't we? Loyal sidekick, animal companion, leader of primates in his own right, a bit of a troublemaker, apt to throw a you-know-what-wrench into the works even when he just drops by to visit, but all in all, rather loveable, wouldn't you say? And not to hold too much of a mirror to the scene, but please indulge me, and let me intro-duce Harry Kumar. Hari Kumar. Caught between names, between places, yet even so, the lord and master of all he surveys. Isn't that what you've been doing, Harry? Dropping in for a cultural visit and then going away with all this new-found knowledge, exciting, isn't it, won't it be, to impart news of this exotic wilderness back home at the credit union? Harry the sap, Harry the metropolitan citizen, Harry the intro-vert, and Harry the warrior, the mountain man, the prince in a shining armoire, such as it is. Harry, may I introduce, Harry Kumar, unlikely hero of the story. I think those are all the players. That is, unless, what's that Harry, oh yes, of course, forgive me, how could I. Might I introduce myself, my liege, my king, your honour, your worship, myself: Anna Varre. Madam, I'm Adam, as the palindrome goes. No, really, call me Anna. Or annA, either way. I've been here before, though, you know, been here forever after and always before, and the story just keeps play-ing itself out. Madam, I'm Anna. Pleasure to meet your acquaintance.

So, now that introductions are out of the way, where to now? Here's the four-one-one, dearest Harry Kumar. Sita disappeared, not quite, but pretty much, before your very eyes. And your suspicions are right, I am the one, the only, the one who was the very agent, the provocateur, the evil child who disappeared her against her will. Now, let's see, Han, loyal canine with the will of his human colleague but not his opposable thumbs, throws down the challenge. The Watson to your *schlock*, Harry. The magnifying glass that does not miss a fingerprint, were I ever to leave one. You owe it all to him, Harry, to Han. Congratulations. Your history together is a testament to all that is holy on this firmament. Sita, he finds her, Han allows her to reappear to your very eyes, Harry, though truth be told, she never truly disappeared, either to me or to her humble self. We had a good time, Harry, travelling from island to island, you not around to pester or posture. But you followed in our footprints, indeed you did, thanks in part to loyal and tongue-lolling Han. G'boy, Han, g'boy. So here we are, an odd set of quadruplets, no?

Oh, and Harry, whatcha gonna do about it? See, I have no intention of letting things run their course as you, no doubt, would like them to, as they always have. So, once again, I ask you, whatcha gonna do?

C'mon boy, what's it gonna be? I need to know right now, before we go any further, before the light on the dashboard goes dim, where do we go from here? You and me forever, Harry, will you do that for me? I need to know right now.

testing the waters

Rather less unusual than talking, but still unusual, is the act of a dog kneeling. But that is precisely what Han is doing before Harry, and Harry hasn't the slightest idea why.

'What are you doing, Han?' Harry asks quietly.

'I'm offering my allegiance to you,' mumbles Han, matter-of-factly, 'my allegiance and undying friendship.' Han punctuates this final word with a quick lick to the toe of Harry's right boot.

'Oh,' says Harry. 'I see,' which, of course, he doesn't. What he does see, however, is the cause of Han's mumbling, which is a bright blue rubber ring that only drops out of Han's mouth as he licks Harry's boot.

'That's the Sita-ring,' says Harry, without a hint of excitement.

'Indeed,' says Han, his voice now clear without the hindrance of the ring. 'I brought it back after showing it to Sita.'

'You found her,' says Harry, stating the obvious.

'Obviously,' replies Han.

'Then let's go get her,' says Harry.

'Um, sure,' says Han. 'Thing is, you should know, I made a bit of a mess when I left.'

'Is Sita all right?'

'Oh, yes, no problem there, I just kind of mussed the place up is all. Couldn't help myself. You know how I feel about sticks. Piles of sticks. Nice, neat piles of sticks. I just can't leave them alone, so chewable and disturbable. And flammable.'

'Ah,' says Harry. 'That's fine. We're going to go there and do more than light up a few sticks, believe me,' surprising himself with his own violent rhetoric.

'Woof,' says Han.

'I beg your pardon?' says Harry.

'Sorry,' says Han.' 'A brief regressive moment. I was saying, perhaps you should send an emissary. You know, if you rush in there, guns blazing and all, it's going to be quite a mess.'

'Hm,' says Harry. 'I've got no idea what you're talking about.'

☾

It is late in the evening when they check into the Royal Lakeside Hotel. Athnic may not be too clear on what role he has taken on, but he has not lost his flair for finding the finest lodgings in town. Harry is looking quite preoccupied. Han is looking for food, although lately his tastes have swung from dog biscuits to fresh fruit.

'Yes, sir?' says the hotel clerk without looking up.

Harry looks at the man blankly and then looks to Athnic for assistance.

'We'll take a suite,' says Athnic. 'Born to Party Jacuzzi if you have one.'

'Why, yes, we do, sir. And that will be under which name?'

'Athnic Long.'

Harry notices that Athnic is once again surrounded by admiring hotel staff, all peppering the hotel hero with questions about his career, his ambitions, his interests. Harry, Athnic, and Han are swept up by a small entourage which escorts them to the specialized suite on the top floor of the hotel. But they have barely entered the suite and Athnic has disentangled himself from his admirers when Harry swings open the drapes and looks down, swallows hard, and points at a building below them on the shores of the lake.

Athnic comes over to the window and squints at the small complex on the ground far below, spewing what appear to be sulphurous fumes from hell. At the front of the building is a small, stylized sign that reads, 'The Polynesian Spa.'

'Aha,' says Athnic. 'Let's go.'

'Now?' asks Harry, wishing he could explore the suite before they head off on another adventure.

'Now?' asks Han, his mouth somewhat full of a small bunch of grapes that he has just discovered in the complimentary fruit basket.

'Yes,' says Athnic, beaming. 'Now.'

'So, do you think Sita is down there?' asks Harry hopefully.

'You think they'd send up more grapes?' asks Han.

'It's our penultimate stop,' says Athnic. And he heads off toward the lift, leaving the door ajar so that his friends can follow. This they do and not a word is spoken by any of them, not inside the lift, not when they exit on the ground floor, not when they cross the promenade to the building spewing smelly vapours. In fact, no one says a word until Athnic has purchased entry vouchers and rented swimsuits for Harry and himself, and all three of them – Han able to avoid detection by swinging from his tail across the i-beams above the attendant – are inside the changing room.

'So,' Harry repeats. 'This is where we find Sita?'

'Nope,' says Athnic. 'Like I said, it's our penultimate stop. But we'll find her soon.' They change in silence and then walk into the dimly-lit spa area which features eight rectangular pools, bordered on the furthest side by the lake. Han decides to sample the drinkability of the closest pool and screeches his distaste. Harry and Athnic climb into the hot pool. Their toes sink into its pebbled bed and the warmth fills their bodies. But no sooner have they entered the first pool than Harry feels strangely compelled to heft himself out and over the small siding that separates them from the second pool. By the time Athnic has joined him, Harry is already moving into the third pool, and then the fourth, fifth, and sixth in quick and more feverish succession. Athnic decides not to try to keep up. Han decides to scamper up and down between the pools, sniffing wildly and making odd grunting noises.

As soon as Harry has plunged into the seventh pool the vapours begin to rise so swiftly that visibility, owing to darkness and density, is reduced to nil. Athnic calls out to Harry, but hears nothing in return. He holds his hand in front of his face – he can barely make out its outline, and when he extends his hand to arm's length, it disappears into the mix of dark and mist.

'Harry!' Athnic calls out trepidatiously. '*Harry!*' he repeats with more alarm. There is no answer. But Athnic thinks he sees a flash of light, or perhaps no more than a flicker, but a light nonetheless, cutting through the darkness from one of the distant pools.

In the seventh pool, Harry turns his body around slowly. He can feel an odd and disturbing presence somewhere near – but he can also feel the presence of friendship, loyalty, love, and they are all so close, so intermingling, Harry cannot distinguish where one begins and others leave off. He walks slowly through the density of water, air, sand, and darkness toward the eighth pool. He does not know how close he is to the edge until his knee bumps up against the smooth side. Carefully, he pulls himself onto the siding, lets his leg slip over into what he knows to be (but cannot see as) the eighth pool. It is the hottest one yet. To his right he can hear short, nervous breathing.

'It's all right, Han,' he says, bringing his other leg into the eighth pool. 'We're in this together.' Han whimpers and smacks his lips.

Harry allows the weight of his legs to draw him into the pool. His toes outstretch for the pebbled floor beneath, but find nothing but hotter and hotter water. Without so much as a splash, Harry is pulled underneath, into bubbling, boiling, swirling, sulphurous waters, a primal broth that scalds his face and invades his lungs. That could be a wave of extraordinarily hot water now brushing across his chest, wrapping itself around his neck, or it could be a powerful arm, flexing its muscle into his windpipe. That could be the corner of a step, pushing into his lower back and causing him to arch his spine in response, or it could be rounded, ornate, gold-plated knee armour. That could be the gurgling of mineral-laden water cuddling his eardrum and entering his brain, or it could be the crude, raspy whisper of an age-old adversary telling Harry he is about to die, not in battle, never in battle, but in the battle that comes after all is said and fought over.

Harry breathes his last. He thought this was just an expression, but this is exactly what happens. Harry feels no desire to take another breath, perhaps because he can feel his lungs are already full of water, perhaps because he *knows* his heart no longer beats. Eyes wide open in the wet blackness, Harry is unable to close his eyes, cannot even muster a quick blink. This is what it feels like to die, thinks Harry, surprising himself by his own perfect calm. This is me dying. His arms float above him. Everything feels absolutely still and Harry realizes that, apart from seeing nothing in the lightless water, he can hear nothing and feel nothing. This is me dead. Harry stays like this, floating without the sensation of floatfulness, still without the sensation of stillness, for what might be a very long time had Harry any sense of time which, at this moment, he has not. At the very least, thinks Harry, he should be able to see his life flash before him, but such is not the case. However, after what might be a millisecond or a thousand years, Harry has no idea which, he *does* see something, a flash of light, or perhaps only a flicker, the sort of light he was used to seeing, in recent days, emanating from Athnic, but now, at this time, Harry feels that flash or flicker coming from behind his own eyes, from deep inside his head, from a place deeper than his own head. And following the flash or flicker comes a wealth of sensations: desperately loud gurgling noises, enormous pains from deep inside his chest, the feeling of heat and wetness across his face and chest and limbs, and an incredible and forceful sense of motion, of swirling movement.

Then, what could be a rope that once wrapped around Martha Rendell's neck now coils around Harry's, furry and wiry, tightening, pulling, lifting, so that Harry is wrenched from the water with such force that the cool lake air feels like an immersion in the lake itself. He spits out huge quantities of hot liquid, gasps and sputters, grabs with both hands and vainly attempts to loosen from his neck the tail that rescued him from the ravenous demon's jaws, hears a whisper full of arrogance telling him the battle is nigh, hears the whisper overwhelmed by Athnic calling out to him through the darkness and the vapour, falls to the siding exhausted and semi-conscious.

Han's tail slides off from Harry's neck. The dense mists lift and, for a moment, everything seems clear. Athnic holds Harry's head in his hands, asks him if he's okay. Harry nods weakly.

'What did I say,' says Han, 'about sending in an emissary? Hey, what did I say?'

Harry smiles. His face glows. When he speaks, it is warm wind, soft rain, blue sky, and rich earth that come out of his mouth as words: 'I guess I should have listened to you, my friend.'

Han snorts, shows his teeth, then licks Harry on his cheek.

Athnic looks down on his friend. For the first time in a very long time, Athnic feels quite helpless. He feels like he is waiting for something but he does not know what that might be. Athnic is no longer in control and feels like he has never been in control. In recent times, if he ever felt anything like this, the feeling would dissipate in, quite literally, a flash, and Athnic would have all the answers he needed. Not so this time. Athnic, helpless, looks down on his friend. Then, without any hint or warning, with all the suddenness and immediacy of a lightning strike but with the subtlety and grace of starlight, a flicker passes from behind Harry's eyes, out through his pupils, simultaneously sprinkling and bathing Athnic in a glow that is both remarkably stark and undeniably soft.

'So, I need an emissary.' Harry looks up at Athnic. 'Got any ideas?'

Athnic the emissary

Emissary, solicitor, counsel or, *agent, procureur, avocat-conseil, mandataire ou émissaire*, however you say it, it's a role in-between. A role of wisdom. A role of neither-here-nor-theredom. An emissary, however much he may be a direct agent, must ever act the diplomat, someone to bring two adversaries closer together, bring their bodies and minds together. He is, of a kind, a matchmaker, attending to two opposites. And Athnic is the emissary that Harry sends to meet me.

Athnic agrees to act as Harry's emissary. At first, Athnic was a bit stunned by all of this turnabout. He was the one who directed the game; he was the one who decided what to do next and when to do it; he was the one who was helping Harry to find Sita even if Athnic had no idea how he was doing this. But then, there was Athnic, staring down at the water-logged, back-to-life Harry, and there was Harry, gazing up calmly at Athnic as if this was a position he had been in a thousand times before. His body reclaimed from the sulphurous murky depths only moments before, and yet here he was, the man with the plan.

It would be too pat, too coy, for me to suggest this was all my doing, that I had given the light to Athnic and now had taken it away from him and passed it along to Harry. Too pat. Too coy. And what would I have to gain by endowing my enemy with such power? A new play with the same old ending. No, that's not it at all. No, the story has to be told, you see, but told from a different slant. The tip of a pinnacle clipped by pre-dawn light, is that the same tendentious tip that swelters in the noonday sun? Or that cools off under the blue light of a full moon? No. You see, Athnic had to be for Harry what he was – but now the story comes full circle and Athnic has to take his rightful place, not in front of Harry, leading the charge, but beside him, his loyal second. Too sudden, you think, too pat, too coy? Okay, perhaps. But that's what happens in stories. Characters change, they do the unthinkable, they turn themselves inside out and upside down. They exchange thoughts, feelings, bodily fluids with one another. They change. They interchange. Athnic-the-irrepressible-pointman is now Athnic-the-docile-emissary; Harry-the-selfdoubting-yesman is now Harry-the-warrior-chieftain. It's learning to trust in the unthinkable, to trust the untrustworthy, *that's* where the story changes. There, if nowhere else.

So Athnic, still full of bluster but now also topped up with wonderment at Harry's new regal pose and his own necessary back-seat position, is only too willing to play the diplomatic role. This close to Sita, their goal after all, Athnic is willing to do whatever it takes to win her back to the safe and trusting folds of home. And of course he knows exactly where to go since I have been far from frugal with the clues. Kakahi Falls, Sulphur Lake, the land of Hurutini, these are all names and places that seep deep into the consciousness of the Harrys and Athnics and Hans of the world. Come and meet me, Athnic, at this place they call Hell's Gate.

And so here he comes to negotiate the release of Sita from the mud-pools and sulfurous geysers of Rotorua. He is gone, Harry calculates, exactly three hours and twenty minutes, just long enough to sit down for a hot cup of cocoa with the offending kidnappers and find out, much as is to be expected in matters such as these, that there will be no truck with diplomatic missions. That, of course, is the way the story goes.

It's about time you showed up. It's getting rather late in the day.

'I'm here to negotiate the release of Sita Simpson,' Athnic says rather formally.

Uh-huh. And what do you have to negotiate with? I think this will somehow stump him, but I must give him credit for not missing a beat before his response.

'If you set her free,' he says to me sternly, 'we'll let you go unharmed.'

Oh? And if not, little man?

'Then prepare for battle.'

Battle? With you and, excuse the expression, whose army?

Now he is silent, perhaps a bit confused. How, indeed, does he expect to rescue Sita? I haven't prepared him for this part. Ah, yes, truth be known, I've been helping Athnic along the way. He may be smart, able, and magnificently magnetic, but like everyone else, he needs a guiding hand from time to time. So it was my not-so-little voice popping into his head every once in a while, telling him where to head to next, informing him how to get to the next stage of this wild Sita chase, giving him just that iota of knowledge that would help the sad trio find the object of their affection. And Harry trusted him just as Simpson asked him to. I have to give him credit, I didn't think this would work. I felt for certain Harry would back out when the going got tough – why go to Toronto Island and put up with crazed travelling companions? Why take an intercontinental journey to Australia on a whim? Why, for heaven's sake, take a private jet flown by, for all Harry might have known, a madman, all the way down here? But trust seems to go a long way. And speaking of a long way, we are a long way from birthplaces like London and Ayodyha, a long way from serendipitous islands that retell death after death. So what does it matter that the life of Harry Kumar was short and, the loosest of all possible terms, happy? It might have been happier, I suppose, had I not sucked the breath out of him in a sulphurous pool, drained him of life's energy as one might squeeze a dishrag dry. But, truth be told, one life ends and another is resurrected in its very body. Harry Kumar, dead or alive, come and get me. And maybe this final battle will not incur the same false endings.

Then a battle there will be, fair emissary. Go tell him to prepare.

Athnic turns his back to me and walks away. Off he goes to do my bidding – and not for the first time, but the first time he is conscious of this fact.

Off you go, little man. Do my bidding.

(

Athnic reports back to Harry dutifully.

'Anna Varre prepares for war,' he tells Harry. 'Anna Varre went on at considerable length about backward plans and lost trusts. And for a moment it looked like a negotiated truce was possible. But then Anna Varre's face went like thunder, an arm shot out and showed me the exit, and that was that.'

'No final words?' asks Harry.

'None but a mysterious parting growl, "See you yesterday,"' reports Athnic.

'Indeed,' says Harry and he shakes his head sadly. He sighs. Han sighs. Athnic, not fully knowing why he is doing this except that, like yawns, sighs can be infectious, sighs.

'Guess that's it,' says Harry to no one in particular.

'Yes, guess that's it,' says Han knowingly.

'Suppose that's it,' says Athnic, completely baffled by what 'it' might be.

But when he looks over to Harry he has a good idea of what 'it' actually is. Harry has transformed from his normal appearance of a meek credit union teller into, into, into … something quite else.

Harry is wearing a chain-mail chest protector that is coloured with a rainbow of silky reds, yellows, and magentas. While Athnic and Han gaze on in amazement, Harry is perfectly self-assured, although he has no idea why. He thinks back to one of the last conversations he had with Sita before she disappeared:

'Look, I'm thirty-five years old, I have no family since Mum died six years ago, I work as a non-descript teller at a non-descript credit union …'

Harry is wearing kneepads that are somewhat reminiscent of what skateboarders wear, except Harry's knee apparel has the distinct appearance of something utterly regal, although making kneepads look regal is quite some task.

'… I never travel anywhere, I'm not like you or Athnic, you guys have lots of friends and do lots of things …'

Harry is wearing an unusually luxuriant face guard that makes him look princely and warrior-like all in one glance.

'… I'm just – I'm just Harry Kumar, ordinary guy who holds out promise to do ordinary things for the rest of his ordinary life …'

And through all this gladiatorial regalia, Harry is smiling a deep, peaceful, serene yet stern smile.

'… and I just realized that I despise ordinary.'

Harry turns to Athnic and Han, nods cordially at them both. He thinks of what it means to be ordinary and what it might mean to be extraordinary. And, for some reason, he thinks about how living out his life in a prison or an island somewhere could be both ordinary and extraordinary, depending on which tack he took. Harry thinks about his recent conversations with Simpson about trust – trust in others, trust in himself. Harry thinks all of this and then makes an announcement.

'Let's go do this thing,' says Harry, gesturing with a golden staff he holds in his left hand.

'Yes,' says Han, 'this thing is long overdue.'

'Agreed,' says Athnic, eager to find out what thing they are about to do.

the great battle

The battle itself lasts only a mere thirty minutes by Athnic's estimate. But it's all the preparation, the singing, the recitation of poetic calls to arms, the body painting, the posturing with opponents (and, oh, what extravagant posturing there is) that takes all the time. Yes, fully eight or nine hours of pre-battle rituals before the first blow is struck and the first warrior fends it off successfully, before the first assaulting arrow is fired and deftly split in half by a defending arrow. But amidst all the hullabaloo, no one really cares about any of the matches except the centre-ring, no-holds-barred, main event between the colourful and now-downright princely Harry Kumar and his opponent, well-booed from all quarters, the evil and demonic Anna Varre. When the two step up to each other, dramatized by what seem to be excessively greater shows of force by geysers and steam jets and bubbling pools of various order, the terrain goes quiet. The assembled warriors, and heaven knows from whence *they* came, an assorted lot of monkeys, humans, demi-gods, and demons, their members made all the more confusing by their penchant to go invisible from time to time, hush as Harry and Anna square off.

We meet again, hey? Let's at it then.

'Sure enough. The same battle, though, the same ending.'

Endings are always the same. It's the angle of the dénouement that matters, ha!

'Angles aside, if the end result is the same—'

Whose end, Harry, whose end? Mine, surely enough may not differ. It's you, though, you and your damnable inability to trust, that's what stays the same.

Harry parries with his staff and Anna adeptly avoids contact.

'All this talk of trust. You, Athnic, Simpson. I can trust. How else do you think I got this far?'

This far? By radical indecision-making, that's how. By following blindly. By playing out the story as if you had no control, that's how. That's not trust. You'll see.

'You confound me. But I don't have to understand you to defeat you.'

Anna swings a roundhouse kick in Harry's general direction and Harry easily deflects the blow.

Ha. I'm already beaten. I'd never have it any other way.

'Then why this charade, this acting out, this ridiculous chase?'

Why? Ha. To see if you could learn. To see if you could trust. Really trust.

'And somehow you think I haven't?'

Ha, the tense is all wrong. Not have you, but will you?

After several moments of such feckless activity, conundrous conversation, Harry and Anna become locked in an embrace. The spectators can swear they hear ribs cracking and organs grinding to a halt. The two could be lovers, thinks Athnic from the sidelines. When they part and stagger backward, thinks Athnic, it is as lovers do when separating after harsh words or strong emotions.

Thunder and lightning and steam abound. Harry and Anna, two steps apart, look one another over, and then only when Anna leans into Harry's face, close enough to suck the moisture from his breath, leans over and whispers, *It's done then*, before keeling over in apparent lifelessness, do the assembled warriors break into cheers and lift Harry onto their shoulders, no matter which side they were on. The battle is over. Anna is not dead, it becomes clear, but clearly defeated. Tended by comrades, Anna raises a finger and weakly addresses the throngs.

As before, so now. And maybe again and again and again. But you – *a finger points straight at Harry's heart* – you will push her back and fail again and again and again.

Harry has broken a sweat, to be sure, but is smiling and in good form. He looks at Anna Varre, now collapsed into unconsciousness. Harry, who has now made something of his life, who has gone on the adventure that others may only dream of, who has reversed his fortunes and tendencies and attitudes so dramatically he is hardly recognizable as the tepid character who inhabited his body mere days before, smiles at his adoring fans.

From the shadows of a smouldering boulder, a figure appears, dressed in jeans and a tanktop. It approaches the victorious warrior, appears to begin to genuflect, then in a change of mind, stares Harry right in the eyes.

'Hello, Sita,' says Harry.

'Hello, Harry,' says Sita. 'Good to see you.'

'And you,' says Harry. And he reaches out and Sita reaches out and their palms touch and steam escapes from every imaginable crevice in the place, one huge, sulphurous, noisy, wet, splendorous sigh.

YVR, reprised

'And how long were you out of the country?' asks the immigration officer. Harry, Sita, and Athnic stare at him blankly. Finally, Athnic manages to mumble that it's been a while, though truth be told, none of them actually remember how long they have been gone.

'Oh,' says the immigration officer. 'Well, welcome back.'

When Harry, Sita, and Athnic pass into the international arrivals area, there is a lone figure standing near the escalators. He holds a single flower in his hand, a tiger lily, and he is smiling broadly. Sita turns to Harry and Athnic.

'Please,' she says, 'wait here.'

Sita goes up to Simpson and they hug for a very long time. Looking on, Athnic thinks this pose looks familiar but soon dismisses the thought and drags Harry over for a coffee.

'So,' says Simpson still smiling. 'Have a good vacation?'

The absurdity of the question, the whole predicament, makes Sita laugh.

'I don't – I don't even know what happened, Dad. Am I going crazy?'

'No,' says Simpson, his smile giving way to a more serious, if not entirely grim, look. 'No, you're fine. And listen, you did what was meant to be.'

'Me? I didn't do anything. I just was – I mean– '

'I know, I know,' says Simpson. 'What I mean is that you made it through and things are going to be all right now.'

Sita is silent for a moment. 'But things are going to be different now, aren't they?' she says finally.

Simpson looks at his daughter and smiles again. 'Yes, things will be different or else the same all over again.'

Sita turns to look at Harry and Athnic in the coffee shop. 'Come on,' she says to her father. 'Let's go get them and find Han.'

But before they get over to the coffee counter there is a shout from the table next to Harry and Athnic. A woman and small child are trying to shoo away a wiry looking animal who is proceeding to eat their banana bread with great eagerness. Harry and Athnic leap into the fray but Han is too quick for them, leaping off the stool he used to access to the morsel on the table and skittering off to a far corner of the coffee bar to finish his snack. Amid cries of 'My god' and 'Was that a mongoose?'

and 'Somebody call security,' Harry's voice rings out trying to calm the crowd, explaining that Han has never done anything quite like that before. And as the melee continues, if a soon-to-be-airborne passenger were to look past the coffee counter, past the jade bar and the shops, and up to toward the skylights, this hypothetical person might see a plethora of images igniting across a series of video screens, messages and messengers, exploding through history and video technology. A seasoned ferryman caught between Homer and the power of myth, a hippie with no way home, a pregnant woman seeking escape and redemption through alcohol and flight, a dog-walking Australian wondering why girlfriends pop in and out of her life, a neckless prison guard caught up in the intrigue of mistaken identity, a thousand religious zealots burning down a mosque and building a temple or razing a temple and building a mosque, a pair of wizened hotel clerks just waiting to make a traveller's life miserable, another hotelier misnamed through history and culture and trying his best to live up to his future, a thousand, no, hundreds of thousands of wrongfully accused and willfully imprisoned, clamouring to get out of jail cells and off island exiles and away from varieties of incarceration too numerous to fathom – images upon images upon images of characters and messengers and stories all shouting their existence onto a mirage of screens high above the transitional goers and comers below. This is what someone might see if everyone within earshot were not so concerned with catching up with a strange-looking dog with supple legs and arms and a supine tail, laughing as he evades everyone who tries to capture him, contain him, restrain him.

re-teller

Harry counts out four-hundred-and-sixty dollars for the client at his window. The woman takes her money, smiles at Harry as if she were about to say something, but then nods and exits the credit union. Harry looks up at camera no. 8, smiles, and blows it a kiss. He hears a harumph coming from Mr Peabody's office followed by the sound of an old oak chair being pushed back. Harry turns to the manager's office and sees Mr Peabody appear. Mr Peabody's eyes narrow and he walks confidently over to Harry.

'Mr Kumar, trouble on the floor?'

'Sir?'

'You were – gesturing toward the surveillance equipment. I surmised you might have a message of sorts.'

Mr Peabody had carefully instructed the entire credit union staff in a set of signals more complex than those used by major league baseball coaches, all intended to safeguard the credit union. Tugging twice on one's ear meant a suspicious client was approaching; pressing the back of a wrist to one's forehead, femme-fatale style, meant a hold-up was in process; two fingers to one's lips meant a fraudulent cheque was being passed. However, a blown kiss was not on the repertoire of emergency signals, so Mr Peabody was a bit confused.

'No sir, no message,' Harry says assuredly, adding under his breath, 'just peace and love.'

'Yes, well then, Mr Kumar. As it happens I was wanting to talk to you about your unexcused absence. You know, of course, that I called in numerous favours for you to keep your job. Yes. I mean not only was there the matter of the absenteeism, but that was preceded by your poorly thought-out scheme to integrate under-rated voice-recognition software into our whole communications system. I don't have to tell you how upset upper management was when they found out about this, do I Mr Kumar?'

Harry looks around him. Daphne, Arlene, and Agnes are all within earshot and are pretending to do their work, although Mr Peabody knows they are listening and is announcing this lie in a public manner for the fourth time this week purely for their benefit. When he is finished gloating, he will retire to his office where he will telephone his wife and tell her of his exploits, giggling and chortling all the way through.

'No, sir, I realize that was an egregious error on my part. And I am extremely grateful for retaining my job.'

'As you should be, Mr Kumar, as you should be. But I'm afraid to inform you, young man, that while you may continue to work here, it will be a long way off before you are considered for promotion, you realize that?'

'Yes sir, Mr Peabody. A long way off.'

'Yes, Mr Kumar, when I placed my trust in you and gave you your own office to update our, uh, computer files, well, you violated that trust didn't you?'

'I suppose so, sir.' Harry can see that Daphne is close to tears and that Agnes is gritting her teeth. They don't like to see Harry maligned this way, but they have told Harry they fear for their jobs if they speak in his defense. Perfectly understandable, he has told them.

'Well then, carry on, Mr Kumar. And let's have no more thoughts about voice-recognition nonsense, shall we?' He slaps Harry on the shoulder and struts back to his office.

Daphne sidles up to Harry. 'How can you stand being lied to like that? You shouldn't have to be the fall guy for Peabody's bad judgement.'

'No, I suppose not,' says Harry. 'But what can I do?'

Daphne shakes her head. Agnes glowers in the general direction of the manager's office. Even Arlene purses her lips in disapproval of this mistreatment.

'I think I'll take lunch,' Harry says aloud. He looks down to the tiny handheld computer that sits by his wicket. He taps open the program that reveals itself as 'Kiwi: the ultimate banking voice-recognition software,' a recent gift from Sam Churchill.

'Mobile audio-recording on, office no. 1,' says Harry. 'Voice-recog broadcast from no. 1 to following e-mail addresses: self, President, Vice-President, CEO. Confirm.'

The tiny handheld computer bleeps and spits out a phrase: 'Audio-recording on, office no. 1, simultaneous translation and transmission to Credit Union President, Vice-President, CEO, cc-ed to Harry Kumar.'

Harry turns to look at Mr Peabody's office. Mr Peabody is on the telephone, his feet up on his desk, obviously having a good time.

Across Harry's tiny handheld computer screen appear a series of expletives and invectives, all aimed at credit union upper management. 'Stupid arseholes … President wouldn't know a good manager if one bit him on his testicles … CEO is really a buffoon who happens to be the son of an idiot tycoon … VP believes everything I tell her about hapless Kumar,' and so on. Harry smiles, flips his tiny handheld computer shut, and thinks about how running things backwards can sometimes be a good thing.

you can check out anytime you like but you can never leave

The uniformed concierge is busy multi-tasking. He is directing a bellboy to take a couple's inordinately heavy suitcases up to the twelfth floor; he is in conversation with a grumpy old Texan who wants to know where he can find a really good martini; tucked at the back of his mind in his "things-to-do file" is a mental note to make dinner reservations for the family in sixteen-oh-two; and in front of him an impatient middle-aged man in a dark suit, mirrored sunglasses, and a bus driver's cap, paces furiously, his every step shadowed by two younger men, identically clad but for the cap. After quickly assisting the Texan, instructing the bellboy, and speed-dialling the restaurant, Athnic Long looks up at the pacing man and says, 'Yes, sir, can I help you?'

The man stops in mid-pace, turns on his heel and, in one motion, flips his cap back high on his head and tears off his sunglasses. The two younger men also stop pacing, but retain their sunglasses, fold their hands in front of their crotches and stand at attention.

'You bet you can,' says Director Merrick.

'You!'

'The same.'

'I thought – I thought we'd seen the last of you.'

'Things change,' says Merrick, smiling. He looks at the young man to his left, then to the one to his right. On cue, each smiles and snickers.

Athnic holds up his hand as the restaurant hostess answers the phone. 'Rosa? Athnic. Fine. Table for four tonight, seven PM, by the window. Yah, kids, so near the washrooms would be good. Bye Rosa.'

He looks back up at Merrick who is near to snarling.

'I suppose you think you're good at your job,' he says, shoving his sunglasses back on his face.

Athnic nods. After all, he is.

Merrick's attendees sneer.

'But there are some jobs you fall down on, aren't there?' Merrick continues. 'We depended on you, Long, and you let us down.'

'I might remind you,' says Athnic patiently, 'that I never agreed to work with you. You came to me and said you needed my help. I said I'd do what I could. But that was before I found out what you were all about. How could I help you at the expense of Harry?'

'Dammit man, you could have helped us both. We needed to rewrite history, is that so hard? And your Kumar friend, he was trying to do the same, wasn't he?'

For effect, or perhaps out of habit, Merrick turns to the young man to his right and backhands him on the shoulder. The young man stares at his shoulder, then at Merrick, and finally at his colleague, now stifling a laugh, on the other side of the director. The young man struck by Merrick steps behind the director and punches his colleague, hard, in the left shoulder. A pushing match ensues, something Merrick tries hard to ignore.

'You know,' says Athnic. 'I'm not sure what Harry was trying to do. I know he went after Sita because he wanted to change himself, and I know I was somehow meant to be part of that. But beyond that – look, I'm a concierge. That's what I do. I do it well, but that's what I do.'

'The junta is disbanding,' Merrick says with some finality. 'The BPJ is no more.'

The two young men cease their pushing match to stare at Merrick.

'I never knew it ever was,' mutters Athnic.

The pushing match resumes, now escalating to a competition to see who can grab sunglasses from his opponent's face.

'Oh it was, young man, it was, let me tell you. And just because it's faded from view, doesn't mean its principles are lost. *We're* still out there, all of us who believed in it, who needed it – and all of you who don't want to believe in it, don't think you need it, yes, we're still out there, and we shall come back again. Wherever people need order, we'll be there; wherever folks are getting too uppity and out of hand, we'll be there; whenever things are running backwards, we'll be there to set things right. We'll be there, do you understand, to keep the inside inside and the outside outside, the top top and the bottom bottom. You had the chance to be with us but you failed, miserably at that, and now, dear Mr Long, you really and truly have seen the last of Director Merrick.'

One of the young men has managed to dislodge his partner's sunglasses and, as both men struggle to gain possession of the sunglasses, they become entangled and fall to the floor with a thud.

Merrick looks down at the pair; the men look up at Merrick.

'Can't you two just give it a rest?' asks Merrick, exasperation apparent in his voice.

'Sorry, sir,' says the young man with the dislodged sunglasses.

'Yes, sir. Sorry, sir,' says the other, then mutters, 'but he started it.'

'I don't care who–' Merrick begins, but then realizes any further discussion is futile. He clears his throat, turns back to Athnic, smiles, adjusts his sunglasses.

'Good day, sir,' he says, tipping his hat. 'Till we meet again.'

And with that, Merrick performs a respectable about-face, and marches out the front door of the hotel. His attendees gather themselves to their feet, brush themselves off, and jockey for position behind the director. If Athnic were not so busy, perhaps he would follow the vaude-villian trio out of the hotel, down the street and around the corner, through a small green space, over a guard rail, and finally on to a no. 3 bus, where Director Merrick would plop himself down in the driver's seat and admonish his attendees for their utterly unprofessional behaviour before slamming shut the bus door and resuming his route. And if Athnic were to make it this far, perhaps he would see a look of resignation on Merrick's face, a type of look that indicates the bearer has lived neither wisely, nor well, and is now forced to live out his life wishing for things that might have been. Perhaps Athnic might see, behind the frown Merrick wears underneath his sunglasses, a desperate fear signalling a loss of control, a loss of command, a loss of personal integrity. And if, indeed, Athnic had been so bold as to pursue Merrick to his new-found job, he might have seen, beyond the tinted windshield and over-sized wipers, that distinct look of unrequited love, of missed chances, of dashed dreams; Athnic might have seen his own future in the familiarity of two black-clad passengers who might one day become paramedics, or in the becapped and bespectacled visage of a driver who just did not know when to stop.

But Athnic does not leave his post; instead, he watches the trio disappear out the front door of his hotel, and he thinks back to all that has transpired over the past weeks – Sita's disappearance, his odd encounters with the BPJ and the director, soliciting him to join a cause Athnic knew nothing about and still doesn't, his decision to island-hop with Harry with no clue as to where he was getting his directions, the mass illogic that surrounded Harry's transformation into some sort of warrior-king and Athnic's own switch from leader to follower. All so much, thinks Athnic, and now here he is, happy again, doing what he does best, reclaiming the position he knows most about, aiming to be content from now until the day he dies. Yes, thinks Athnic, all so much.

'Yes, ma'am,' he says to an over-dressed matronly sort who has just come over from reception, 'can I help you?'

Harry and Sita debrief

'I know that, but what exactly did you do together?'

'Together? We travelled between islands. We seldom talked. We – listen, Harry. This little travelling roadshow was not my idea. What are you getting at anyway?'

'Nothing. Nothing, of course. I was just … concerned for your … safety. And I wanted to make sure, well, that, everything was okay.'

'Well, everything's okay. But not okay, because, listen, Harry, something weird happened here. I was at my desk on Granville Island and the next thing I know I was inside this, like, liquid glass bubble. It was – it just was not okay.'

'Not okay. That's what I expected. So what happened between you?'

'I told you. Nothing. This Anna Varre took me, somehow took me with him, her, I don't even know that.'

'And you never even talked?'

'Talked? Talked, yes, of course we talked. I asked Anna why I was being detained, I asked where we were going, I asked what all this was about, and at first all I got were answers in riddles and rhymes. "I don't know and I don't carra, or my name's not anna varre," that sort of thing.'

'And that's all?'

'No. Then I got offers of – of everything.'

'And you said?'

'And I said no.'

'You said "no" to everything? Everything?'

'Yes. No to everything. Everything.'

'And you never…?'

((

Sita and Harry are, quite unremarkably, sitting in a coffee shop on Main Street, having this remarkable conversation. If nearby coffee drinkers were eavesdropping at all, they would think that Harry and Sita were concocting some sort of dramatic screenplay, but no nearby patrons think it worthwhile to listen in on this fairly ordinary-looking couple. But after Harry's last comment, and after Sita's deep, dark, narrowing of eyes that catch Harry in a deathly stare, one or two of the people at adjacent tables do peripherally gaze into this scene, but only momentarily, only until Sita's hands slam down hard on the table and she speaks in short, staccato tones.

'So that's what this is all about? You want to know about whether Anna Varre and I, whether we were intimate? How can you ask that, you of all people? Is that what you want to know, Harry?'

'Well, no, not exactly. No, that's not it. I mean, no. I mean, did you?'

Sita is out of her seat and out of the coffee shop in one movement. Tears are brimming in her eyes, but she won't let Harry see this, won't let him be pleasured by finally seeing her cry. She begins to walk down the hill, but then changes her mind after several paces and does an abrupt about face and starts walking up the hill. By this time, Harry has had the presence of mind to follow Sita out the door, and he looks uphill, sees no sign of her, then turns to look downhill just as Sita has performed her about face and has now launched herself in the opposite direction. As fate would have it, Sita is looking down at the ground and Harry is looking up toward the distance, and Harry and Sita collide with one another, bodies attempting to perform the impossible, to occupy the same space at the same time. Both are alarmed, but both do what comes most naturally, encircling the other with their arms, locking on tightly, both breaking into heavy sobs, Harry's tears as always more fountain-like and forceful than Sita's faint dribblings.

'I'm sorry,' blubbers Harry. Sita says nothing but holds on. 'I'm so sorry,' continues Harry, 'sorry sorry sorry.' They stand like this for mountains of time, Harry sobbing and repeating apologies, Sita almost silently sniffling tears down her cheeks. They stand like this until the rain starts, great big drops, and until they are both soaked to the skin, standing there, crying, holding each other.

'Let's go home,' one of them says to the other, and the other nods and reaches down to hold an offered hand and the two of them proceed to walk home in the now-pouring rain.

☾

Harry and Sita sit across from each other in front of the television. They are draped in large white beach towels, the kind Harry likes to buy for his bathroom. Their hair is now only damp after they have taken turns rough-towelling each other's heads. And, oh yes, in case you are interested, which you most likely are, they are not naked, but are wearing various renditions of Harry's ratty and torn sweatpants and t-shirts. They sit across from each other, crosslegged, and their hands rest in front of them, the fingertips of Harry's right hand touching the fingertips of Sita's left hand, the fingertips of Sita's right hand gently sensing the pulse of Harry's left wrist. They do not speak but, and as romantic and melodramatic as this sounds, it's the honest truth, they listen to each other's thoughts.

It's a matter of trust. And you don't trust me. No, it shouldn't even be about trust, for why should you have such expectations? It's about strange possessiveness, goddamn patriarchal ownership.

I don't feel I own you. Nor do I feel you owe me anything. I just feel like there's a piece of this whole puzzle missing. You, me, Han, this Anna Varre, Athnic, all of us, like we're connected and goddamn falling apart.

Let's say I slept with Anna Varre. No, let's say I seduced Anna Varre, that this whole thing was my idea, the travel, the bubble, the islands, the messages. Let's say I created Anna Varre and seduced Anna Varre. What then?

Then, I don't know what to think. I must admit, if I thought you weren't the victim here....

I'm not the victim here, Harry. There's nothing victimy about me and you knew that from the first day you met me. So if I'm not the victim – and I'm not – does that make me your enemy? Can you be my hero if you're rescuing me from nothing? If your rescue is all to defeat me?

If that were true, yes, maybe. But Sita, it was all Anna Varre, you know that, I know that. Han knows that even.

Maybe we made up Anna Varre, you know, Harry, made up Anna because we needed Anna. Maybe you are Anna Varre, I am Anna Varre, Han and Athnic and everyone we know is Anna Varre and you and I , you and I, we're just players in the game. Did you ever think of that, Harry?

No. Not until now. Not even now

Then once again, you don't believe me?

I do. I do, really. That night, Sita, that night you came by after your date and you kissed me.... Everything changed, maybe not that night, but soon after. What were you thinking, Sita, what were you thinking?

I was thinking of freedom, Harry. Of not having to explain myself by your rules, or abiding by rules that some great lord or master has created for me. I don't mean, of course, a crazy individualist thing about being myself; you know I'd never run that game on you. But I mean seeing those archaic rules for what they are and doing something about them, running them backwards perhaps. You must understand that, Harry, you must understand that.

((

Han walks into the room, slightly bored since he has foregone the fine art of conversation, no longer necessary now that he has reverted entirely to canine form and desire and since they are no longer tripping around the world on a major quest. At least, this is the explanation that Anna Varre gave him, but that memory is now deep in the recesses of a monkey's mind, not a dog's brain.

He sees the fingertips of Sita and Harry variously engaged, leaps up on the couch between them and licks their fingers.

'Hi, Han,' says Harry.

'Hey, Han,' says Sita.

Han looks at his main human companion and at Sita, both humans whom he trusts and loves a great deal even if he has not the fullest comprehension of what makes them tick. Here are two people, he thinks, who by all regular standards should be together, should be spending their lives together, should be enjoying what they know about each other and learning what they don't. Yet here these two people sit, enshrouded by towels and their thoughts, and however much they may be inside each other's heads, might as well be a hemisphere away. This is, thinks Han, not just about trust and responsibility, about love and faith, but about completely different ways of being in the world. Not a good place to be, thinks Han, starting from a place of infinite distance so that any approaches are still immense distances apart. Han licks the hands of Sita and Harry again, looks them both in their stony faces, and curls up between them. Instinctively, both humans break their touch with one another and lay a hand on the dog. Han sighs, whimpers, and goes to sleep.

Anna concludes

So, okay, so I suppose it's up to me to bring down the curtain, cue the orchestra, be the fade-to-black kind of guy. So it goes. And here we are with history abounding about us and yet refusing to change even a dollop, funny thing that. Imagine, then, a vista full of islands as far as the eye can see, many many islands, luscious gardens and thick vegetation and stark rock outcroppings, all surrounded by liquid liquid liquid. Islands that trap people, islands that appear to set them free, but all islands that contain those self-same people in oddly different kinds of ways. Islands that are used for refuge are also islands that are used for incarceration. I might abscond with the cash (or a veritable princess as the story would have it) and flee to my island kingdom, Lankan or Rotoruan as the case may be, hole up there and, you know what, the very fact of being holed up, the very notion of me being alone with the princess maiden is really the whole point. You see, it doesn't matter, just doesn't matter what happens inside the story since the story told, unfolded, imagined, is the story that gets written down into stone, impressed in people's memories, entrenched in fables and glories. And what if those islands are more imaginary, what if I decide, or someone decides, that an arbitrary site, say the birthplace of our stealthy hero Harry Kumar (which may be London, may be Ayodhya, may be someplace else depending on how you enter this story) is of such import that the ground upon which he births is held as sacred ground? See, this is where physics comes into play, that insane dog and his rush up and over and through the pinnacles, trying so desperately to occupy two spaces at once, but matter matters and such cannot occur, or so they tell us. Which means this birthplace of Harry, or our lovely yet misguided Director Merrick's beloved watering hole, or prisons upon prisons upon prisons, cannot be simultaneously occupied by the preoccupations of others. Something must give. Something must come down, and if it's not London bridge then it's another structure and if it's not a structure then it's a palace or kingdom or prison in someone's mind. And it doesn't matter, it truly doesn't, how I came to swipe Sita from her comfortable island office, and what transpired between us, well then, that's between us, and it doesn't matter what Harry thinks, but what matters is *that* Harry thinks, and you see, he isn't going to ever stop thinking. He's in between places that Harry, in between races and places, and the spaces in between are so small that he can hardly see through them, and they are so large that he can hardly see where to climb through, and they are so finite and so infinite that Harry just looks out onto the world and shakes his head, unbelievingly, shakes his head while Han's tail wags the canine's entire body and still there is no comprehension about who has won this battle – although I gladly admit defeat myself if that will help at all, yet it's not about winning or losing, it's how you play the post-game show, who do you love and who do you trust? – and in this whole mess is the well-informed, ill-informed Athnic who is now destined to return to his happy job where he is loved by all and in the end, be veritably kissed by a bus, but all this happens not now, not now but in the indiscreet and indeterminate future where all this has already happened, and dogs have already climbed to the top of pinnacles and seen the promised land on the other side and Harrys and Sitas sit for eternities, draped in towels, wondering wondering what might have been if not for bubbly islands that once separated them, that kept them apart as they are now kept apart by each others' voices inside each others' heads, and let's not forget about me (please) poor backwards thinking backwards acting always backwards Anna Varre, playing with people's lives, with their lies and stories (what might be the difference I have yet to figure after aeons of playing this game of history and myth), with their hearts, let's not forget, with their histories both past and future, with their dogs and with their manservants and with their parents and with their children and their grandchildren and their great-grandchildren, all of whom will insist that something be built upon this spot in testimony to something or other and all of whom will, in their turn, tear down that selfsame something in mob-like violence or a theatrical mushroom-capped explosion or by keeping walls and bars and glass and steel as barriers to their futures, to their freedoms, to their loves and their desires, and all of this because islands can only be prisons, and prisons can only exist where islands exist, and separations can only happen when prisons and islands present themselves in the woods, in the air, in the water, and in the imagination. Oh ho. This might as well be the end of the story, the end of my story which is also their story and everyone else's story, but why confuse matters further, why go beyond that image of Harry and Sita, their skin the palest brown, touching the dog between them, towels dampening on their heads and shoulders and torsos and fingers, fingers that are not in touch with canine, touching each other ever so briefly and so fleetingly and so tenderly but always always always signifying that moment just before that union began and always always always always pointing to the inevitability of separation.

Ashok Mathur

Ashok divides his time between Calgary and Vancouver. He teaches critical studies at the Emily Carr Institute of Art and Design. His prose, poetry, and critical writing focus on a variety of social justice issues. He's working on an anthology of critical race theory. He is also active in organizing around anti-racism through creative and critical modes of production. His books include the novel, *Once Upon an Elephant*, and a collection of poetry, *Loveruage*.

PHOTO: COREY TERAMURA